MURDEROUS ACTS

BY

COLIN KNIGHT

ALSO BY COLIN KNIGHT

Some People Deserve to Die

Public Service

Bad Analysis

Escape From Prague

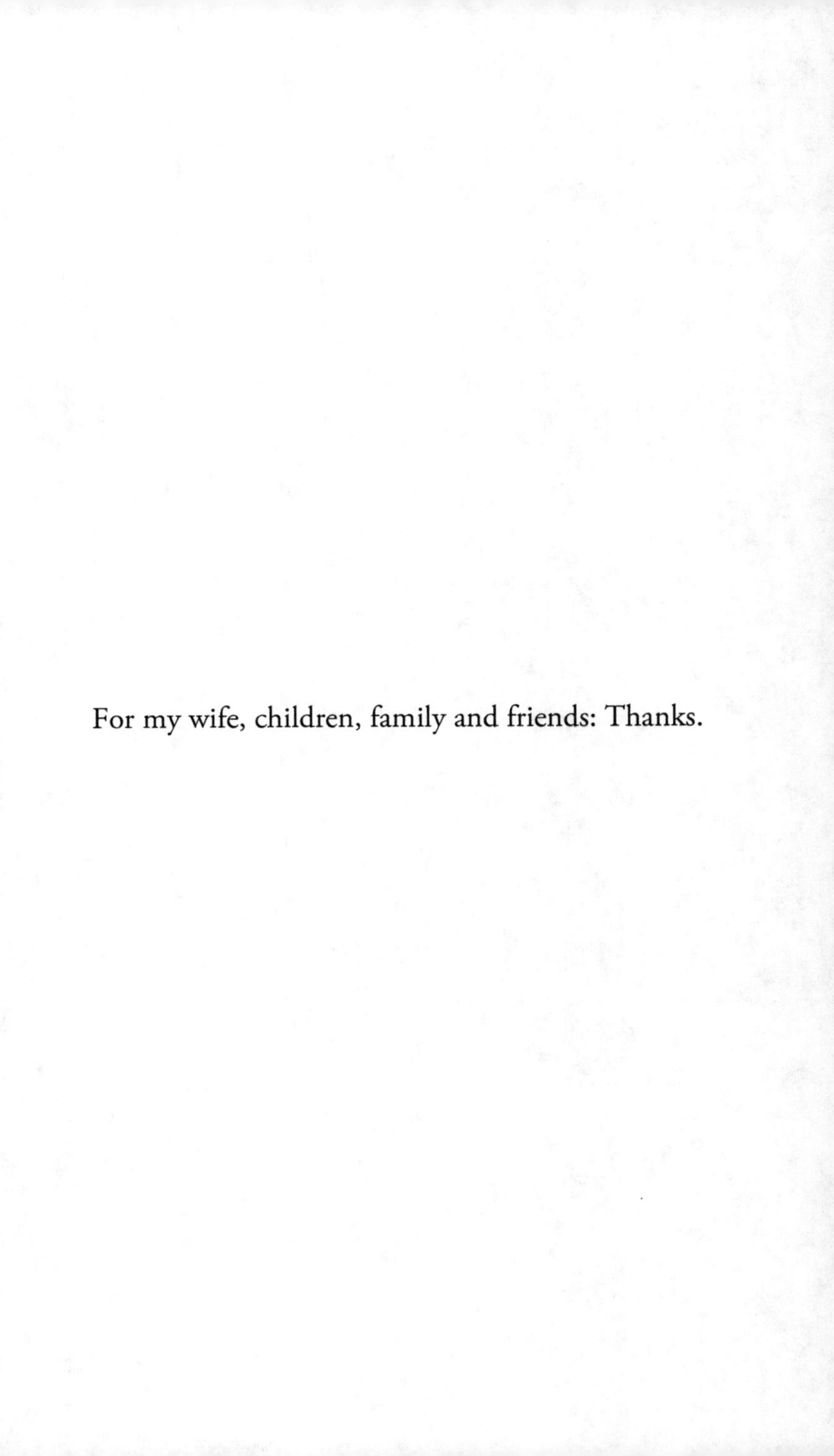

For my wife, children, family and friends: Thanks.

PROLOGUE

Knock, pause, knock, knock, pause, knock.

Blood, dried black and hard to get, resisted coming out as David wiggled and rubbed the wet Q-tip under and around the chipped nail on the little finger of his left hand.

Knock, pause, knock, knock, pause, knock.

Reluctant, but concerned by Robbie's "secret" knock, David rinsed his hands, pulled the sleeves of his overcoat down, and opened the door to his flat.

"What's wrong?" asked David, noting Robbie's pajamas and flushed face.

Robbie brushed moisture from his reddened cheek with a knuckle. Then he visibly swallowed and pushed out an explanation.

"I'm… I'm just glad you're home. I was worried about the police, and what would happen to you and my mom."

"It's alright, Robbie," David soothed as he squatted down to eye level. "There's no need to worry. It's all sorted. Go back to bed before your mom wakes up."

Unmoved by the assurance, Robbie shuffled his feet and fixed his eyes on the worn doormat. Snorting mucus into his nose, hesitant words slipped out.

"I, I, want to say thanks, as well."

"Thanks for what, Robbie?"

"For, you know, getting rid of Troy, and saving my mom."

Raw and desperate, Troy's scream ricocheted off the shuttered buildings as he pulled the knife from his own stomach.

Pushing the image and sound from his mind, David spoke softly.

"I didn't do it, Robbie."

"But I was in the store, and I, I, heard what you said."

"That," David said, thinking back to the confrontation, "was just talk, Robbie. I didn't want your mom to worry."

Dull gray snot had escaped Robbie's nostril, and he dragged the cuff of his pajama sleeve across his nose and mouth as he spoke.

"What about the other bad people?"

Confused, David lowered his voice.

"What bad people, Robbie? What do you mean?"

"It's all in my books."

"What books?"

"The books about the neighborhood. And you."

The wide-eyed innocence of Robbie's young face did little to calm David's sudden apprehension.

"What do you mean? What books?"

"Well," Robbie replied, confident about his achievements, and pleased that David wanted to know. "For the neighborhood, I make notes on people and things that happen. I look out for spies and terrorists, or burglars, or people watching the house. You know, suspicious stuff. And I put everything in my books in case the police need to know."

"Oh," David sighed, momentarily relieved, as he thought of Robbie's well-developed imagination. "But you said you have a book about me."

A shiver shook Robbie's body as the cool air of the unheated entranceway to the two flats leached through his loose-fitting pajamas. A tooth pressed his bottom lip as he debated with himself. If he told what he knew, then David and his mom would know he had snooped in David's flat. But David was a good person, because he had saved his mom, Robbie reasoned.

He decided to confess.

"You know, stuff like when you come and go. What clothes you are wearing, or anything different. When Jenny comes over, and the stuff in your flat. I'm sorry."

"What do you mean, the stuff in my flat?" David asked, with more force than he realized.

"Um, like the new stuff. And the odd stuff that you've been collecting. When I come to play with Shadow, I take photos and put them in my books. I didn't mean to spy on you."

David's right hand slipped into the pocket of his coat. His fingers closed around the smooth plastic cylinder of the spent EpiPen. Past the plastic, he caressed the sharp edge of a business card and the coarse thread on the inside of a metal cap that once closed a hip flask.

With his left hand, he checked the Fairbairn-Sykes, seven-inch, double-edged fighting knife wrapped in a program from a greyhound dog race.

Feigning a smile to hide his anxiety, David whispered his next words.

"Why would you do that, Robbie?"

With pride and confidence in his skills, and unaware of David's tense body, Robbie didn't hesitate to reply.

"To protect Mommy. Now I know you are a good person, so I won't do it anymore. I promise."

A dark grimace flickered across David's face, and Robbie stepped back.

"I won't do it again. Really, I won't. I, I guess I should go now."

"It's OK, Robbie," David consoled the kid, as he adopted a soft tone and relaxed expression. "I understand. It's great that you look out for your mom so much. She told me things have been bad in the past."

Assured by David's calmness, Robbie raised his eyes.

"You're not mad at me, then?"

"No, not at all. Tell me, where do you keep the books?"

"Some on my desk, but the, you know, secret ones, in my treasure chest."

Behind the mask of calmness, David's mind hurtled into a state of uncertainty and fear. He knew Robbie went into the flat every workday morning to feed his cat, Shadow.

What did the kid know?

He would have had plenty of time and opportunity to see things. But Robbie was a twelve-year-old kid, and there was nothing really to see.

On the verge of discounting his anxiety and send-ing Robbie off to bed, David's subconscious lunged and took control.

The kid's a snoop. He has a telescope and a camera. He's been in your flat alone, every day. He's seen everything.

To strengthen its call to paranoia, his subconscious added a restless murmur of agreement from the imagined theatre audience that had, in David's mind, followed and adored his resurrected acting career for the past year.

Now sensing the expectation of the audience and caught in the glare of the stage lights, David succumbed.

"Hey, Robbie. I'm heading out to Bedfont Park. Do you want to come?"

Eager that David wanted him to go, Robbie agreed, even though he had only been to the park before with his mom, or with his mom and David together.

"Yes, please! I'll get dressed right away. Can we go to the lake, as well?"

"Yes, of course. I'll make a flask of tea and a snack."

As Robbie started through the door to the stairs to his own flat, David, prodded by his subconscious, called out quietly.

"Hey, Robbie, I'd really like to see the books you made. Why don't you bring them, and we can look together?"

"OK, I'll bring my school bag."

"And Robbie?"

"Yes."

"Is your mom awake?"

"No, she's dead tired from, you know, being up all night."

"Let's leave her to sleep then, eh? There's no need to tell her where we're going. We'll be back before she's up."

"OK, David."

ONE

"Excuse me," said a hoarse voice from the customer side of the dark marble bar top that delineated the line between customer and server.

Unruffled, David looked up, smiled, and placed a folded napkin in front of the man.

"Good morning, welcome to Sea Food World. What can I get you?"

The man, his bland face puffed and tinged red from his overnight flight from New York to London's Heathrow Airport, rolled his eyes upward over his fingerprint-stained reading glasses and pointed at the menu.

"What's wrong with the Scottish salmon?"

David had heard the question before. With patience and a delicacy, he did not feel, and with a wink to Nancy, his fellow server, he regurgitated company policy.

"The Scottish salmon is excellent and highly praised by connoisseurs. The Balik salmon, as you probably know, is imported, and is six pounds more than the Scottish due to the cost of shipping and taxes."

Four years ago, and every year since, corporate training had taught David the nuances of promoting the product that returned the highest profit margin.

Before his indoctrination into the disingenuous world of marketing, he, like most lay people, had assumed the goal was to sell the most expensive item, and therefore realize the highest profit. "Not always so," the training officer from head office had explained at the time.

In the case of the two salmon choices on Sea Food World's menu, the objective was to sell Scottish salmon at ten pounds, rather than the Balik salmon at sixteen pounds. Scottish salmon cost Sea Food World four pounds per serving, while the Balik cost twelve pounds. Scottish salmon provided six pounds' profit, while the Balik returned only four pounds' profit.

David continued with the corporate script.

"It's true that many people believe Balik is the finest salmon in the world. Its connection to the last Russian tsar makes it more exotic than the others, but many Scottish salmon producers have been awarded a Royal Warrant by Her Majesty The Queen."

The Royal Warrant, David knew, had not been conveyed on the Scottish smoked salmon suppliers to Sea Food World, but as the corporate suit had emphasized, he had not said that it did. Besides, the salmon came with scrambled eggs, and from his own experience, egg did little to enhance the taste of salmon, let alone enable a tongue to distinguish whether the salmon had swum in the cold waters of a Scottish loch or a Russian lake.

David didn't object to the deception. For him, it was all an act, and acting, despite what others thought about his affliction, was what he was good at.

Ninety percent of customers—Russians aside—displayed a preference for the current British monarchy, rather than the former "despotic" Russian tsars, and they opted for the Scottish smoked salmon. They saved six pounds and Sea Food World gained an extra two pounds of profit. Everyone won, according to head office.

True to form, the customer who had wriggled into a degree of comfort on the plush leather of the barstool ordered as expected.

"Well, if it's good enough for Queen Elizabeth, then it's good enough for me. I'll take the Scottish salmon and a Bloody Mary with an oyster."

On autopilot, David laid a drink coaster and a fork on the bar top. The knife, plastic due to security measures, remained in his hand. He weighed it on his palm, then balanced it on the tip of his finger.

"Almost thirty American," blurted the man, "for an egg, salmon, and a drink, and I get plastic to eat with?"

David, who was irritated by the contradiction of another customer who was stupid enough to pay thirty "American" for a simple breakfast and yet become indignant about its cost, forced a sympathetic smile onto his face and gently placed the knife beside the fork.

The man, content to have managed the ordeal of human interaction required to secure his meal, propped an iPad on the counter and traded the real world for the internet.

~

David's application for the position of server at Sea Food World had been an ironic and comedic attempt to secure a job where he could work without fear of discovery and ridicule. At the end of the interview, when asked if he minded the smell, and told that he would likely "go home smelling of fish," he had almost choked as he stifled a desire to laugh. With assurances that he could handle it, David had gotten the job.

At thirty-six years old, he wasn't new to the service industry. Schlepping drinks and food had been an integral and formative part of his life since his last year of high school, when he had worked part time at Mandy's, a small cafe on Harrington Road in Altrincham, near Manchester.

In high school, Mandy's had provided David with two important things: first, an opportunity to study and incorporate all the human characteristics, mannerisms, dialogue, and emotion of the many mini-tragedies he witnessed into his passion—acting in the school drama club. Second, waiting tables provided money. Not that he really needed it. His parents were generous to him and his sister Jenny, but David liked to have his own money, and the independence that allowed.

Twenty years on, and here he was again, schlepping food and drink. Only this time, the money paid for the roof over his head, the food in his belly, and the other essentials that people needed to exist. His observation of customers had not changed, though. In fact, his abilities to observe, recall, and apply what he had learned about customers had improved immensely.

The job at Sea Food World had come before his flat in Feltham. It hadn't taken long to realize that his paycheck, London property prices, and the need for an easy and inexpensive commute to work would require cheap accommodations. His dingy flat, thirteen miles west, southwest of central London, and two miles south of Heathrow Airport, was the product of that reality.

A one-bedroom, ground-floor affair with an open-plan kitchen, it contained an airplane-sized bathroom and a communal garden shared with the occupants of a two-bedroom flat on the upper level of the converted house.

Four years later, with his affliction hidden by the heavy scent of seafood on his person, he deftly placed the Scottish salmon and egg in front of his customer.

Two

Five forty-five a.m., and as always, a squeak and a rumble echoed through the concourse. One loud and one erratic, they announced his arrival. The dirty, dishevelled man, ironically responsible for cleaning the seating section of the public concourse and emptying waste stations on the customer side of the various cafes and bars, knew damn well that the front wheel of his battered black garbage cart wobbled and squeaked. And he wasn't deaf.

David knew the man could hear because they had exchanged words several times. Each conversation had become increasingly tense as David sought to first encourage, then demand, that the man fix the wheel of his cart. Their first exchange, from David's perspective, had been confusing.

"Good morning. That's a hell of a noisy wheel. You might want to fix that."

"Na, don't want ta do that, lad."

"Why not? You can hear the cart a mile away."

"That's the point, lad."

"The point? What point?"

"Being heard, lad. That's the point."

The man, called Larry, as David later learned, had then emptied the two garbage stations and shuffled away without any further explanation. David also discovered that Larry, one of only five unionized cleaners remaining on the payroll, had been an airport fixture for over twenty years. He'd begun work at the original Terminal 1 in 1997, and had progressed through various terminals and areas until he'd been assigned to David's section three months after David had started work.

Despite the noisy wheel, Larry enjoyed much popularity amongst the concourse employees, store workers, security guards, and even the customers. For David, it wasn't about the wheel, or Larry's soiled uniform, rough-shaved face, dirty fingernails, or worn shoes.

David's problem was Larry's smell. And when he allowed himself to admit to it, his jealousy of Larry's popularity, despite all his shortcomings—but especially the smell. In addition, Larry, who was sensitive to David's hostility, only supplied terse and pithy responses to David's comments and demands about his cart, clothes, and appearance.

~

With Larry fifty meters from the bar, David checked his watch. Flight AF1381, Heathrow to Charles de Gaulle, departed daily at 7:20 a.m. Two passengers, men in their mid-thirties, took the flight every Monday. The men hadn't known each other prior to the early morning flights until David had introduced them.

Now Andrew and Dean shared Monday breakfasts together, as well as the occasional dinner in Paris.

Andrew, a product manager with Siemens, always arrived before Dean, a design and test manager with Atkins. Both men were technical experts, pushed into management roles they didn't want. But they were affable, friendly, and tipped David more than they should for a bagel, salmon, and a coffee.

Before he had introduced the two men, each had been a "bar sitter," eating alone, watching the news channel, and exchanging all manner of information with David. This was how he learned of their mutual interest in kitesurfing.

This morning, as usual, Andrew had arrived at 5:50 and Dean a few moments later. At the bar, after a few greetings, Andrew challenged Dean.

"OK, Dean, how about five pounds today?"

"Five pounds!" Dean exclaimed as he gestured playfully to David and pointed at Andrew.

"Did he ask you for an easy one today, or did he offer you the five pounds to tell him who it would be?"

David, used to their banter, pursed his lips and eyebrows in mock thought. Dean, an avid movie watcher, was three bets up on Andrew, so it was time to even the results. Andrew, much more a techie than he liked to admit, needed help.

Reforming his face into a neutral expression, David lifted and extended his arms outward in front of his chest and looked into the distance, as though addressing a crowd. After a short pause, he gulped, tensed his nostrils, and spoke.

"They won't know what they're looking at, or why they like it, but they'll know they want it."

Dean immediately spluttered, "That's too easy."

"Steve Jobs," Andrew said over Dean.

"Yeah, well that's fine. But who was the actor?" countered Dean.

"Mark—no Michael Fassbuder, or something like that. Am I right, David?"

"It's Fassbender," David corrected him," but that's close enough for me."

Andrew and Dean argued amicably for a moment until Dean handed over a crumpled five-pound note.

David, a former actor and an avid movie buff, knew Fassbender more for his movie roles in *Band of Brothers* and *Macbeth,* rather than his recent portrayal of Steve Jobs, but he smiled at Andrew's win. The men, engaged in animated talk of their respective weekends, then carried their breakfasts over to a table.

Facing the men's backs, David's upturned mouth leveled out and drooped downward with the unwanted memory of his own Shakespearian performances, and the acrimony and resentment that accompanied the premature end of his own acting career. Statue-like, his vision and memories lost in the dark marble of the bar top, the absence of the squeaky wheel meant he didn't immediately notice Larry's return.

"What ya so glum about, lad?"

Jolted, David snapped back, "What the hell, Larry? Where did you come from?"

"Same as always. I come from m' home in Hounslow."

Ignoring Larry's sarcasm, David searched past Larry and asked, "Where is your cart?"

"Busted. That's why I'm here."

"What?"

"I said she's busted. Gettin' it fixed at lunchtime."

"Thank god for that. About time the bloody wheel was fixed."

"Ain't the wheel. That's fine. It's the handle."

"The handle?"

Larry, one foot on the bar rail, leaned a dirty elbow on the bar top and sighed.

"Yeah, well, more the bracket on the side of the cart."

Flicking his hands for Larry to get off the bar, David spoke to him with resignation.

"What do you want, Larry?"

"Nowt. I came to tell you that I can't empty the waste until this afternoon on account I don't got m' cart."

"Come on, Larry. The bins will be overflowing by ten."

"Union and safety rules say that all garbage must be conveyed in carts in public areas. Can't do nowt about it. Don't want to lose m' job, now do I?"

On the edge of a rant, David sucked in air, but paused as Larry lifted a hand and smiled.

"Don't worry. Eddie from level two will come by around eleven and empty the bins."

"But you said…"

"Nah," Larry chuckled as he stepped back from the bar to leave. "I said 'I' couldn't empty the bins 'cause I won't have m' cart. But Eddie has his, so he's gonna do it. We cleaners stick together, you know."

Exasperated at having been "had" again by Larry, David turned his back to the bar, sorted glasses and cups on the counter, and kept one eye on the wall-mounted mirror that enabled him to monitor his customers and the general concourse area.

THREE

Robbie, eleven years and 312 days old, closed his left eye and squinted with his right to peer through the clear glass of the finderscope to aim his Levenhuk Skyline 50x600 AZ telescope at the spire of St. Mary's parish church.

The church, founded in the eleventh century, sat on the edge of Bedfont Green, about a crow mile from the bedroom window of Robbie and his mom's second-floor flat on Cedar Street in Feltham. In June, sunrise began around five a.m., and despite the speckled, drab-blue clouds, Robbie had a clear view of the church and surrounding area by seven a.m.

The scope, equipped with three Barlow lenses, a 5x24 finderscope, three eyepieces, and an erecting eyepiece, had been last year's "big" Christmas present.

With the spire in view, Robbie pressed his right eye to the main eyepiece and traced a line from the tip of the spire to the edge of the rooftop. After a small focus adjustment, he made several slow left and right sweeps along the dark slate tiles in search of rifle barrels and dark-suited figures.

Assured the church roof was unoccupied, Robbie refocused and followed a disciplined fifteen-minute grid pattern search of his neighborhood, ending with a maximum depression angled scan of his own street. Despite disappointment that he had yet to discover any rooftop-mounted snipers, camouflaged spies, or "suspicious" objects in the vicinity, Robbie continued his daily surveillance.

Positioning the telescope to ensure he could see without being seen had taken several hours and half a dozen trips outside to stare, without being noticed, at his own bedroom window from as many different angles as possible.

The problems were that the telescope had to be high enough to see over his window ledge, recessed back in the shadow of his room to avoid being seen from the street, and precisely situated to allow maximum left and right views. His loft bed had provided the solution.

The bed, up high on four posts to accommodate a desk and chair underneath, also had side panels to prevent the occupant from falling out during the night. After much analysis, several rough sketches, and much trial and error with string and Scotch tape, Robbie had solved the problem. With two C-clamps "borrowed" from the school's woodworking class, he mounted the telescope halfway along the side panel of his bed.

Clair, Robbie's mother, had reservations about the telescope. Despite concern that it got in the way of the ladder, that he would bang his head, and that it made it difficult to kiss him good night, the telescope had remained in place. Also, Clair hadn't wanted to stifle Robbie's resourcefulness.

Satisfied with his surveillance, Robbie capped the lens, cleaned the eyepiece, secured the optical tube with a bungee cord to the bedside panel, and climbed down the ladder from his bed.

Perched on the edge of his well-worn, three-wheeled leather chair, reclaimed from someone's curbside discarded household contents, Robbie considered his collection of spiral notebooks arranged numerically on the back of his desk against the wall. Decided, he pulled notebook number 3 from the pile.

Opening the book to the end of previous day's notation, Robbie recorded the date, time, the results of his surveillance, and returned the notebook to its place between numbers 2 and 4.

Between pajama bottoms off and school trousers on, his mom's voice sounded through the thin walls of the cramped, two-bedroom flat that they occupied on the second floor of the converted house.

"Robbie, are you up? Breakfast is ready."

"Coming, Mom."

Seated at one of the two places set on the small wooden table pressed up against the wall, Robbie shoveled cornflakes into his mouth while his mom buttered toast and added sugar to his hot tea. Placing the tea and toast on the table, Clair looked at him lightly.

"All clear outside, Robbie?"

When her son nodded and smiled with his mouth full, Clair inwardly released the tension that had accompanied her every morning since Christmas Day, when Robbie had conducted his first neighborhood surveillance.

She had been uncertain about purchasing the telescope, but Robbie had been persistent, polite, and logical. An approach that Clair could not combat with any good reasons when he had pointed out that "lots of kids have telescopes." Despite her reservations that the telescope would feed his tendency to be a little obsessive and his preoccupation with keeping his mom safe, "Santa" had delivered the telescope, and Robbie had monitored the neighborhood ever since.

What, thought Clair now, *would happen if Robbie actually did "see" something?*

With his cornflakes done, Robbie dipped the corner of a slice of toast in his tea as he spoke.

"Have gym today, Mom. And geography and science. Mr. Wragg, the science teacher, is going to show us how to make a volcano. He was going to show us about smoke bombs, but he said that it probably wasn't the right time, what with the terrorist bombs in Manchester. Anyway, I can't wait. It's going to be great."

"Do you have your gym clothes?"

"Yeah, I packed them last night."

The skin on Clair's thin, pale face pulled taut in a wide grin. *Of course* Robbie had already packed his bag. He always did. Being prepared was another aspect of his personality, along with his knack of noticing when things were out of place, or new, or didn't belong.

"Good. Your lunch box is on the counter. I've made you a ham sandwich, and put in an apple and a juice box."

Robbie's eyes were wide with hope. "Grapes?"

"Yes."

"Thanks, Mom."

A loud slurp signaled the end of Robbie's sweet tea. With a wipe of his sleeve across his mouth, he pushed back from the table.

Clair watched with pride as he tucked his white shirt into gray pants, straightened the blue tie under the blue V-neck sweater, and wiggled gray-socked feet into shiny black shoes.

"I'm gonna go down and check on Shadow before school, Mom."

"Make sure you double-check you lock the door behind you, and bring the key back up, OK?"

"I always do, Mom. Don't worry. David told me a hundred times already."

Robbie, tall for his age with curly dark hair, sad blue eyes, and crooked teeth, both melted and hardened his mother's heart. He was so like—and unlike—his father.

"Back soon!" Robbie called over his shoulder as he took the key to David's flat from the hook by the fridge and rushed out the door.

Clair sighed at the closed door. Then there was David. He was kind to her and Robbie, and had helped them get settled when they'd moved into the flat last year.

Robbie, insecure and fearful for her, and about men in general, had begun to trust David. He was good for her, also. Their "dates" had been gentle and gradual, and he had the patience she required, but she wasn't sure she was ready to trust *any* man again.

FOUR

With Larry gone, and Andrew and Dean seated with their breakfasts, David regarded the airport shopping and eating area. As usual during the early hours, travelers were thinly spread along the terminal concourse, or clustered in small bunches around coffee stands and food kiosks. With his "one-eyed" surveillance from the mirror above the bar, a blurry image of two men walking toward him merged with the sound of a man shouting.

"I don't give a *shit* what you think."

The voice, loud, self-important, and raspy, bled across the hard tile of the sparsely occupied concourse.

"I pay you to screw the filmmakers and get me the best deal. You're my agent, not my mother. I need a bloody drink."

The man shouting was tall and broad, with styled dark hair. He wore designer jeans, a shirt, and a jacket ensemble prevalent on most upmarket men's health and fashion magazines.

He continued his oratory.

"What a great night. I could have anyone of them, you know."

"Indeed. Indeed you could, Jason," a restrained, polished voice replied with a hint of resignation.

Edging a barstool aside with his hip, the man with the loud voice placed a hand on the bar. David turned to welcome them, but was cut off before he began.

"Scotch," the man demanded. "Single malt, with lots of smoke and peat, and two ice cubes."

The man squinted to read the labels of the dozens of bottles arranged on the second shelf of the display that ran the length of the bar.

"I don't suppose you have any Caol Ila or Ardbeg from Islay?" he added pompously.

Three-quarters of the way into his usual "welcome smile," David's face and the skin of his cheek pulled backward toward his ears, contorting and twisting as recognition and emotion collided with professional habit.

The second man, compact, well-groomed, and tastefully dressed in business-casual blacks and grays, reacted to David's facial expression and leaned in.

"I see you recognize Mr. West," he said quietly.

West, impatient and hungover, interrupted them.

"Look, it's all very nice to be recognized, but could someone get me a damn drink?"

Using his acting skills, David reshaped his face into a compliant bartender and gestured to the bottles.

"I'm sorry. We don't have Caol Ila or Ardbeg, but we do have Octomore and Lagavulin, which are also from Islay."

"Yes, yes, either one will do. And put it over ice, but only *two* ice cubes." He pointed his thumb to the left.

"My friend here will have black coffee and water. That's all the bugger ever drinks."

With his back to the men, David reached for the Lagavulin. Sweat leeched from his body. He had indeed recognized the obnoxious man. Not as Jason West, but as Steve Rooke. A two-faced, deceitful, vain, and manipulative little bastard who had—for a short time—attended the same secondary school and drama classes as David.

Struggling to maintain his composure, David set the Scotch and a glass of water on the bar before he moved to the coffee machine. As it ground the beans and heated the water, thoughts of Steve Rooke rushed into David's mind.

Steve had been a year older than David when they had both participated and competed in the high school drama club. Steve, who had transferred to David's school toward the end of his last high school year, had taken a lead role from David when he had gotten into trouble for using a knife in a fight. After high school, David attended Manchester University, and Steve the University of Kent. Their paths hadn't crossed again for many years.

After university, Steve had renamed and rebranded with the stage name Jason West, and had gained some decent parts in made-for-TV dramas and supporting roles in one or two movies.

David's last recollection of being in Steve's proximity had been at a drunken post-event party that had followed a show during the London Fringe Festival in 2008. He didn't recall Steve so much, but he did remember how badly the party had ended.

The coffee, black and freshly brewed from a Venezia espresso machine, steamed as David placed the slim glass cup on the paper napkin in front of the quiet man.

Jason, his glass empty save for two misshapen ice cubes, tapped it with a finger and pointed at the menu, which David had provided with his first drink.

"Another Scotch would be good. Fresh glass and ice, if you don't mind. And I'll take a bagel and smoked salmon. But the bagel has to be peanut-free."

"You have a peanut allergy, sir?"

"Yes, otherwise I wouldn't be asking for peanut-free, would I?"

"I'm afraid I can't guarantee the bagels are peanut-free, but we do have some Jacob's crackers specifically for customers with a peanut allergy."

"Those bloody things. Oh, alright, but double up on the salmon will you, so I can drown the taste of the crackers."

"Certainly," David replied.

"Anything for you, sir?" he asked of Jason's companion.

"No, thank you," the quiet man answered with a disdainful glance at West.

Preparing the drink, David reluctantly recalled the summer of 2008, Jason West, and the beginning of the end of his own acting career.

In July, at the height of the summer, he'd had the lead role in *Hamlet* at the Duke of York's Theatre in London's West End. The part, complex and demanding, with over thirty thousand words of dialogue, had taxed David's acting abilities. In addition, the theatre, built in 1892, with limited air conditioning, had been stifling in the summer heat and compounded everyone's stress levels.

With the combined pressure of performance and environment, David had sweat like everyone else. Except in his case, an unexpected and inexplicable pungent aroma of fish had accompanied his perspiration.

David pushed the painful memory away, served Jason his second drink, and fetched the crackers and salmon that had appeared in the pass-through hatch that connected the out-of-sight food preparation area to the bar.

Relieved, but not surprised, given Jason's narcissistic nature, that the man had not recognized him, David added the crackers and salmon to the counter. Turning away to attend to another customer a few seats away at the bar, he caught the first words of a story Jason had begun to relate to his agent.

"Did I ever tell you about Wanda?"

At the mention of Wanda, David, along with his welcome smile, menu, and napkin, all choreographed to perfection, froze in front of the new customer. Face taut and shoulders hunched with tension, he took the customer's order and lingered by the terminal as Jason's agent responded without enthusiasm.

"Probably, but I don't recall. Is she another one of your conquests? If so, I don't want to hear…"

"No. Nothing like that. It's this place. You know, the smell of the fish. It reminds me of Wanda."

"Wanda. That's an uncommon name."

"That wasn't his real name. His name was Duncan, or Drew. We went to school together for a few months. Anyway, his name isn't important."

"Alright, go on then, but we have to be going soon."

A beep from the terminal demanded David tap the "order complete" icon on the screen. Instead, to maintain his proximity to Jason, he tapped the "cancel" button and re-entered the order.

Warming to his story as if he were on stage, Jason drew air and puffed out his chest.

"Back in 2007 or 2008, I'm not sure exactly, this guy Drew had a lead role in *Hamlet* at the Duke."

West's agent sipped his coffee and feigned interest in his client's story.

"Mm, *Hamlet* at the Duke. That's a good role. Did he…"

"Shut up. I'm telling the story. Anyway, as I said, he had the lead role and he was doing alright until the middle of summer, when he suddenly began to smell."

"What do mean, smell?"

Jason chuckled cruelly, distorting his handsome features.

"Smell, stink, give off an odorous aroma."

"You mean he had B.O.?"

"God, no, it was much worse than that," Jason replied smiling. "He stank."

"Stank?"

"Yes, it was awful. Things got so bad that the other actors complained and threatened to stop working with him."

"Oh, come on, Jason. Surely all he had to do was wash?"

"That's what pissed people off. He said he did, but halfway into the performance, he would stink again."

David's teeth compressed as his finger stabbed the terminal screen. Anger he hadn't felt for many years churned in his stomach and climbed into his chest.

"Poor fellow," the agent said. "I expect he must have eaten something. Maybe a bad curry?"

"No, no, it wasn't curry. It was fish. Yeah, fish. Can you believe it? And it got worse. The play ended a couple of weeks after he started to, you know, smell, but that wasn't the end of it. You see, word got around about his smell, and I heard that when he auditioned for a part, the producers actually had people sniff him."

Incredulous, the agent put his half-empty cup on the bar as he addressed Jason.

"Oh, give me a break. You expect me to believe that people actually sniffed him at auditions. Really, Jason."

"Look, it's the truth. I'm telling you, he got sniffed, and guess what?"

The agent waited, his face impatient as a chaperone with an unpleasant child.

"He stank. It was incredible. I mean, he wasn't a half-bad actor, and might have even made a living at some point, but the man just didn't do anything about how he smelled. It's as though he didn't know, or just didn't care."

Without any further comment, the agent pulled money from a pocket and placed it on the bar.

"Anyway," Jason continued. "That's why we called him Wanda. You know the movie with John Cleese, *A Fish Called Wanda*? Pretty funny, eh? Guess what else? People started leaving little goldfish in plastic bags for him. One time, I was at a party when someone put a goldfish in his wineglass. That was hilarious. Everyone fell about the place. Of course, we were all hammered, but anyway, it was still pretty funny."

The agent got down from his barstool, straightened his coat, and gave his client a cool stare as he spoke.

"Actually, Jason, no, I don't think it's funny at all. You know there was a movie a few years ago, called *The Boy Who Smells Like Fish*."

Jason, ignorant and insensitive as his narcissism demanded, laughed as he spluttered, "Oh, my god, really? I don't believe it. I…"

"Shut up, Jason. I'm not telling you this to bolster your adolescent sense of humor. The movie is about a schoolboy who has a rare disease that makes him smell like dead fish…"

"Ha ha, you're even worse than me. That's a good one."

Resigned, the agent stepped away from the bar.

"I don't suppose you know what happened to the actor? What was his name?"

"Like I said, Drew or Duncan, or something like that. I've no idea. Anyway, the best part is, you know the goldfish in his drink at the party…"

"Don't tell me it was you, Jason."

Off his barstool, leaving his agent to pay, Jason grinned widely as he chirped an indifferent response.

"You'll never know. Anyway, the guy really lost it on everyone. Broke someone's jaw, smashed the place up, and got arrested. The schmuck probably works in a fish and chip shop or something."

Rooted in front of the terminal, David's vision blurred as he watched the fuzzy shape of Jason West saunter across the concourse toward the departures area.

~

Andrew and Dean, their breakfast over, exchanged concerned glances as they paused in front of David to say goodbye.

"Are you alright, David?" Andrew asked.

Forcing a smile to his flushed face, David managed a soft reply.

"Yes, thank you. Have a good flight. I'll see you next week."

"Are you sure, David?" Dean asked. "You're a bit pale, and sweating."

"Yes, really, thanks," David stammered as he gripped the bar for support and watched Dean and Andrew leave to catch their flight to Paris.

Embarrassment and humiliation surged through him, fueling his anger and rage, which in turn, triggered his stress. If David had suffered from asthma, he would have reached for a puffer. But his disease had no cure, and there was no inhaler to provide relief. Unrestrained, his condition exploded, and his body exhaled sweat. And with the sweat came the odor.

Since his diagnosis in late 2008, a balance of routine, disease management, and therapy had governed David's life. The scientific community called it Trimethylaminuria, or in his case, secondary Trimethylaminuria, or TMAU2.

Laypeople called it Fish Odor Syndrome. To David, the disease was a burden that had ended his acting career, limited his friendships, and foiled his attempts to form intimate relationships.

His routine involved avoiding stress, specific types of food and taking medication. Personal hygiene regulated the worst physical manifestations of his disease, and therapy subdued the dormant violence that his resentment of Trimethylaminuria brought to the surface.

"What's wrong, David?" Nancy asked as she struggled with an armful of discarded plates and cups from several tables. "Are you going to faint?"

Between rapid breaths, David used his "standby excuse."

"I'm OK. It's my bloody anemia. I must have forgotten to take my iron supplements. I have some pills in my locker. I just need a few minutes to sit down. Can you manage, Nancy?"

"Of course, David. Take your time. It's been quite a while since you forgot your pills. Almost a year, isn't it?"

"Yeah, about that. A year older, a year more forgetful," he joked to cover his fury inside. "I won't be long."

Perspiration sucked his clothes to his body as he squelched across the concourse to the staff room located through the maintenance door that housed Larry's cleaning cart and supplies. Small and windowless, it was cramped but well-ventilated by large vents. It housed staff lockers, a sink, and a toilet.

With his forehead pressed against the cool metal door of his locker, beads of sweat fell from the tip of his nose. The droplets splattered onto the floor, each impact amplifying his anger. Rage fed on the anger until he pounded his fists on the metal door to obliterate the mocking, arrogant image of Jason West from his mind.

FIVE

The second-floor, third solid-steel door on the right marked "Personal Services" fronted Dr. Rachel White's counseling and support practice. Operating alone, save for Rupert, the receptionist and office administrator, Rachel had served Feltham's psychiatric community since 2010.

David, a sheen of sweat on his cheeks, slammed the door behind him and glared at Rupert. The longtime employee sensed David's palpable anger and sought to soothe him with a sincere smile and soft tones.

"Hello, David. You're a little early today. Rachel is in the bathroom. She'll be with you in a moment."

Rupert had several tactics to stall agitated patients. The "in the bathroom" line was only for extreme cases, but in Rupert's judgment, David's demeanor made this one of those times.

David's fists clenched and unclenched as he paced the room. After a few minutes, when Rupert judged David's mood had tempered a little, he signaled for him to enter Rachel's office.

Inside, David unloaded.

"Right in front of me, as though I wasn't there. The bastard laughed as he told his bloody agent about me.

You know what he said. He told him about how they used to call me Wanda. A fish called fucking Wanda. You know how many times I heard that whispered behind me?"

Rachel, fiftysomething, trim, well-dressed, and compassionate beyond what was good for her own mental health, listened closemouthed to David's every word. Horrified by his anger and rage, she struggled to project a calmness she did not feel.

While he vented, Rachel lamented with sadness as her patient returned to the bitterness and loathing she had seen in him during their first sessions back in 2011.

Initially, all David had needed was to rant and rave. And he had. For three months, three times a week, he had ranted and Rachel had listened. Gradually, with coping mechanisms, a strict food regimen, and counseling, he had made progress.

For the past year and a half, Rachel had reduced the sessions to once a week. But now, in front of her eyes, David had regressed to the primitive stage he had been at their first session.

Eyes downward, David strode from door to window and back. Words, harsh and vile, spat from his mouth.

"And you know what else? That bastard West. Jason fucking West, for god's sake. The goldfish. Yeah, that one. *The* one. It was him. He told his agent that he put the fish in my glass at the party. You know the party, right?"

Rachel did know. A fight, people sent to hospital, and David sedated and arrested.

"Yes. Course you do. That was the end, wasn't it? No more work for David after that. Not just that David stinks like dead fish. No, David's violent. Unstable. Goddamn them all."

With his coat still zipped and his pace frantic, his perspiration accelerated and the odor strengthened.

Rachel, struggling to ignore the smell, thought as she listened. For David's first months of therapy, she had used Noxzema under her nose and held the session at the end of the day to allow the room to air out. She had even put a blanket on the sofa. Unaware of what had happened earlier that day, and having not used Noxzema, or a blanket, for years, Rachel gritted her teeth now to check an urge to gag. As he continued his rant, Rachel mentally reviewed the causes and treatment for David's disease.

Emotional upset, stress, and sweating were three key environmental factors he needed to avoid to help manage his condition. Medical factors included low doses of antibiotics to reduce gut bacteria, activated charcoal to decrease free trimethylamine in his urine, and vitamin B2 supplements, three to five times a day, to enhance FMO3 enzyme activity. Washing with body soaps with a pH between 5.5 and 6.5 was another. Regimented adherence to a program that included all these factors had enabled David to successfully manage his Fish Odor Syndrome for several years.

An abrupt halt and a shouted accusation startled Rachel from her analytical review.

"You don't need to pretend, Rachel. Your nostrils are straining to close. I can see it in your eyes. I know I stink. The whole fucking world knows I stink."

Emotional and physical exhaustion forced David to sit. With his head in his hands, a growl leaked through his fingers.

"I'm gonna kill him."

Despite the smell, Rachel drew a deep breath. Now was the time. Twenty years a registered counselor, graduated from this and that, and a member of all she needed to be, Rachel was qualified. But much more than that, she could read her patient. Body language, posture, and a final statement of action or intent were her signals to engage. Ready, Rachel began.

"And what will you do after you kill him?"

"What?" David asked, his fingers splaying slightly to reveal his face. "What do you mean? I don't know. Who cares?"

"What I mean, David, is that even if you do kill Jason West, would anything really change? Would you be any different?"

He hissed out a snarl.

"I don't care. He would be *gone*. That would be different."

"You won't always be like this, David. It seems hard now, and maybe even impossible…"

Rachel paused. As expected, David remained silent. Like most patients, he wanted to be helped.

"Do you remember when we first began working together?"

A slow nod indicated his acknowledgment.

"I remember. You were a lot like you are today. Filled with anger and hatred. But you're not that person anymore. You found your way back to yourself. Who you really are."

Hands down from his face, David's voice cracked with defeat and resignation.

"What's the point? There's no cure. Special soaps, special vitamins, watching the foods I eat, no stress, changing my fucking clothes three times a day. Working in a sushi bar. I'm sick of it."

Rachel leaned toward him.

"There is your sister, Jenny, and your mom and dad. They all love you, David. And there is Clair, and her son, Robbie. You've told me how well that's going."

"Doesn't matter, does it? They've never smelled me like this. It's not going to work out now. It never does."

Rachel, aware of David's failed relationships, had high hopes for Clair, who from his account, seemed different from other women he had dated.

David's calmness, Rachel knew, could leave at any moment, so she chose her next words carefully.

"You have made things work out, David. You've succeeded better than many in your situation. You have a job, a home, a close family. You have a social life with the quiz team at the pub, football matches, and from what you tell me, things are going very well with Clair. And don't forget, you've already told Clair about your condition, and it hasn't seemed to make any difference, has it?"

Rachel, still on tenterhooks despite David's outward calmness, continued to focus on the positive.

"You asked me what's the point. Jenny, your parents, Clair, Robbie, and you, David. That's the point. All your hard work these past years. Your successes. You have a life, David. One that continues to improve."

Leaning close, Rachel gently took his hands in hers and looked him in the eye.

"Revenge isn't the answer, David."

Breaking eye and hand contact, he looked past Rachel at some unseen entity, held his arms wide, and projected in a menacing voice an excerpt from Niccolo Machiavelli's *The Prince*.

"'If an injury has to be done to a man, it should be so severe that his vengeance need not be feared.'"

SIX

Unable to work on Tuesday or Wednesday, because the anger he couldn't calm made him sweat, which in turn, made him stink, David stayed in his flat to seethe in isolation and darkness. Despite pleas from his sister, Jenny, he cancelled their regular Wednesday night dinner. Instead, he dug in his closet for the well-worn copy of *The Prince* he had first read in high school as background for the play *Othello*.

With a boost of supplements, careful diet, many showers, and an undefined emotion after reading *The Prince*, David regained some composure and went back to work on Thursday.

Despite a return to his regimen, both Thursday and Friday required two changes of clothes. He also avoided his evening social activities at the Bell on the Green pub, as well as his budding relationship with Clair and her son, Robbie.

All week he had thought about Rachel and her words. Her assessment and advice, he knew, were true. Yet, he wanted another way. Why, he asked himself repeatedly, should Jason West endure no hardship or consequences for what he had done? How many others had West hurt? How many had suffered his abuse and ridicule? How many more people still suffered in silence to satisfy the insecurity of West's narcissism?

Saturday and Sunday went well. By Sunday evening, he felt calm enough meet and talk with Clair. She knew about his condition, but had never witnessed a real breakdown. David didn't mentioned Jason West, and instead said that his lapse was due to work stress.

On the following Monday, David went to work, even though he was agitated and a little sweaty. Like most service industry workers, he lived paycheck to paycheck, disease or not, and work was a necessity, not a hobby. Adherence to his nutrition, supplements, and hygiene routines provided a good start to the day, and he arrived at work with relative confidence.

However, when Andrew and Dean stopped by for breakfast and asked if he felt better than the previous Monday, thoughts of West immediately soured David's mood. An encounter with Larry, who had commented that the bar area smelled a bit off, and a suspicion that Nancy had flinched when she squeezed past him, added to David's stress. By 9:30 a.m., he had to change his clothes and apply large amounts of deodorant. By the end of his shift at noon, his clothes were so damp, his armpits, bottom, and nipples chaffed with every step he took.

He returned home as quick as possible, closed the front door, drew the curtains, and began his routine all over again. First, he stripped naked in front of the washing machine and added baking soda for the wash and vinegar for the rinse cycle. After downing several B2 supplements, he took a cool shower using Neutrogena Extra Gentle Cleanser. Then he donned loose-fitting shorts and sat on a dining room chair with a fan blowing gently across his body. He drew deep, slow breaths and opened a cold can of Foster's lager.

Unlike 95 percent of other sufferers, who could not tolerate alcohol without it producing significant odor, David was thankful for the small mercy that his body allowed him to consume beer in limited amounts without the consequences being too severe. As he savored his drink, Shadow, his charcoal-gray cat, purred and wound himself between David's legs. A resident for six months, Shadow had become attuned to his master's routine and waited expectantly for his afternoon snack.

He hadn't wanted a cat. It had appeared on the front step of the main entrance to the flats on a cold February morning as David was leaving for work at four a.m. He had shooed it away, but the next morning, it was back.

After three mornings, he relented, macabrely telling himself that the cat must be drawn to his condition. He gave the cat some milk before shooing it on its way again. Of course, it returned once again. By the end of the week, it had taken up residence.

An unexpected benefit of Shadow's arrival was that Robbie, Clair's eleven-year-old son, volunteered to visit the cat in the morning before school. As David left for work at four a.m., Robbie's play-with-the-cat visits around eight a.m. kept Shadow happy.

Shadow had soon become a catalyst for David to interact with Robbie and form a friendship that drew him closer to Robbie's mother, Clair. All having arrived within the previous twelve months, Shadow, Robbie, and Clair gave him a sense of belonging and purpose that he had been lacking since the brutal and traumatic end of his acting career.

Together with Shadow's purr, the clunk of the washing machine as it switched from wash to rinse nudged David from his seat and into the kitchen. After feeding Shadow, he assembled ingredients for his midafternoon lunch.

Guided by the need to avoid foods containing the chemicals trimethylamine, choline, and trimethylamine N-oxide, David gathered chicken breast, white rice, green peppers, and tomatoes. Half an hour later, he poked at his stir-fry and tried to dispel the thoughts of Jason West that stabbed his consciousness. A chirp from his phone, and the recognition the caller was his sister, Jenny, finally edged Jason West from his mind.

"Hi, Jenny. What's up?"

"Hi, David. You know nothing's up with me. I'm just calling to check up on you. How did it go at work today?"

Jenny was his rock, anchor, and best friend, and had helped him more than any scientifically proven food regimen or highly qualified therapist. His sister, aside from Rachel, was the only other person who knew about Jason West's airport visit. One thing Jenny had gotten him to agree to was that he would never lie to her about his condition or his feelings, especially if he felt like he wanted to do himself—or someone else—harm.

"Not so good, Jenny."

"What happened?"

"The day started well, but then someone asked me about last week."

"You told someone at work what happened?"

"No, no, never. When it happened, two regular customers noticed I didn't look too good, and they asked if I was OK. Well, this morning, they asked me if I was better. Their question set me thinking again. Then that bloody Larry started on about the bar smelling funny, and I'm pretty sure Nancy could smell me, so everything…"

"Oh, David, I'm so sorry. Shall I come over after work? I could be there by five."

Torn between wanting Jenny's help and needing to be alone, he declined.

"It's alright. I've done all the things I need to and I'm feeling better. I think I'll just watch a movie and have some quiet time."

"If you're sure. I mean, I really can come over. I have no plans tonight."

His sister, David knew, rarely had plans, and in sympathy, he almost changed his mind.

"Thanks Jenny, but I'll be OK."

"Hey, David," she said brightly. "It's Monday. You have your appointment with Rachel today, right? She's just what you need right now. You always feel better after talking with her."

"Er, yes, that's right" David answered, uncharacteristically unsure if he wanted a session with his therapist today. "The appointment is at four thirty."

"You should go, David," Jenny encouraged him, her voice filled with care and compassion.

"Of course."

"Good. Now, we're still on for Wednesday, right? We can't miss another one."

"Yes. I'm looking forward to it. I'll see you at five thirty, as usual?"

"Alright. I love you, David. You won't forget to go to see Rachel?"

"I won't forget, Jenny."

"Promise?"

"Yes, promise. I love you too. See you Wednesday."

David pressed the end call button, but still deep in thought, he kept the phone in his hand.

His sister was right. Rachel had certainly helped him over the years, but something had changed. He didn't know what it was, but he sensed a need for a different kind of therapy now. A kind that would address an undefined or an unacknowledged premonition of something to come.

Shaking his head at the ambiguity of his feelings, David put the phone down and checked his watch. Three thirty-five. If he left now, he would just make it to his session with Rachel. Indecision and guilt weighed on him as he paced and debated with himself. Swayed by his promise never to lie to Jenny, he quickly got dressed.

SEVEN

Mondays and Fridays were Robbie's favorite after-school days because his mom finished work at three in the afternoon. After school, Robbie walked to Singh's variety shop where she worked, and after his mom let him select a treat, they walked home together.

On the other days—Tuesday, Wednesday, and Thursday—his mom ended work at six, and Robbie walked home alone, or with other kids from the next street over. Because his mom didn't get home until late, Robbie had to check in with David when he got home from school. Today, Robbie was extra pleased it was Monday, because he hadn't wanted to check in with David. Well, he did, and he didn't.

He did, because he liked David, and his mom liked him. He was also fairly sure that he and his mom had kissed. To Robbie, this meant that "it" was pretty serious. Plus, David's cat was really smart and very fun to play with. And he was sure that David liked him. But all this liking each other, that was actually the problem.

Something had happened last week. David had changed. That was why he was glad it was Monday and he didn't have to check in with David. He just needed to figure out what was wrong, which was what he was about to do.

Under his loft bed, seated at his desk, Robbie selected spiral notebook number 7b from the neat line of books ranged against the wall. Number 7a was stored in the closet for future reference, should he need to verify or check any previous event. Robbie opened the book and flipped about halfway through the 175 A4-sized lined pages, and stopped at the ones headed with the current day and date.

This page, like all the others, had been divided into four columns: "Time," "Action," "Comment," and "Unusual." Robbie paused and considered his most recent entry:

4:00 a.m. / Left for work / Maybe he is better / Nil.

Then he flipped back to the previous Monday and began to read his entries for his observations on David's life for the past seven days, one line at time. As he read, Robbie noted on a separate piece of paper any entries he had made under the headings "Comment" and "Unusual."

Monday: Didn't answer door at 3:15 p.m. / Left at 3:45 p.m. / Came back later than usual / Looked angry / Why?

Tuesday: Didn't go to work / Heard him moving around—didn't answer door in morning—didn't see Shadow / Didn't see him / Knocked on door—but he didn't answer / What's wrong?

Wednesday: No work again! / Checked in after school, but didn't let me in to see Shadow / Didn't open door—said all OK / Jenny DID NOT come for dinner!!!

Thursday: Left for work as usual / Fed Shadow / Flat smelled of fish / Checked in after school—he said hi, but not like normal / No date with Mom for their quiz night / Why?

Friday: Left for work / Fed Shadow / Still a bit fishy smelling in flat / Didn't see him / What's going on?

Saturday: David home / Didn't answer door / Why?

Sunday: 9:00 p.m. / Mom goes to see David / I fell asleep.

Back at the current day, Robbie read his most recent entry.

Monday: 8:00 a.m. / Fed Shadow / Mom quiet / Said we will talk tonight after school.

Concerned and worried, Robbie set the paper aside and added a new entry:

3:30 p.m. / Didn't answer door to me / I can hear him on the phone / He had better not hurt Mom!!!

A tear slipped from his eye as he wrote the last entry. Men had hurt his mom before. And he wouldn't let that happen again.

Then there was a light knock on his bedroom door, and his mom's voice asking if she could come in. Robbie tucked the piece of paper out of sight in the notebook.

"Hi, Robbie. Are you doing your homework?"

Not wanting to lie, he answered honestly.

"No, I'm thinking about David and you. What's wrong, Mom? Has he hurt you?"

Clair, her nametag from the store still pinned to the right side of her brown-and-black work shirt, spoke softly as she moved toward him.

"Oh, Robbie, no. Not at all. David would never hurt me, or anyone."

Stifling more tears, Robbie ceded his chair to his mom. When she sat down, he squeezed onto her knees and eagerly accepted the arms that embraced him.

"Why would you think David had hurt me?"

" 'Cause something has happened," he blurted out. "Last week David didn't go to work and he didn't answer the door, even though he was home. Jenny didn't come for dinner on Wednesday. You didn't go for your quiz night date on Thursday, and he doesn't want to see me anymore. And his flat smells like fish!"

"Oh, Robbie," Clair murmured as she nuzzled in. "Nothing is wrong with me and David, and he still likes you very much."

"But you talked with him last night, and now he won't even open the door again today. And I can tell that you are sad."

Loosening her arms, Clair turned Robbie to face her and held his eyes with hers.

"Yes, I am sad, but not because he hurt me. I'm upset and concerned because David has been unwell. He got sick last Monday and took a few days off, then went back to work. He just needed some time to get better."

"But why did he ignore me today, Mom? I mean, we could help him. Make him food and stuff."

"I don't know for sure, but I guess that David must have gotten sick again at work today and he probably just wants to be alone."

Robbie hugged his mom tightly.

"What's wrong with him? Is he going to die?"

"No, nothing like that. It's, well, kind of difficult to explain."

Robbie eased back and waited.

Clair studied her son. Always observant and analytical, and "older" than his years, Robbie would not be satisfied with a white lie, and besides, she didn't *want* to lie to him.

She had lied to him before, to hide the truth about his father, the drugs, and the violence. After that, she had promised herself that she would not lie to her son ever again. Even if it meant breaking her promise to David to not to tell anyone. Surely he would understand the need to explain things to a child.

"*Mom*," Robbie urged her, impatient and wide-eyed.

"Well, I can't pronounce the name of it properly, but David has something called Trime-thylamin-uria," she replied, sounding the letters and syllables out slowly.

"What?"

"Trime-thylamin-uria. Anyway, it's also called Fish Odor Syndrome."

"That must be why his flat smelled of fish last week!"

Halfway between a grimace and a smile, Clair tried to explain.

"Well, er, yes, that is probably why. Look, David has a disease that makes his sweat smell like dead fish."

Amused by what his mom had said, Robbie grinned.

"No way, Mom! You're joking! That's just weird. What's really wrong with him?"

"It's not funny, Robbie. If he gets stressed out, or hot, or worried, or anything at all that could make him sweat, he, well, you know…"

"You mean he smells like fish?"

"Yes, and when he does, he just gets more stressed and worried, which makes him sweat more, and it just keeps getting worse."

"Why doesn't he go to the doctor and get a pill or something?"

Somber and serious, Clair held Robbie close.

"There is no cure for it."

"But how can that be?"

"I'm not sure. David says it's a genetic disease, but he has another version called TMAU2, and…"

With his mind fully engaged and working overtime, Robbie moved to his desk and turned on his computer. As he moved the pointer and clicked, he challenged his mom.

"But there *must* be a cure. I mean, David doesn't smell of fish *all* the time. I don't understand."

"If he eats certain foods, washes with special soaps, and takes vitamins, then most of the time he is OK. But sometimes, it gets really bad, and he gets very upset."

"Is it new? I mean, did he catch it from someone?"

"No, I think he's had it all his life, but it seemed to sort of begin in his twenties. I'm not really sure. He told me a few months ago about it, and that it had something to do with him losing his job as an actor."

"David is an actor?"

Robbie was surprised and impressed.

"Well, he used to be. Now he sometimes does voices for commercials."

"Was he in any movies?"

"No, he mainly acted in plays, on the stage. Anyway, that's not what it's about, Robbie. The thing is,

David has to be careful, and if he is, then he doesn't have the problem."

Robbie was thinking about David's flat and how clean it was. There was never any dirty laundry lying around, and the windows were open all the time. Now it all made sense.

"So, Mom," Robbie said, brightening up as comprehension set in. "David was just sick, right? So he's not mad at you or me, and everything will go back to normal."

"Yes, that's right, but it might take a few days to settle down, so we need to be patient."

"OK, Mom. I'm going to Google it."

Clair, relieved that her son finally understood, got up from the chair and spoke quietly.

"Robbie, don't tell David that you know OK? He will tell you in his own time, I'm sure. Let's just say that you know he's been a bit unwell, OK?"

Robbie pulled the chair under his bum and began typing.

"OK, I get it. I'll find out more and see how we can help."

Clair paused in the bedroom doorway to watch her bright, intelligent, caring son. Robbie would research David's disease and know more about it than she did.

She wondered where her relationship with David would lead, if anywhere. Truthfully, his odor *was* noticeable, but not always, and not always so bad. Anyway, there was a lot more to him than his disease, and he was very good to Robbie. Sighing with the weight of a single parent, Clair closed the door.

From downstairs, the sound of David's door closing echoed through the building.

EIGHT

Lulled by the heat and rhythm of the bus on the way to his counseling appointment with Rachel, her impact on his life filled David's thoughts.

Rachel had never asked, "How are you feeling today?" and David liked that. When he had "gone off the deep end" in 2008, well-meaning friends, his agent, his colleagues, and even his parents had asked him that question.

He *hated* that question, mainly because he couldn't answer it. More accurately, he was afraid to tell people about the hate and rage that consumed him. That he felt helpless. That an urge to hurt those who had mocked and ridiculed him burned inside.

In late 2008, unable to cope with a disease that had yet to be fully diagnosed, David found himself unemployed and living alone in his central London flat near Hyde Park. He had hidden his true feelings. Untreated, he began to make moral judgments and construct self-righteous rationales for killing competitors and fellow actors. He had placed his well-being above all others, and demanded loyalty, all the while expecting betrayal.

Shunned by his profession, he was isolated, ashamed, and hurtling toward depression. His inevitable breakdown led to a twenty-four-hour sedation session at the Charing Cross Hospital A&E, a psychological evaluation, and a call to Jenny to take him home and "get him some help."

Throughout 2009, three therapists who all asked how he felt had preceded Rachel. Then, in January 2010, he had found her. She listened, formed her own opinion about how he felt, and articulated and expressed "his" feelings in ways he could finally understand. Three months later, Rachel gradually encouraged David to discover what might be at the root of his desire to hurt—and even kill people.

Shepherding him through a review of his formative teenage years, Rachel helped him consider that his violent thoughts had likely been seeded through a combination of two things: a need to "fit in," and the influence of a well-meaning teacher, who after witnessing David's behavioral "talents" and problems, had introduced him to acting.

Mimicking other people had been David's ticket to acceptance in a rowdy gang of high school boys. Pupils, parents, and teachers could not escape his knack for copying a person's voice and mannerisms.

Often, David's antics led to fights, which led to bruises from the other boy—or boys—and a sore ass from the headmaster's cane. But that was the price he paid for a certain "popularity." Neither bothered him as much as the stupidity of having to stand under the clock in the school entrance "for all the school to see" what a "bad" pupil he had become. Thirty minutes of taunts, finger pointing, and snickers was a waste of time, despite the headmaster's views that "a little humiliation might bring some humility."

By David's thirteenth birthday, the cycle of misbehavior, fighting, punishment, and humiliation had become firmly entrenched, despite interventions from school councillors and his parents. The consensus in the staff room was that despite above-average grades, David would inevitably "come to a bad end."

The possibility that he was a child with high-functioning abilities, under-challenged and misunderstood in the mainstream school environment should have been apparent. They should also have considered the likelihood that he had unconsciously channeled his high-functioning abilities into misbehavior and disobedience. If viewed together, authorities might have recognized that such characteristics were common attributes of a potentially psychopathic personality.

Fortunately, or so it seemed at the time, Ms. Cook, a newly graduated, enthusiastic and innovative drama teacher armed with the latest teaching techniques, arrived at the school at the start of David's fourteenth year. Ms. Cook's long blonde hair, fair skin, well-developed breasts, and slim figure, combined with her flamboyant clothes and a ready smile, did not go unnoticed by David, or the other testosterone-laden high school boys.

Initially attracted as a result of his adolescent lustful desire, David attended the first meeting of Ms. Cook's after-school drama class. Accompanied by friends who only came to "ogle Cook's tits," David soon mocked the boys who bravely attempted to read lines from various Shakespearian plays. A few weeks into the term, when the "fun" of ridiculing "drama queens" had worn off, David, without telling his "friends," had decided to attend more drama classes.

Unknown to him, Ms. Cook had noticed his quiet observations from the back of the gymnasium. After learning of his mimicry skills, she bade her time until the day he shuffled his feet as he hung around after the others had left for the "chance" encounter he really wanted.

David's transformation didn't occur overnight. An ability to derogate and insult through mimicry, no matter how accurate the verbal and physical imitation, had little to do with the creation of an animated fictional character based on the written word. However, gradually Ms. Cook's patience, professional skill, and her belief in David's natural talent steered him onto a different path.

By the end of the school year, he had ceased to be a frequent fixture under the clock at the school's entrance. Fights and conflicts were few, and a new group of "artsy" friends fed and nurtured his newly discovered passion and interest in acting. His three minor roles and one supporting role in Ms. Cook's four short, one-act school plays had whetted his appetite. To the relief of his parents, he joined the Altrincham Youth Drama Society, an amateur group headed by Ms. Cook and her "friend," Ms. Smith.

David wasn't the only kid from his high school to join. Steve Rooke, now known as Jason West, had been a year older than David. Insincere, egocentric, and cunning, he had also caught Ms. Cook's eye.

David and Steve had vied for acting parts—as well as Ms. Cook's attention—throughout the last term of the school year. At the end of the year, with Steve/Jason pursuing self-discovery during a "gap" year prior to university, David had a clear field with Ms. Cook and the Altrincham Youth Drama Society.

In the first week of the summer holidays, Ms. Cook addressed the twenty-five members of the Youth Drama Society and informed the eager group that the theatrical objective for the summer would be to perform William Shakespeare's tragedy, *Othello*, and that for background, the first step was to read Machiavelli's *The Prince*.

The directive to read a treatise written five hundred years ago by an Italian political theorist received mixed reviews from the drama society. Until, that is, Ms. Cook's use of excerpts and characters from *Othello* connected and outlined *The Prince*'s themes of free will, virtue, human nature, hatred, and statesmanship and warcraft. This comparison animated and encouraged the young actors. None more so than David, who was soon seduced by the ruthlessness of *The Prince*.

Ecstatic at the news that he would play the antagonist, Iago, who adhered to Machiavelli's ruthless ideals, David had worked and studied harder than ever.

According to Rachel, much of David's post-breakdown morality, self-righteousness, desire to kill competitors, and fixation on loyalty and betrayal began with his adolescent exposure and immersion in Machiavelli's *The Prince*, as well as his study of the character Iago.

In Rachel's opinion, and unbeknown to David, the philosophy of Machiavelli's *Prince*, as expressed through the ruthless and devious machinations of Iago in *Othello*, had entered the matrix of David's mind and etched itself into a corner in the recesses of his nascent psychopathic character.

~

Without remembering the bus ride, or how he had entered the building, David suddenly stood before Rupert.

"Ah, David," he exclaimed with surprise. "I guess you didn't get my message?"

"What?"

Well-groomed and impeccably dressed, just like the stereotype of his sexual orientation demanded, Rupert stood with open arms.

"I'm really sorry, David, but Rachel has a personal emergency and had to leave the office. I did try your cell phone."

David checked his phone and saw one message waiting.

"Rachel really does want to see you, though, and she asked me to assure you that she is very sorry that she couldn't be here. We have managed to free up some time tomorrow at four. Could you come then?"

David's mind shrouded in the fog of memory, and with unbidden lines from *Othello* pricking his thoughts, he waved a hand at Rupert.

"Yeah, OK, I mean, it's probably karma that Rachel's not here."

Rupert, encouraged by his boss to observe and report any "out of character" behavior by patients, made a mental note to tell Rachel of David's fatalistic comment.

"We'll see you tomorrow then, at four?"

"Yes, alright," David replied, without conviction.

He had just decided that he needed a different kind of therapy, anyway. He needed to watch a movie. And he knew exactly which one.

NINE

Strangely relieved by Rachel's sudden unavailability, and eager to be home, David impulsively took a taxi. Despite guilt about avoiding Robbie, he hurried into his flat. Closing the front door, he reassured himself that his talk with Clair on Sunday had explained things, and that she would find a way to tell Robbie without revealing his disease. Anyway, he would make it up to the kid when he felt better. Right now, he just needed to be alone to escape into one of his favorite movies, one he had been thinking of for several days: *Sleuth*.

As a teenager, in the mid-1990s, David's interest in movies had matched those of his peers with blockbusters, such as *Under Siege, Lock, Stock and Two Smoking Barrels, Trainspotting, Braveheart, Face/Off*, and others.

Success with the school drama club, which included assignments to watch movie and TV adaptations of Shakespeare's tragedies *Othello, Hamlet, King Lear*, and *Coriolanus*, significantly changed his tastes and understanding of movies. In his late teens, David's interest in films had become a hobby, and in his mid-twenties, at the peak of his budding acting career, they had become a passion.

His ardor wasn't for the action or the story line, but for the acting. How the actor portrayed the character, and if, in his opinion, he or she succeeded or not. It was this focus on the acting that first drew David to the movie *Sleuth*.

Originally a 1970s stage play, *Sleuth* became a 1972 British mystery thriller film starring two of David's favorite actors: Laurence Olivier and Michael Caine.

Made more than a decade before his birth, *Sleuth* had become one of David's top ten favorite movies since his first viewing at the Curzon repertory cinema in his hometown of Altrincham. He had gone to watch the onetime screening of *Sleuth* because it was widely thought to be the basis for another of David's favorite movies, *Deathtrap*, a 1982 American thriller which also stared Michael Caine.

Sleuth, a murder mystery centered on a duel of intellects with unexpected twists and turns, pitted a thriller writer, who reveled in his own cleverness, against a man engaged in an affair with the writer's soon-to-be murdered wife. Replete with deceit, shams, betrayal, conspiracy, and disguises, David had been awed by Caine and Olivier's performances.

Luxury wasn't part of David's life—not because he didn't appreciate or want luxurious things, but because serving overpriced seafood to weary travelers provided little more than a living wage. Even in the depressed and undesirable outskirts of London's Feltham town, his income did not stretch that far.

However, he did have one indulgence: a fifty-inch Samsung HD flat-screen TV, and Samsung 5.1 Channel HT-H5500W home-theatre system, complete with wireless headphones. Acquiring the system had taken fifty-two weekly payments, and David treated his prize possession with care. A bed-sized black cloth covered the TV, stand, receiver, and front speakers. Under the living room window, out of sight, a matching cloth covered the rear speakers.

In front of the cloth-covered Samsung system, a small twenty-inch TV with rabbit ear antennae sat on a worn rectangle IKEA coffee table gathering dust. Paranoid that his system, which could be seen from the window, might be stolen, David used the table and small TV as a decoy. Only Jenny, Clair, and Robbie, who had all watched movies with him, knew about the TV system.

With the decoy TV out of the way, stir-fry dishes in the sink, and a cold can of Foster's lager, he settled into his worn vinyl sofa and pressed play. Shadow, familiar with the routine, snuggled beside him.

The movie, as always, filled his mind and pushed away unwanted thoughts, if only temporarily. Soothed by the familiar scenes and awed by the acting, David followed passively along until he sat up to savor his favorite scene.

As the movie concluded its elaborate and twisted plot, Andrew, played by Olivier, shot Milo, played by Caine. When Milo died, he told Andrew to be sure to tell the police that it was "all just a bloody game." As the credits rolled, thoughts of murder—or more precisely, the process of murder—entered David's thoughts.

Motive, David thought to himself. Ninety-nine percent of the time, it all came down to motive. Or more accurately, the ability of the antagonist, usually a detective of some kind, to distill from the murder victim or suspects a reason for the person's death that eventually resulted in the killer's capture.

Opportunity, related to the time and place of death, often followed motive and means. Then method and knowledge appeared in time for the antagonist to put them all together into a compelling narrative.

Physical evidence, such as CCTV, ticket stubs, and of course, DNA, was also gathered to support the motive, opportunity, and the means. Add witnesses to the evidence, and a case was made, the killer caught, and a conviction secured.

Unnoticed by David, as he continued to muse about the mistakes killers made, the credits ended and the screen went black, then blue, and then reset to the "play" option.

Cryptic messages, thought David, that weren't that cryptic, that led the authorities right to the killer's door. Clues were often revealed so that people knew why the person had been murdered—as though justifying why the act was committed—again leading to the killer's motive.

Murder in their "own backyard" allowed authorities to narrow their search area. Murder committed while using drink or drugs often bolstered the killer's courage or enhanced the experience, which frequently led to mistakes. Then there were cell phones, computer records, and revisiting the scenes of the crime and using the same vehicle with out-of-date plates, tax, or overdue tickets. Sometimes the killer would even taunt the authorities.

Because David had watched the movie at least a dozen times before and knew every scene, he couldn't be sure if he had watched the second half or not. Either way, he knew that the murderer in *Sleuth*, played by Olivier, had been caught because his own cleverness had done him in.

"I wouldn't make *any* mistakes," David said to the screen.

Movies, plays, books, and acting had taught him a lot about killing people. In the darkness of his room, an idea formed in David's subconscious and clamored for acknowledgment. It attached itself to his ongoing feelings of frustration, resentment, and loathing, which it channeled into physical expressions of heat, sweat, and tension. Then his subconscious took over, mixed the toxic ingredients, and made the target a real person: Jason West.

Afraid of his thoughts, David stood, dislodged his protesting cat, and gulped air as he stumbled to the kitchen sink in need of water.

TEN

With a serenity borne of an idea that his subconscious kept beyond reach, David had gone to bed and slept deeply for the first time in a week. The next day, refreshed, he made his usual four a.m. bus ride to work and arrived with an optimism and lightness of attitude that he didn't understand.

Typically, on Tuesdays, fewer travelers and customers graced the airport concourse and Sea Food World. With time on their hands, David and Nancy usually restocked the bar, cleaned surfaces, and arranged tables and chairs.

Nancy, a middle-aged "professional" food service employee with years of experience reading people's moods, had initially given David plenty of personal space when she'd arrived. But with a sense that he had gotten better, Nancy spoke to him in an easy manner now.

"How was your weekend, David?"

Afraid to share the unsettling thoughts that had begun to form in his mind, he hesitated before remembering that she would dominate most of the conversation anyway.

"Pretty good, Nancy. How about you?"

After a deep breath, Nancy used up almost three minutes recounting the mundane details of her weekend before David could insert a short reply.

"Sounds like you had fun."

"Yes," she said, and continued talking until she sensed his attention had wandered.

"David, are you, um, feeling better?"

Keeping to his cover story about his anemia, he reassured Nancy.

"Yes, thanks. I took my iron supplements and I'm feeling very well today."

The sound of high heels clicking on tile interrupted his contented feeling. Above the three-inch heels of the bright red shoes, slim, pale ankles led to well-developed calf muscles. Up out of sight beneath a fitted black dress, he saw the outline of taut hamstrings and firm buttocks.

The dress, designer and expensive, hung from her shoulders, and dipped just enough at the front to allow a good, yet tasteful, view of breasts that had retained their firmness by never having held milk for a suckling child.

On top of a slim neck, a high-cheek-boned face moisturized day and night to fend off inevitable wrinkles featured professionally styled eyebrows, overly round eyes, full lips, and a perfect nose.

Joyce Margaret Ogden owned the face, the dress, and the shoes, and she was coming toward David. The world knew her as J-MO, or "Just My Opinion," the tagline for her massive social media presence. A freelance professional gossip who had built a following of millions by destroying the lives of thousands, she relentlessly badgered David for snippets of any overheard gossip.

David, himself a victim of gossip, disliked J-MO and all she represented. As such, he generally avoided all social media, sensational headlines, "insider entertainment" shows, and reality TV.

Back in January, when J-MO had first graced the Sea Food World bar, she, along with her equipment, had sprawled over two barstools and a good chunk of the bar top.

David bristled now as she blazed a perfume-scented trail across the concourse. With nowhere to hide, he pasted a welcome smile on his face as she sallied to the bar and addressed him in her overly affected voice.

"David, David, *please* tell me you have a juicy story for me today."

"Good morning, Ms. Ogden."

"J-MO, please. How many times do I have to tell you? Call me J-MO, everyone does. Now, tell me, what do you have?"

"Only fresh coffee, multigrain bagels, and smoked salmon, like always."

Four cell phones, each a different color, hit the bar top in succession as J-MO disgorged them from her shoulder bag and aligned them side by side like gaudy coffins. The phones, she had once explained, were linked 24/7 to different social media sites, and they vibrated and flashed in constant competition for the attention of their owner. With both eyes on them, J-MO challenged David the same way she did every time she stopped by.

"How come you never tell me anything? This place is a travel hub for Europe, and I can't believe you don't hear things."

Tired and annoyed by her constant demands for dirt, but unable to speak his mind to a customer, David shrugged and repeated his defense.

"I'm too busy to notice, and people really don't tell me things. And," he added more forcefully than he intended, "I just don't make a habit of listening to other people's conversations."

Deaf to his principles, and convinced everyone had a price, J-MO tried bribery next.

"I could, you know, leave a really big tip, one of these days."

Saved by the ding of the kitchen bell, David retrieved a plate of salmon and caviar from the pass-through and delivered it to a customer at the far end of the bar.

Another customer, a man straight from the cover of *GQ*, took a seat, exchanged pleasantries with David, and ordered lox and bagel. A couple arrived after that and kept David away from J-MO's clutches for a few more minutes, until he was forced to deliver her food.

"Here you are, Ms. Ogden," he said tersely, as he placed her plate on the bar.

But before he could step away, J-MO spoke again.

"Thank you, David. I'm going to need this. I'm off to Berlin today. I'm meeting a young girl who says she's carrying the baby of a famous soccer player. I'll bet you can't guess who?"

"No, I probably can't."

"Well, I wouldn't tell you anyway. You will just have to wait until I expose the bastard. He's married, of course."

Despite being an accomplished actor, as well as a professional server, a snarl briefly distorted David's face as an urge to slap her welled inside him.

J-MO, focused on her phones, only caught the end of David's slip, and interpreting it as a mild frown, murmured with fake piety, "If I didn't know better, I'd think you didn't like me."

Unbidden, the recent encounter with Jason West, which had been occupying more and more of his thoughts, synced with J-MO's presence, and he suddenly imagined Jason telling her the story of Wanda.

A professional smile and a quick turn away from the bar to collect another customer's breakfast from the pass-through hid the surge of vehement ill will that burst into David's skull. He purposefully lingered with other customers to delay his return to J-MO, trying to regain some sort of composure. He also hoped it would lessen the perspiration he felt gathering on his body.

Focused on typing a one-handed tweet and oblivious to David's emotions as she was to everyone else's, J-MO tossed her credit card on the bar and gathered her cell phones. After keying in her PIN, she held onto the wireless card reader to force David's attention back to her as she made another attempt to coerce him.

"Anything you told me would be completely anonymous, you know. I never reveal my sources."

"And I never reveal mine, Ms. Ogden," David quipped, back in control.

Unwilling to accept rejection and compelled to have the last word, J-MO simply tossed her head and spoke with condescending certainty as she slipped off the barstool.

"We shall see, David. We shall see."

Peas in a pod, thought David, about Jason West and J-MO. Destroyers of lives for their own gain. People without empathy or sympathy. *Parasites.*

The memory of high school biology and a lesson about parasites drifted into his mind.

An organism that lived off and harmed its host in order to live, grow, and multiply. He recalled that there were two ways to get rid of most parasites. One required a person to make their body a less hospitable host, which either killed the parasite or made them leave on their own. The second suggested toxic methods to simply kill it.

As the corridor to the departure gates swallowed J-MO, David calmly noted that both methods required getting rid of the parasite.

ELEVEN

One umbrella wasn't enough. David's left shoulder, and Clair's right, were soaked. During the ten-minute walk from their building to the Bell on the Green pub, the rain, cold and abundant, had run off the umbrella in torrents. They weren't the only wet patrons. Several others had also been caught in the downpour from the purple clouds that had hovered over Feltham all day.

It was a Tuesday night, at seven p.m., and with the threat of rain, few people had felt inclined to come to the Bell, so David and Clair had their pick of places to sit. Away from the bar, at a two-person round wooden table, she arranged their half-sodden coats over chair backs while he stood at the bar chatting with the bartender, Kev. With a pint of Foster's in one hand, and a vodka and orange in the other, David joined Clair and set the drinks on the table.

"There you go. That should warm you up."

"Thanks, David. I've been looking forward to this all day."

After a clink of glasses, they both took a good swallow.

Setting his drink down, David sympathized with Clair.

"Tough day?"

"Yes. Same as every day. People are so dammed rude. I don't make the food, package the food, or decide what price it is. I just ring the price on the till, and put it in the bag."

After another quick swig of vodka, and unaware of how David watched and enjoyed the way her nose wiggled when she drank, Clair continued.

"The old people are the worst. I swear they only come in to argue and complain. Today it was Mrs. Chapman, the old woman with the walker with wheels, who lives off Dunkirk Crescent. She came in three times. Soap, carrots, and a newspaper. Weird. I mean, how can you need those three things separately? And you know what? The soap was too expensive, the carrots too soft, and the newspaper only had bad news in it. I…"

David, a low, warm laugh slipping softly from him, touched Clair's arm.

"She's probably just lonely. I bet she comes in so often because you're kind to her."

"Yeah," Clair answered, her natural empathy reasserting itself. "She's not *so* bad. Although, I have to tell her to stop pulling wads of five-pound notes out of her bag, and that she should only bring what she needs to the shop. Bloody thugs and druggies are everywhere, but she takes no notice."

Then she stood and motioned with her empty glass. "Same again, David?"

They had been going Dutch on entertainment costs since they'd begun going out together six months ago. Both had low-paying jobs, and neither adhered to the outdated convention that the man should pay or always get the drinks from the bar. And more importantly, Clair valued her independence.

She was slim, almost thin, and walked with confidence, her worn, once-dark blue jeans snug on her hips, and her white shirt tucked into her trim waist.

David sighed as he admired the curve of her bottom.

His hands had wandered over those curves, held her torso, and stroked her hair. His lips had also kissed hers. However, nothing more than what would have passed as making out in the 1950s. Ever so slowly, as each of them dealt with their own issues, David and Clair were inching closer together. To what end or future, he did not know.

Lost in a pleasantly undefined fantasy, Clair startled him when she returned from the bar.

"Kev is certainly chatty tonight," she said, as she set David's pint down and took her seat.

"That's because his girlfriend Lizzy is coming home from university on the weekend. He asked if we would be in on the weekend, because he'd like to introduce us. Maybe have a drink together."

"That would be nice. I wonder what she's like."

"Shall we come on Saturday, then? *Danger Street* is playing."

"The cover song band, right?"

"Yes. They were here a few months ago. They were pretty good."

An audible groan from several pub patrons, synchronized with the bang of the front door, announced the entry of four men into the pub.

The leader, Troy, noticeably older than the other three, paused, looked around, and conveyed contempt for the disdain of the groaners.

Well known and disliked, Troy and his "crew," Izaak, Daxon, and Brogan, were the local "chavs," who, despite law enforcement efforts, remained free to roam and disrupt the local community at will.

"Bloody hell," Clair murmured as she nodded toward the men. "That's all we need."

"I'm surprised they're allowed in here after last time. I heard that Troy had a right argument with the darts team about something."

"Yeah, I remember, but I don't think there was fight or anything."

"Bloody chavs ruin everything."

Chavs, and Troy in particular, in keeping with the characterizations attributed to them, cared little for the opinions of "non-chavs," which in practice meant 99.9 percent of the population.

Considered amoral, thieving, bling-laden, and illiterate, they favored hip-hop and R&B, held no jobs, followed no rules, and took whatever they wanted. For some reason, they saw themselves as cool and glamorous.

Often the product of dysfunctional homes, chavs viewed themselves as tough rebels who relied on intimidation and violence to get what they wanted. They were inherently cunning, and had an unhealthy obsession with cars, Vin Diesel, smoking, and alcohol.

Troy was in his late twenties, and a classic chav from an earlier decade, he had neither the sense nor ambition to leave his adolescence behind. He dressed in trademark chav clothes: Adidas sneakers, baggy black sweatpants with a white stripe up the side, a gray hoodie over a white T-shirt, and shiny fake baubles on his fingers, wrists, and neck. A grubby knee-length overcoat, the only departure from classic chav dress, completed his anti-establishment costume.

With little variation from their leader's clothes, Izaak, Daxon, and Brogan followed Troy with what they thought was a tough swagger.

Far enough away to dull the sound of the chavs' overly loud and incomprehensible slang, David and Clair enjoyed their date, discussed the upcoming quiz night, and made plans for Saturday. He had tried to apologize and explain again for his behavior over the last few weeks, but gracious as ever, she simply waved his apologies away and offered her support, encouragement, and understanding.

Almost nine months had passed since Clair had moved into the flat above David, and it had been six months since their first date. Yet, their relationship had progressed slowly as he wrestled with his fear of rejection, while Clair, burnt by past relationships, had resisted any sort of commitment.

"I'm just going to the bathroom," said Clair, pushing back her chair.

"OK, you want another drink?"

"Yes. But wait till I come back," she answered.

Unseen by either David or Clair, Izaak, Troy's "lieutenant," nudged and winked at Troy as she crossed the floor and entered the women's washroom.

Troy, who had noticed and badgered Clair several times while she worked in the shop, stared at the taut fabric across her bottom and turned to Izaak.

"I'll be shaggin her ass soon, yeah."

"Innit," Izaak replied, in affirmative chav slang.

In anticipation of Clair's exit from the washroom, Troy moved himself and his followers away from the bar so that she had to walk right past him.

When she came out, he inflated his chest and squared off directly in her path. Undaunted, and not one to back away from confrontation, Clair stepped up to Troy.

"What do you want?"

"Me and m'crew," Troy said, smiling as he indicated to his disciples, "think you got a nice ass, yeah. Bout you be givin me a bit, yeah?"

"I doubt you could manage my ass. Now get out of my way."

Izaak stepped closer to Troy and snarled.

"Don't be disrispectin the man, yeah."

"He ain't no man, and you're just a boy. Now move."

Izaak, agitated, looked to Troy for leadership.

He spread his arms wide as he spoke.

"No need to be dissin me, Clair. Anyway," Troy continued as he nodded in David's direction. "What you doin with that loser? I make you come like you never did, yeah?"

"Yeah, then we do ya, too," chirped Daxon as he bounced on the balls of his feet.

David, his back to the pub, hadn't seen Troy confront Clair, and turned just as Kev, who had at one time been a friend of Troy, crossed the pub and confronted him.

"Time to go, Troy."

As Kev spoke, Clair, seeing David get up from his chair, stepped past Troy to head him off.

Troy, who would later recount to his crew that Clair's sidestep had been a victory, and that he would "'ave her soon enough," gave Clair's body one last leer, drained his pint, and left the pub with his crew in tow.

David, his face flushed and body tense, met her in the middle of the room.

"You alright?"

Holding his arm, more to prevent him from walking toward Troy than from any real need, she smiled.

"Yes, of course. No problem."

"What did that fuck Troy want?"

"He's a jerk. It doesn't matter," she said as she steered him back to their table.

"What did he say?"

Clair thought for a moment. If they had a future, then it needed to be based on truth.

"He said I had a nice ass, and that he would like some of it."

"The fucker. I'll kick *his* ass if he comes near you again."

"It's no big deal, David. I can handle him. He's been in the shop before. He's all talk in front of his little boys."

"What? He's been after you in the shop?"

"Just the odd stare and comment. It's nothing, really. I mean, I don't like it, but he's just a jerk, and he doesn't scare me."

Back at the table, David leaned in close and whispered with flat certainty, "If he bothers you again, Clair, I'll take care of him."

Unnerved by a side of David she hadn't seen before, Clair only nodded.

TWELVE

Three turns left, one turn right, several kneads with his paws, and Shadow finally coiled and pressed himself against Robbie's right thigh on the cool vinyl of David's sofa. As Robbie's right hand stroked Shadow's back, his left worked the universal remote control for David's entertainment system.

On screen, a still image of a blood-soaked Benedict Cumberbatch, playing Sherlock Holmes in the 2012 adaptation of *The Hound of the Baskerville,* stared back at him. With his finger over the pause button, Robbie compared the remaining run time for the show with the actual time on his watch.

His mom and David had left for the Bell at ten minutes to seven and said that they would be back by nine p.m. Previous experience had taught Robbie that his mom and David would actually return at 9:10.

Robbie had to check the time, because instead of starting the ninety-minute show at seven, he had spent too long snooping around David's flat. He knew that snooping, or as Robbie preferred to call it, "investigating," because it sounded more professional and legitimate, was wrong.

But his mom's safety was more important, and it was his responsibility to look after her. Besides, after his mom had told him about David's fishy problem, Robbie had researched the disease on the internet, and he needed to check that David really did have the disease.

His investigation began in the bathroom, where Robbie compared his internet notes in his spiral binder with the labels and descriptions on packaging and bottles. Soap, with a pH between 5.5 and 6.5; activated charcoal and copper chlorophyll in supplements; shampoo, conditioner, and shaving cream "specifically formulated" to help manage body odor, as well as various body talc and deodorants were all present.

After chastising himself for not having previously noticed the difference between David's bathroom stuff and his mom's, Robbie checked the laundry, which had appropriate pH detergent, before heading to the kitchen.

The contents of David's fridge and cupboards had looked much the same as anyone else's, Robbie recalled, but this time he noticed a list taped to the inside door of the cupboard over the sink. It had two headings: Good / Bad. Under each one, there was a list of foods, which after Robbie crosschecked with his notes, conformed to the food guide for people suffering from Trimethylaminuria.

Satisfied David did indeed have the disease, and that it wasn't some kind of ruse to trick his mom, Robbie took photographs of the bathroom items, laundry detergent, and the food list on the cupboard door. The photos would be added to the rest of the photos of David's flat that he kept in a binder locked in a treasure box in his closet.

The confirmation of the disease, and his struggle to deal with it, increased Robbie's respect for David and increased his growing attraction as a role model.

Pleased with his investigation, and happy that David was still a good person, Robbie put his camera in his bag and settled down to watch—and reluctantly, fast-forward—through the remainder of *The Hounds of Baskerville.*

THIRTEEN

Thirty-nine minutes. Eleven to walk from his flat on Cedar Street to bus stop #74313 outside the Bell on the Green pub on Staines Road. Eight for bus H25 to take him to Hatton Cross Station. Eleven on bus X26 from Hatton Station to Heathrow Terminal 4, and a final nine minutes to walk through the terminal to the "staff only" room located across the concourse from Sea Food World.

Dressed for the early morning chill and the ubiquitous London rain, David shrugged off his raincoat as the warmth of the terminal heated his body and threatened to induce sweating. Since his encounter with Jason West, his body temperature regulation, linked more than most to his emotions and moods, had become erratic and difficult to control.

He expected to change his clothes at work once, or perhaps twice during the week, but the anger, resentment, and the memories caused by West had greatly disrupted his routine and regimens.

During his first full week back after the West encounter, David had needed three changes of clothes. The following week it had been two, then three again last week. This week, six weeks after the West airport incident, and his fourth full week back at work, he had successfully reached Wednesday morning without the need to change clothes during his shift.

This progress toward "normalcy," David attributed to positive sessions with Rachel, support from Jenny, and several good dates with Clair. Yet, despite his outward progress, he still had a problem. Inside, where no one could see, his reaction to people and situations he would normally have shrugged off had become increasingly uncompromising and judgmental.

The first instance had been Clair's run-in with Troy in the Bell. He had, of course, been incensed that the thug had insulted Clair, even though he knew she could take care of herself. But he had become even more enraged when Clair had mentioned that Troy had bothered her in the shop. Nothing had really happened, beyond a few crass, juvenile words, and it should have been left at that. But it hadn't. In fact, David had found himself fixating on Troy, and the debased chav lifestyle he represented.

The more he thought about the man, the more he began to question Troy's contribution to society, as well as how many people had Troy insulted, disrespected, and hurt. What in fact, was Troy's purpose for living?

A similar thought process had attached itself to his recent interaction with J-MO, the "professional gossip" who destroyed people's lives without mercy, or morality. What was her function in life, and why did she live?

Even stranger, and more disturbing, David had begun to place both Troy and J-MO in an imaginary

Machiavellian context, in which he was The Prince charged with deciding their respective worth and fate.

Paradoxically, in David's fanciful construct, the stress of being The Prince, who decided a person's fate, did not induce sweat or odor. For him, in his role, in which he thought of himself as being an actor, he was free of his disease. It was as though the role of acting had cured him.

Despite his dark thoughts, his week had begun well. Even though he had brought two additional changes of clothes to work to add to the one already in his locker, he had a bounce in his step and a smile on his face as he entered the staff room to hang up his coat.

Unfortunately, reality pushed back when he recalled that it was Wednesday. This meant that Mr. Taylor, David's least favorite customer, would come in for breakfast. The thought of Taylor dispelled David's positive mood and threatened to increase his temperature.

Fifteen minutes into his shift, Larry, unhurried behind his cart, arrived and turned up the heat.

At his obnoxious best when David motioned him to empty one of the waste stations in the bar area, Larry toyed with him.

"What ya want?"

"The waste bin," David said, pointing to the stuck open flap of the fake brown wooden housing around the plastic garbage can within. "It's full."

"It is."

"Can't have it like that."

"No," Larry answered, leaning on the cart.

"Well, are you going to empty it?"

"Can't."

"What? Why not?"

"No bags."

David pointed at a wad of white plastic bags on a hook on the side of Larry's cart.

"What are those?" he shouted.

"Bags."

"Well, then."

"Wrong bags."

"What's wrong with them?"

"Nothing. Very good bags."

"Stop messing around, Larry, and just empty the f-ing garbage."

"Now, now, no need to swear at me. I'll get the union on…"

"Oh, for god's sake."

"It's no good. I don't have bags. I mean, *proper* bags. These 'ere bags are only for dry paper and such. I have to use black ones if there is food mixed in. Which there always is at this place."

"But it's overflowing! Can't you just use a white one, then transfer it to a black one and…"

"You expect me to handle that stuff, all that stinking fish? I'm not supposed to touch *anything*. I'll have to talk to the union if you are telling me I have to do that."

"I'm not telling you, I'm just suggesting that…"

"Ah, well then, you'll have to wait till I get the right bags."

"How long will that take?"

A broad, triumphant smile filled Larry's face.

"Two minutes. I'll be right back."

Leaving his cart in front of the waste station, Larry sauntered across the concourse, opened a door marked "Staff Only—Maintenance," and disappeared. The door swung shut.

~

Exasperated, David checked his watch. Mr. Taylor, or "Mr. Clean," as he thought of him, would arrive in about ten minutes. Always on Wednesdays, between 9 and 9:15 a.m. For the past sixteen weeks, Taylor had frequented Sea Food World for a light breakfast.

Chalk and cheese. Apples and oranges. Shit and sugar. Larry and Mr. Taylor. The two men could not have been more different. Larry epitomized sordid squalor, while Taylor espoused cleanliness and virtue.

Back behind the bar, David nodded to Paul as he poked his head through the pass-through. He was one of several line-cooks who liked to be called a chef, despite the fact that 80 percent of his work consisted of assembling precooked or raw products.

"Larry winding you up again, David?"

"He's a lazy bastard."

"What's it this time?"

"Said he needs black bags to empty the waste station. White ones won't do."

Paul's eyebrows rose as he nodded his head toward Larry's cart.

"He's right. New policy last week. Same for the kitchen. The white bags aren't strong enough or something like that. All waste with food in it must be in black bags."

David groaned.

"Yeah, well, he just likes to piss me off. One of these days…"

"You gotta relax, David. Larry is a good guy. He's always helping people. You just need to get to know him," Paul added as he retreated from the hatch and back into the kitchen.

David, unmoved by Paul's suggestion, glared at the still-closed maintenance door. Overhead, the god-like PA system warned people about what would happen to unattended bags and paged passengers to "go immediately" to various gates. Resigned, he broke his stare and panned the airport concourse.

An ever-changing parade of humans, with differences in height, gait, color, girth, hair, age, clothes, bags, accessories, and posture filled the concourse with constant movement and noise.

Acting had improved David's ability to observe and learn. Mentally adopting the mannerisms and appearance of passengers had helped him get a number of voice-over jobs, and he never tired of the variety and diversity of the subjects he could study and use.

Anticipating the imminent arrival of Taylor, he polished a glass, selected a crisp napkin, and double-checked that the label on the Evian water had not become damp and soggy. After sixteen weeks of interaction, David disliked Taylor. A lot. He recalled their first meeting with apprehension as Taylor's arrival time approached.

Their mutual dislike had begun one minute into their first exchange, when "Mr. Clean," holding a glass to the light, had tutted and requested a "fresh, clean, and preferably cool" glass for his sparkling water.

Sometimes glasses from the dishwasher were a little spotted and warm, and the request itself for a fresh glass hadn't bothered David. However, the superior manner and condescending tone of the request *had*.

David's disdain had become more difficult to hide with each visit.

Spotty glasses had been the precursor to a litany of complaints and acrid remarks about Sea Food World that punctuated Taylor's sixteen weeks. Criticisms that focused on two things: dirt and odor.

The dirt complaints were usually about imperceptible dust, grease, or fingerprints found on menus, glasses, the counter, display cases, chairs, tables, the floor, and anywhere else Taylor could think of.

The odor complaints were made about burnt coffee, other people's scents, the cleaning products used on surfaces, the waste station, and the one subject on which David actually agreed with Taylor: Larry. Despite the common ground concerning Larry, Taylor had soon become David's most disliked customer. Even more than the gossip columnist, J-MO.

On Taylor's fourth visit, David's dislike had changed to fear when Taylor had wriggled his nose and claimed he could smell an odor of rotten fish. Hypersensitive, David had immediately perspired, explained that he needed to check the waste station bins, and hurried away to apply deodorant.

Shaking off the memory, he served a middle-aged man, who felt compelled to explain that the reason for the early morning hot flask of sake was because his body time was actually five in the afternoon.

At 9:14, Taylor arrived, perched himself on a bar-stool, and pushed out a perfunctory "good morning."

"Good morning. Usual?"

"Yes, thank you."

"Any coffee today?"

"No. Just water, no ice."

Taylor's nostrils wriggled. Real or imaginary, David could no longer say, such was his paranoia. Wary of Taylor's sensitivity, he kept his distance, in case he did what he really wanted to do, which was punch "Mr. Clean" right on his fucking nose.

FOURTEEN

Rachel twiddled her pen and put her notepad, which had her day's plans on it, away.

"I think, in light of recent events, we should use today's session to revisit something important that we agreed had a strong impact on your teenage years. Would that be alright, David?"

"Yes, sure. Whatever you think will help."

"Good. Well I want you to take us back to the events that happened when you were fifteen. I want to consider the links between those past events and what is happening now. I want you to explain, contextualize, and neutralize your current thoughts. Do you know what I'm referring to, David?"

He nodded agreement. He had shared those experiences with Rachel many times before, but this time, while his words recounted an abridged version to his therapist, his mind replayed the events in detail.

After Ms. Cook selected David to play the antagonist Iago, who adhered to Machiavelli's ideals in Shakespeare's Othello, *David had studied harder than ever before. But with four weeks of the summer school break remaining, and three weeks before the first performance of* Othello, *his former life as the school mimic and member of a despised gang caught up with him.*

Around seven p.m., after a long rehearsal session, David was tired but energized by the intensity of the scene in which Othello promotes Iago to his lieutenant and gives him the order to kill Cassio.

His walk home from the local community center followed the pathway along Sinderland Brook to Woodheys Park, across the park, and on to Clough Avenue and his home.

As he stepped from the pathway onto the grass of the park, David was reliving the scene and repeating the lines to himself. He did not notice the boys loitering by the play structure. Alternately sucking on cigarettes as they passed a bottle of vodka between them, they paused as one, like a wolf pack, as David approached.

"Eh, look who we got here," the tallest and ugliest of the four boys announced with mock enthusiasm as he lifted his ass off the seat of the swing made for ten-year-olds.

Pulled from his concentration by the familiar voice and tone, David halted about twenty feet from the group, all of which had stood to flank their leader.

"Whot? Ya got nothin to say to your mates, eh, Davey? You too good for us now?"

Deano, a budding career criminal who attended school to exploit the opportunities to sell weed rather than receive the benefits of education, nodded to his followers as he spoke. The pack, responsive to Deano's lead, took a step forward.

David regarded the group with apprehension. Until the arrival of Ms. Cook, David's penchant for mimicry had secured him a prominent place in Deano's gang, and he had participated in many instances of bullying and intimidation. Sensing he was about to become a victim, and experienced enough not to trigger a predictable response by running, David opted for engagement.

"Hi, Deano, what you guys up to?"

"Why? What's it to you, nancy boy?"

"Just wondered, that's all. I haven't, er, seen you lot for a while."

"That's 'cause you been dressin up and puttin on makeup with the rest of the queers. Or have you been gettin a bit with Cook?"

Ignoring the homophobic staple retort of Deano, David attempted levity.

"Ha, chance would be good, but Ms. Cook never…"

"That's 'cause she's a lesbo dike. You ain't never gettin any of that."

While he knew of Ms. Cook and Ms. Smith's intimate relationship, and the muddled fantasies it had spawned in his dreams, he did not want to soil her reputation with the likes of Deano.

"Well, I don't know about that. Anyway, it's, er, good to see you guys, but I gotta get going."

"Not so fast. The boys would like to hear some voices. We've all missed them, haven't we, lads?"

"Yeah," grunted Gerbil, the runt of the pack, but the most violent when under the influence of drink or drugs. "Let's hear you do that wanker, Mr. Lyons."

"Look, guys, I'm really tired and my throat is sore from rehearsals. I…"

"Rehearsals! More like it's sore from swallowing the cock of the "leading man," Peanut put in, so called for the odd shape of his head.

Laughter spilled from the group, until Deano took charge.

"No, not Lyons. Let's hear you do Cook and Smith getting it off together. Eh lads, want to hear that?"

Unanimous, like bleating sheep, the "lads" endorsed Deano's demand.

Unable to resist the instinct of the trapped to seek an escape, David tensed, braced his feet for flight, and leaned toward the gap between Deano and Gerbil. Too late, the pack moved in and the gap closed. Peanut, behind and to David's left, shoved David at Deano, who pushed David back. Gerbil, on David's right, weighed in and pushed him at the fourth and silent member of the gang, Bilko, an asexual, goth-like teenager obsessed with silent movies and mimes.

After a few shoves and pushes, Deano stepped back.

"Go on then, fuck off, David," he said, with an exaggerated flourish.

David, who should have known better, smiled and stepped past Deano, who returning the smile, kicked David's legs out from under him. The instant David hit the floor, Peanut, Gerbil, and Bilko kicked at his torso. After a few more kicks, Deano, in keeping with his preference to extend the event by offering victims false hope, called his dogs off and motioned David to stand.

Familiar with the routine, instead of waiting for the next assault, David dug in his jeans pocket for his small Swiss Army knife that he carried for protection.

Thumbing the blade open, he stabbed at his attackers. The first lunge caught Peanut in the arm, and the second, mostly as a result of Peanut's thrust forward to defend himself, passed right through Peanut's hand. Peanut screamed, blood sprayed, and David let go of the knife and ran.

Three hours later, after Peanut's parents had taken their "innocent" son to the hospital, the police knocked on David's front door. Charges were laid. However, with character references from Ms. Cook, sympathy from local police officers familiar with Deano and his gang, and on the condition that David agree to immediate anger management counselling and a hundred hours of community service, the charges were dropped.

David's anger at the injustice of the consequences was dwarfed by the rage that swept through him when he learned that the anger management counseling and community service hours would prevent him from further participation in the production of Othello.

Incensed, but wily enough to hold his tongue, David took his punishment and plotted. A week before school resumed, Peanut's house, aided by a gallon of gasoline poured through the letterbox, burnt to the ground. Fortunately, smoke alarms sounded and no one was harmed. Accusations about David were soon made, but without any evidence, neither David nor anyone else was arrested.

"David."

He rubbed his face, blinked, and focused on Rachel's faraway voice.

"Yes?"

"Thank you for sharing your experience. I know we have explored these events before, but as I suggested earlier, in light of recent events, and your reaction to them, we should clarify and remind ourselves of what this means, so we can better manage any situations."

Used to Rachel's soothing voice and inclusive manner, David simply nodded.

"You remember how we learned together that unbeknownst to you, the philosophy of Machiavelli's Prince, as expressed through the ruthless and devious machinations of Othello, had likely entered your subconscious? Also, we agreed that the ruthlessness of Machiavelli's Prince in dealing with his enemies had probably taken your anger toward Peanut and suggested the use of gasoline to address your grievances."

"Yes, I remember."

"Do you also remember that you never really wanted to harm Peanut? Also, how the realization you might have also killed his mother, father, and younger sister horrified you and made you ill?"

A bead of perspiration broke out on David's forehead as memories of the sound of the whoosh the gasoline had made through the front door to Peanut's house surfaced. He also recalled how he had lingered for a moment, placed his hand on the door, and smiled as he felt the heat. He hadn't told Rachel about that part. He hadn't told anyone. He felt that same heat now, and the corners of his mouth twitched in recognition.

Interpreting his twitch as an indication of remorse, Rachel continued.

"This is what is happening to you now, David. I believe that the encounter with Jason West has acted as a kind of catalyst, and triggered thoughts of Machiavelli. Now, Troy, J-MO, and I suspect to some degree, "Mr. Clean," as you call him, have offended and upset you. And to deal with these offences, possible solutions are being provided by your internalization and connection to Shakespeare's *Othello* and Machiavelli's *The Prince*."

Although Rachel's client sofa conformed to the most up-to-date ergonomic specification for comfort and posture, David squirmed with discomfort as she fixed a compassionate yet professional eye on him.

"What kind of resolutions or determinations have you made for West, Troy, J-MO, and Mr. Clean?"

In truth, David hadn't actually gotten that far. Disparate and irrational thoughts of imprisonment, torture—and for West, some kind of horrible death—had flitted in and out of his thoughts, but he had reached no real conclusions.

With uncharacteristic wariness concerning Rachel, David suddenly decided to lie.

"Banishment. That's what should happen to them. They should be banished from society."

"Well," Rachel answered with a trace of relief, "that is a very positive approach to take, David. Together, we can take conceptual and emotional control of these people and banish them from your consciousness."

On one level, he participated in the breathing, word association, and problem-solving exercises that followed, but on another, his mind focused on the trip down memory lane. Especially the thoughts about Deano and the gang, which spurred David to ask himself the same questions he had about Troy and J-MO: What was their purpose in life?

Then there was the issue of burning down Peanut's house. Had he really wanted to kill him? Had he really felt horrified and ill that the deaths could have included members of Peanut's family? Hadn't the Prince some advice about dealing with the entire family of a person who caused you problems?

On the bus ride home, David reflected that Rachel had been right and wrong. The philosophy of Machiavelli's Prince, as expressed through the ruthless and devious machinations of Iago in *Othello*, had indeed entered his subconscious, except that he no longer thought that The Prince only existed in his subconscious.

As if in proof, David's very conscious mind asked if his enemies—West, Troy, J-MO, and maybe even Mr. Clean—might need a more tangible solution than conceptual and emotional banishment.

FIFTEEN

Reassured that David actually did have a disease, and that it was probably the reason he had been acting weird and a bit rude to him and his mom, Robbie settled in at his desk to review and catalog the photographs he had taken in David's flat.

Beside each photograph, printed on one half of a plain, A4-sized paper on his printer, Robbie added handwritten notes on where, when, and why he had taken the photo. When complete, he numbered each page, punched three holes in the margin, and inserted them into a one-inch three-ring binder labelled with David's name on the spine.

After adding the last page, Robbie turned to the beginning of the binder and flipped through the pages. The "Book of David," as Robbie thought of it, had begun three days after he and his mom had first moved into the flat above David's. The first photograph, taken during the night when he had sneaked downstairs, showed David's front door. Beside the photograph, Robbie had noted after the date, "David, lives downstairs, seems OK."

Photographs of the outside of the house and blurred views through David's windows followed. On page fifteen, David, without his knowledge, made his first appearance. Taken in the late afternoon, at a high angle from Robbie's bedroom window, the photograph, to Robbie's imagination, suggested sinister surveillance that did not, Robbie later accepted, do David justice.

The next dozen pages contained sketches instead of photographs. Invited into David's flat with his mom for tea, and to "get to know each other," Robbie had drawn the layout and contents of David's flat. Beside the sketches, he had noted such things as, "old stuff, worn, one toothbrush, double bed, dusty, old TV."

Underlined with red ink next to the sketch of the living room, Robbie had written, "What's under the black cloth with the old TV on it?" An additional note, in blue ink beside the red ink, said, "Solved. See photo of room on p.41."

"Hey, Robbie!" his mom called from the other side of the bedroom door. "Brian and Joey are here to play soccer in the park."

"OK, Mom. I'm just finishing something. Tell them I'll meet them there in ten minutes."

Back with his binder, Robbie paused at the first photograph he had taken of David's cat, Shadow. Charcoal-gray, with two off-white front paws and vibrant yellow eyes, he had immediately fallen for the cat. Encouraged and allowed to play with it by David and his mom, Robbie and Shadow had become fast friends. After a few weeks, as mutual trust and friendship between Robbie, David, and Clair developed, David asked if Robbie could "look in on Shadow" before he went to school each morning.

After some guilt and soul-searching, Robbie used his mornings with Shadow to snoop and photograph David's entire flat. He rationalized that protecting his mom outweighed David's privacy. The snooping also included an inventory of David's clothes, books, music, movies, shoes, jewelry, and even the occasional rummage in the garbage. Pages of photographs and comments on the minutiae of David's life almost filled the binder, and Robbie thought he would soon need a second one.

Carrying the binder to the "treasure chest" in the bottom of his closet, under where his clothes hung, Robbie stopped. He desperately wanted David to be a good person, and 99 percent of everything Robbie had discovered said he was. But, no matter how hard he tried to ignore it, David had one secret that he had still not uncovered.

Crouching on the floor, Robbie opened the binder about midway and thumbed to a page he knew well. He had taken the photograph on the second morning he had looked in on Shadow.

The notes beside the image had been added to many times since the day he had taken the photograph. "What is in the box?" "Why does he have it?" "What is his secret?"

They had been the first entries. Later notes included: "Where is the key?" "Only bad people keep secrets." "Is it treasure?" and "I need to open it."

Perhaps David's secret was his disease, Robbie thought as he focused on the lock. But, if that were true, what would he keep in the box? His medicines, soaps, and stuff were in plain view, and Robbie hadn't even noticed they were different from regular cleaning products. So David couldn't be hiding something about his disease.

The knowledge that David had something to hide had worried Robbie for a long time. Yet, because everything else seemed normal, and his mom was happier than she had been since the other man, he had forced himself to ignore the locked box.

But now, as he placed the book in his own "secret chest," Robbie resolved once and for all that he needed to discover David's secret, and that meant finding a way to open the lock on David's box.

Sixteen

Revisiting his teenage years with Rachel had not been therapeutic. Instead, a melancholy impotency had descended upon David. Lying on his bed, his mind drifted to the corner of the room and the dirty laundry basket beside the wardrobe. Only clean laundry had ever piled up in the basket. Mostly towels, linens, and old clothes he never used. His dirty clothes stank too much to sit in a basket until "laundry day."

But there was something else in the laundry basket. Something he hadn't opened for a long time.

Up off the bed, David removed two towels and a few shirts from the top of the basket and withdrew a small wooden box with a hinged lid and a Yale-type door lock. With the box under his arm, he went to the kitchen and set it on the table.

He retrieved a chipped teacup from the back of the top shelf of the kitchen cupboard above the fridge. Turning the cup upside down, a key fell into his palm. Despite knowing what lay inside, and the likely outcome of looking at the contents, he inserted the key anyway, opened the lid, and took out his scrapbook.

Unlike most people, David's scrapbook began at age fifteen. Not because he had any ill feeling about his life before that, but because for him, fifteen was the year his acting career really began.

The first entry was amateurish, pasted to the left-hand side, and spotted with illegible handwritten notes. It featured what David considered his first playbill. Five by eight and a half inches, the playbill, produced and "printed" by the high school art class as a favor to Ms. Cook, announced the Altrincham Youth Drama Society's August 25-28, 1995 production of *Othello*.

Highlighted in bold, black letters, it also listed David Thomas Edwards as Iago, the intelligent and crafty villain of the play, who embodied the Machiavellian stereotype of a man who used evil for his own sake and desires.

With too much glue applied, the playbill paper had bubbled, dried, and turned a dirty off-white color. In the right-hand margin, where the five-inch-wide playbill left a space, images, names, and objects in blue, black, and red ink had been hand drawn, connected, and scratched out.

The ink scratching had been David's teenage expressions of anger, retribution, and violence toward those who caused him to lose his part in the play. Decapitated torsos of Deano, Bilko, and Gerbil, each with swords through their chests, lay below a blazing fire with Peanut tied to a stake, screaming for help.

Police officers, community councillors, and the school headmaster, all writhing in agony, populated the rest of the space. Up on the top right-hand side of the page, a four-by-four-inch coffin, with the name Steve Rooke/West in the middle, teetered on a cliff edge.

David's 1997 A Level certificate, his acceptance letter to Manchester University's undergraduate drama program, and a small facsimile of his 1999 University BA Drama certificate occupied the next three pages. Several pages of playbills, programs, and ticket stubs for amateur performances put on by the university drama club during David's undergraduate years followed.

He smiled as he recalled his attempts to pull off something comedic, try his hand at singing, or portray weak characters in plays such as *The Comedy of Errors* and *The Tempest*. By the end his first year, his ability to play dark, sinister, and duplicitous characters had been acknowledged, and to his delight, future casting matched his strengths.

The next entry was another acceptance letter, this time from the prestigious London Academy of Music and Dramatic Art, followed by his 2002 Classical Acting for Professional Theatre MA graduation certificate. On the adjacent page, a glossy photograph filled with the confident, smiling faces of his graduating class, complete with signatures and expressions of future luck, reflected the optimism and hope of the time.

The next dozen or so pages detailed what David thought of as his real formative years.

In 2003, his first real paying performance was the part of Sebastian at the Open Air Theatre in Regent's Park in a production of Shakespeare's *Twelfth Night*. While the comedy of mistaken identities, unrequited love, trickery, and drunken reveling had not been David's first choice, he had embraced it with energy and had been rewarded with very positive reviews.

Next, he had played Edmund in *King Lear*, a consummate schemer and Machiavellian character eager to seize any opportunity, and willing to do anything to achieve his goals. With qualities similar to Iago in *Othello*, David had excelled in the role and received critical acclaim.

Macbeth followed *King Lear*. Macbeth's driving ambition, encouraged by his ruthless wife, to assassinate the current monarch to realize the prophecy of three witches that he would become king, suited David's abilities and interests. Significant accolades and recognition in London's theatrical circles had ensued.

Then he had played Iago, and was considered by many to be a "natural" for the part. He had reveled in the character's evil acts, his support of Othello's suspicions, and his demonic scheming. To David, Iago symbolized many human characteristics that defined him as Machiavellian.

In 2005, David had decided that he needed to express some acting diversity, and had starred as Reverend Samuel Parris in *The Crucible*, by Arthur Miller. Reveling in the narrative tone that compelled characters to make the choice to conform to survive or uphold one's beliefs whatever the consequences, David again excelled and gained more recognition.

In 2006, he had made his "West End" debut portraying another Machiavellian schemer, Claudius in *Hamlet*.

Revisiting his past glories lifted his spirit as memories of after-show parties, romantic liaisons, and overtures from directors and writers flooded him with endorphins.

Turning another page brought David to July 2008, and up to his highest acting achievement. The playbill, inserted in a plastic wallet and carefully attached in the scrapbook, detailed his lead role as *Hamlet* at the Duke of York's Theatre in London.

Several pages of positive media reviews, photographs, and peer comments followed, with a final article in *The Stage* with the headline: "David Edwards to play Macbeth at the Royal National Theatre in 2009?"

His body now limp, David lingered on the page, savoring the past limelight, his old friends, and his old life.

Then his face reddened, and he ground his teeth. His eyelids blinked rapidly, and his throat constricted and dried. Reluctantly, David turned another page.

No playbill, no photographs, no reviews or accolades; only cold, dispassionate facts. A single sheet plotted the barren points of his more recent life.

December 2008: I have Trimethylaminuria. I stink like dead fish.

January 2010: Rachel—support group!

2011: UKvoices—voice-over parts in commercials. Hate them.

2012: Airport job at seafood bar—the end.

2013: SFW and some voice-over work.

2015: Still at SFW—still the end.

He stared at his last entry. That had been two years ago. He'd had nothing to record since then.

Looking back on his career, he realized something significant. He had excelled at playing Shakespeare's Machiavellian characters because he hadn't really been acting. He had acted with conviction because he *understood* Machiavelli's prince.

The conclusion filled him with a sudden wholesomeness. *Perhaps he should implement the ways of the prince now? Why not?*

There were plenty of candidates for judgment. People who plagued society, people who threatened him and the people he cared for. People like Jason West, J-MO, and Troy. Even that prick, Mr. Clean.

The more David tabulated the unworthy, the better he felt. The better he felt, the stronger his imagination became. Unfettered imagination merged with hope. Hope triggered desire, and desire spawned justification. Euphoria entered his mind, the subconscious joined, and delusion took control.

David picked up a pen and mouthed the words as he wrote a new entry in his book:

I am The Prince.

SEVENTEEN

Throughout the rest of the week, Machiavelli's advice, opinions, solutions, and recommendations of how a prince should conduct himself dominated David's thoughts. Interactions and judgments about coworkers, patrons, and commuters were considered by a zealous subconscious that evaluated and positioned each encounter within a distorted and self-serving Machiavellian framework.

By Saturday morning, exhausted by the turmoil in his head, he sought some solitude. Unable to break his Monday to Friday 3:30 a.m. wake-up time, he had woken and eaten. Instead of hurrying to catch the bus to Heathrow and work, he paced his flat until he set out to walk from his home to Bedfont Lakes Country Park on Clockhouse Lane.

It was a twenty-minute walk each way to the entrance. The park had several small lakes, wetlands, wildflower meadows, and woodlands. The land, originally owned by the Duke of Albans in the 1780s, had been farmed until the 1920s and used as a landfill site from the 1950s to the early 1970s. It had been developed into its current existence as a country park by the Hounslow Council in the early 1990s.

David didn't visit the park for the hundreds of plant and bird species, the 124 moths, 97 fungi, or 20 or more mammals. He went for the solitude, the peacefulness, and to think. Bypassing the not-yet-open information center, he stopped at the beginning of the longer five-kilometer loop that brushed up against the park's two larger lakes.

At 5:45 a.m. on Saturday mornings, David often had the park to himself, at least until he returned from the loop. Today, though, four other people—two men and two women—had beaten him to the trailhead. Undecided whether to rush ahead, hold back and wait for them to get ahead, or take the shorter loop, David shuffled his feet and stalled. After some discussion about the distance, the foursome grasped their walking sticks and crossed the gravel path to the head of the shorter trail. Relieved, David entered the longer, five-kilometer trail.

The walks usually diffused his stress: the noise and bustle of the airport, the bus rides, the proximity to people, the cruel irony that the attention he had once craved as an actor had now turned against him.

However, today the stress didn't evaporate as usual. Instead, it coalesced and morphed. Like blood depositing plaque with each flow to the wall of an aortic valve, fragments of Jason West's callous story eddied and swirled in his mind, layering insult on injustice, spite on deceit, and cruelty on malice.

Unaware his pace had quickened to match his racing thoughts, the damp early morning air grabbed at David's throat and swamped his lungs. Hot and sweating, he unbuttoned his coat, slowed to a stop, and leaned one arm on an information board fixed at an angle on top of a post.

Recovered after a few minutes, he studied the large black-on-blue print and the colorful laminated photograph. In it, a small, bright blue and reddish-orange kingfisher dived for small fish from a perch a meter or so above the water. Below the picture of the bird, words informed the reader that, "One of the best places to try and view this behavior is looking straight out across South Lake from the dock, where they may be seen at all times of year."

David, who had walked the dock many times, nodded in agreement with the text.

A meter to the right, another information board drew his attention. In the photograph, a stoat, its yellowish-white underside visible as it stood on hind legs in search of prey, stared at David as he read the caption: "Stoat—a small but voracious predator. A mature male is capable of killing and carrying an adult rabbit. They can live for up to ten years and are able to travel up to five miles/eight kilometers in one hunting session."

More information boards described the red fox and the tern, as well as the amphibians and fish that inhabited the lakes and wetland. Save for a few birds, David couldn't see the inhabitants of the park, but he knew what they were doing: they hunted, they killed, and they consumed. The weak overcame the strong: natural selection.

Rested, but not really calmed, David resumed his walk. Thoughts of the countless life-and-death struggles all around him as nature dictated the actions of the park's inhabitants filled his mind. Images of Jason West pushed into his thoughts. The animals—the stoat and the fox—attacked Jason and gnawed and tore pieces of flesh from his disembowelled body. Bits of bloodied flesh floated in the lake, and the kingfisher pecked at them from above, while unseen, below the water, fish nibbled and tugged.

The fox, his sharp teeth bared under bright dark eyes, swelled and grew until it became a lion. Then the lion and the fox winked at each other, and their forms merged into a towering image of Septimius Severus, the Roman Emperor, from Machiavelli's *The Prince*.

Vivid and violent, the images continued until David sat down on the trail, on the verge of nausea, and placed his head in his hands. As his breathing slowed, the lion and the fox faded from his mind, to be replaced with the Machiavellian assertion that a ruler should be both lion *and* fox.

His memory nudged, and a Machiavellian maxim burst forth: "He who defines his role has more freedom, for people become their roles."

Despite the ferocious and disturbing images, and the accompanying sweat that had dried cold on his skin, David's cheeks dimpled as a tight smile formed on his face.

As he neared the end of the trail, Iago, *The Prince*, and predatory animals merged with scenes from the movie *Sleuth*, and David's thoughts turned to the inevitable mistakes killers always seem to make.

Eighteen

The glass slipped from David's hand and bounced on the thick rubber mat designed to ease back and foot pain for people whose work required long periods of standing. Then the glass rolled off the thick-bottomed mat and stopped at the base of the refrigerator that housed rows of imported bottled beer.

He ignored the glass and acknowledged the man half seated, half standing, on a barstool adjacent to the ordering terminal.

"Sorry about that. You startled me."

"Old habits," the man replied affably. "Not to worry. Can I have a coffee and a menu?"

"Certainly," David said as he slid a menu across the bar.

"Cream, milk, sugar?"

"Black. Just black and hot."

Guiding hot coffee from the machine spout into a white cup, David used the mirror above his head to view the upper torso of his new customer. A clean, pressed navy-blue shirt covered broad shoulders and a deep chest. The man had a thick neck and a close-shaved, ruddy face that blended into close-cropped hair.

David couldn't see the man's eyes, but he felt them on him.

"Hey, David," Nancy chirped lightly as she squeezed between him and the counter. "Food's up for table six. Want me to drop it for you?"

"Yeah, thanks, Nancy."

"How's the Albacore Tuna Nigiri?" the man asked as David placed the coffee on the bar.

"Very good, and fresh. The tuna arrived around half past four this morning on the flight from Thailand."

"Alright, I'll have that. And a glass of water."

After entering the man's order, David asked, "Is this your first time to Sea Food World?"

"No. Well, this is the first time to this one. I used to work out of Manchester, and ate at the one there."

Perceptive, and used to extracting information from customers, David continued in a friendly manner.

"You said you used to work out of Manchester. Will we be seeing you here again, then?"

The man's shoulders tensed at the question.

Sensing the man's discomfort, David added quickly, "Oh, the reason I ask is that we have a draw for free breakfasts for frequent travelers. If you drop a card in the box, you can win. So, if you're likely to come back, it's worth putting your card in."

A thin smile accompanied the slight drop in the man's shoulders as he reached into his shirt pocket, pulled out a glossy business card, and dropped it in the box David had grabbed from the counter behind him.

"Old habits," the man muttered again as David withdrew the box and turned to place it on the counter behind him.

When he turned back, the man had left the bar and seated himself at a table beside the wall. He had positioned the chair sideways, so his back was against the wall to allow a clear view of the eating area, bar, and concourse.

Ten minutes later, with a Tuna Nigiri in one hand and a carafe of fresh coffee in the other, David approached the man's table.

The man watched David's progress and moved some of the papers on the table to make room for the plate.

Placing the plate on the table, David gestured to the man's empty cup.

"I brought more coffee."

The man nodded and sat back while David poured.

As he filled the cup, David glanced at a photograph on top of the pile of papers the man had moved.

"Cup's full," the man said sharply.

"Right, yes. Sorry about that. I, er, just…"

"Pretty good, isn't it?" the man interrupted as he pointed a finger at the glossy, full-color photograph.

A child dominated the foreground. Congealed black blood, brown dirt, and a yellowy tinge obscured the once-white bandage loosely wrapped around the stump of what was left of the child's right arm. Below the child's stump, prostrate in the dirt, lay a woman, her skeletal features conveying the malnutrition and disease that had ended her short life.

In the background, to the right of the child and mother, fatigue-clad soldiers smoked cigarettes and drank cans of Coke, indifferent to the suffering before them. Further back, to the left, more mothers and children waited, huddled together for the illusion of safety.

Flustered, David stammered, "Um, no. Well yes, I suppose so."

"You're shocked. That's good," the man said as he picked up the photograph and placed it in a folder.

Disturbed, and sensing he had been dismissed, David returned to the bar and attended to another customer. The next time he glanced at the table, the man had gone. On the table, various denominations of paper currency poked out from under the white coffee cup.

The man, and the photograph, had unsettled David. Flashes of the child's bloodied stump intruded into his thoughts as he wondered about the child's fate.

He had noticed the man's large camera bag. Why had he presumably taken the picture? And why had he said it was pretty good? *Pretty good for what?* David asked himself.

An hour later, as he tweaked the flow of steam, the coffee machine gave a hiss as it spat out the final drop of a double espresso. Hot, and sweaty, David tucked the remnants of an ice cube under his tongue and carried the espresso to a young, clean-shaven man at the bar who was leafing through a thick pile of typed pages secured in a black three-ring binder.

At his back, a familiar and unwanted voice assaulted David's ears.

"David, did you see my story on ITV's *Veggie Man*? You know, the so-called nutrition expert, who tells everyone how bad red meat is for you and the planet, and that we should all eat grains and green vegetables, while he's busy downing half a bloody cow every week? The pig eats more meat than a rugby fullback. It was wonderful. Everyone said so. Can you believe the bloody hypocrite?"

Pretending he hadn't heard J-MO's boast, David placed the coffee in front of the man.

He was a young, idealistic physician with Doctors Without Borders, who David had learned traveled frequently to desperate places. Now he tilted his head and lifted an eyebrow in a concealed show of sympathy.

After the shared moment, David reluctantly acknowledged J-MO's arrival with a tight smile as he walked the six steps from the doctor to the gossip.

"Good morning, Ms. Ogden," he forced himself to say as he watched her spread the phones—her tools of rumor, innuendo, and lies—on the bar.

"Why, yes it *is* a good morning, David. All the big media outlets have picked up my story. My ratings will rocket."

Disgusted rather than impressed, he managed to be polite but terse in his reply.

"The usual?"

"Yes, but I think a champagne and orange juice are in order as well. I deserve it," J-MO announced, with her chin in the air and a flick of her wrist.

Unfortunately, the orange juice and champagne were in the fridge directly behind David, so he was unable to escape.

"Now tell me, what did you think of the story?"

"I'm sorry," David replied over his shoulder, "but I don't really follow, er, that kind of stuff."

"Well, you should. A man in your business should always have some news to exchange and share with your customers."

A mischievous grin filled J-MO's face as she continued.

"Sometimes I think I should contact your boss, whoever he is, and tell them that you don't really act like a typical bartender."

"Well, when you put it that way," David answered with mock seriousness as he nodded to his left. "The young man at the end of the bar. He's with Doctors Without Borders, and he's going in to Syria next week to help save war-ravaged children, and…"

"Oh, David," J-MO interrupted him. "That's no good. No one is interested in *do-gooders*. Tell me that he's really going because he's having an affair with another doctor, or that he has a thing for children, or that he's selling medicine for profit. That's what people *really* want to read about."

Before he could counter with an indignant response, J-MO continued.

"I'm off to Paris today for another big story. I have a lead on a pro-immigration, women's rights politician who has an illegal immigrant Muslim woman stashed away in a flat for his pleasure! Another bloody hypocrite."

Engrossed in her own press, J-MO gathered her phones, gulped her mimosa, snatched a bite of her bagel, and slid off the barstool. Straightening her clothes, she fixed her eyes on David.

"I can't wait to break this one. It'll kill his career."

David, who had watched J-MO with her unusual detachment, met her eyes.

"What if it's not true?"

"True? That's up to him. I just set the ball rolling. You know, dear, cat amongst the pigeons, and all that."

His sense of detachment continued as he watched and listened to J-MO's heels click and clack across the tiled concourse. As she disappeared from sight, a fatal judgment about her wound its way unchallenged into David's subconscious.

Nineteen

The man with the photograph had unsettled David, but J-MO's loathsome bragging about how her story had exposed and would likely wreck the career of a meat-eating advocate of vegetarianism had angered him.

Later, as he rode the bus home, he reflected again on J-MO and evaluated her contribution to society. As he did, his rage simmered as his mind returned to the thoughts he had had while watching *Sleuth*—and the mistakes killers always seem to make.

Off the bus, David lifted his face to the sun. The early morning to noon shift was his favorite, as it allowed time for being outdoors in the light. Traditional nine-to-five work, especially during the fall and winter months, when daylight was short, kept people in the dark. Besides, Rachel encouraged David to get as much daylight as he could in the winter to help keep his tendency toward depression at bay.

He didn't feel any depression today, though. In fact, an uncommon optimism and sense of purpose had brought a lightness to his step and relaxed his features. In a perverse way, even the morning exchange with J-MO and the uneasiness he'd experienced with the customer with the photograph had brightened his mood.

Even more perverse, or weird, David was currently thinking about death. And that shouldn't really have made him feel good.

Between the bus stop and his flat, there were two establishments critical to David's routine: the Bell on the Green Pub, and Singh's variety store.

The Bell on the Green, locally called "the Bell," had, for David, a lot going for it. With good beer, friendly staff, a decent chicken curry, live entertainment on weekends, and a ten-minute walk to his flat, the pub had quickly compensated for his bleak flat.

In addition, and much to David's surprise when he had first entered the pub, the Bell had an excellent beer garden at the back of the building.

After a brief word with the lunchtime bartender, John, about which band would be playing on the weekend, David took his pint of Foster's lager to the beer garden. Taking a seat at a picnic table toward the center, he tilted his head backward, closed his eyes, and bathed in the weakening late fall sun.

After half a beer and a short nap in the sun, he opened the buckle of his brown, over-the-shoulder satchel. From the inside, he withdrew a black eight-by-five hardcover notepad. Yellow sticky notes, with black ink words and numbers, protruded from different pages, denoting separate sections.

David fingered the sticky notes until he reached the third one with the word *how* printed on it. He opened the page, and a wide, satisfied grin pushed his lips together and squeezed his cheeks. Before him, transposed with neat additions and notes, the lists he had hastily made on the back of a Sea Food World napkins held his gaze and fed his imagination.

It covered several pages. David ran the point of a black pen down the list and turned the pages. He paused briefly at "electrocute," before he stopped at "shoot." Under "shoot," three questions remained unanswered: How to get a gun? How much did it cost? How to learn to shoot?

Internet research of media and police reports suggested that since the banning of private possession of handguns in 1997 following the Dunblane massacre, getting hold of a gun had become very difficult.

Unschooled in the workings of the underworld, David had indirectly broached the subject with a few people in the Bell, as well as some airline passengers. While some said that getting a gun in London was "dead easy, mate," none of them could actually say how to go about it when pressed. Aware that he needed to avoid pushing too hard, in case he was remembered, David had pressed as hard as he dared, yet he still had no idea how to get a gun.

Frustrated, he moved his finger down the list to "poison." Detailed notes on various options, from hemlock and aconite, to mercury, cyanide, and arsenic, filled several pages. Poison appealed to David, mainly because he remained squeamish about the physical closeness and contact required for other forms of murder.

TWENTY

David's day had begun well. His bus ride to work on a crisp spring Friday morning had been filled with pleasant reflections on Thursday's quiz night at the Bell. David, Clair, and his quiz teammates had narrowly beaten the other five quiz teams, and everyone had enjoyed the good-humored competition in the pub.

More importantly, Clair had held his hand under the table and leaned in close several times. David, hypersensitive about his condition and the impact it had had on previous relationships, had sensed that they had moved a step closer. The sensation had buoyed him all evening, and as the bus arrived at Terminal 4, the hope remained.

Unfortunately, his hope faded when he stepped off the bus, and a scruffy, twentysomething male, decked out in a black tracksuit with fake gold and silver "bling" neck chains and bracelets, barged past David, muttered obscenities, and gave a one-fingered salute when challenged by another passenger. The sight and actions of the man instantly darkened David's mood as thoughts of Troy rushed in.

Worse, Troy still had an interest in Clair. The only blot on the quiz night had been him leering at her.

Irritated, and increasingly angry, David had twice made to confront the man, but Clair had told him that he wasn't worth it, and to ignore him. Fortunately, Troy hadn't stayed long in the pub, and the fun of the quiz had pushed the thug out of mind. Until now.

Sour thoughts of Troy led back to Jason West, and for the remainder of the morning, David struggled to keep his composure, and his perspiration, under control. By 11:30, fatigued and confused by his thoughts and emotions about Clair, Jason West, Troy, and a growing perception of his own impotency, David steeled himself to get through the last half hour of his shift.

With compressed lips and a shake of his head, David replaced thoughts of Jason West and Troy with an image of Clair, her slim body relaxed against his as they hugged in the hallway outside the door to David's flat. Her warmth spread through him a second time, forcing his groin to ache, and filling his face with a blushed-red smirk.

Clouded by his thoughts, he didn't notice the arrival of a new customer until the man blurted out with a sly glance, "She must have been a good shag!"

As if caught in the physical act, David's blush deepened into a vibrant crimson.

"What?" he replied sharply.

The man, tattoos adorning both forearms below the white short-sleeved T-shirt tucked in his faded jeans, edged himself onto a barstool and placed a pack of Rothmans cigarettes and a yellow plastic lighter on the bar top.

Unfazed, ignorant, or just oblivious to David's discomfort, the man continued.

"I said, she must have been a good shag. Either that, or you're havin a fucking 'art attack, mate."

"I'm sorry, I was…"

"No need to be sorry, mate. How about a pint? What you got on tap?"

David, his effort to calm himself abandoned, studied the man's appearance and adopted an instant dislike for him. He reminded him of Troy.

"We don't have 'on tap' beer. Only bottles."

"No prob," the man said. "Give me a Stella. Better make it two. Save you a trip, eh?"

David turned to the fridge, took two Stellas out, and reached for a glass from the shelf.

"No need for a glass, mate. Straight from the bottle for me. Less bubbles, and colder. Billy m' name," he added, pointing at the dark tattoo on his right forearm. "I see you're Dave," he said, pointing to the nametag on David's shirt.

"It's David, actually."

"Well, Dave, I'm off to Prague in an hour. Which gives me time for a few more Stella and some of those, how do you say it, aphro-di-si-acs, eh?"

Despite lifelong lessons about how he shouldn't judge a person's status by their clothes or demeanor, David considered Billy an unlikely character to appreciate or afford the seafood—or benefit from whatever sexual enhancement the food may provide.

"Meeting someone, are you?" David asked with disdain.

"You could say that. More like some-many," Billy replied, his dry, chapped lips spread wide across yellowed teeth.

Before David could ask anything else, Billy continued.

"Some-many as in, as many as I want. Prague is full of whores. And cheap, too. I've got me a couple of favorites, ya know. There's a little chink and a black chick that do a threesome thing. F-ing amazing what they will do."

Billy wasn't the first Prague-bound sex tourist David had encountered, and many similar, but more discreet, comments had been passed between other customers.

David, who had never visited Prague, or paid for sex, pursed his lips in disapproval.

"You're a regular then?" he quipped.

"Yeah. Lots of times."

David watched as Billy drained the first Stella and deftly switched to the second.

"I haven't seen you here before."

"That's 'cause I usually have a beer and a burger over at the Prince of Wales pub. Last week, I watched a documentary on Sky 1 about how fish and such is good for gettin it up and keepin it up, eh. So I say to myself, I'm gonna get me some fish instead of a burger and chips. So here I am. What should I have, then?"

David, sensing a way to send Billy back to the Prince of Wales, leaned in conspiratorially and offered some friendly advice.

"Ah, well, Billy, what you really need is salmon and caviar, but it's very expensive."

"Oh yeah," Billy responded with a trace of bravado. "How much would that be, then?"

David placed the menu on the bar, slid it under Billy's nose, and pointed at the most expensive caviar and salmon on the list.

Without flinching, Billy pointed at the different salmon prices.

"Why such a big difference?"

"One's from a farm, and the other is wild. You know, like free-range eggs."

"Which one's gonna give me more lead in the pencil?"

"I can't say for sure, but most, er, discerning people go for the wild salmon and caviar."

"Well, I ain't very decernin, but what the fuck— give me one of each."

Surprised by Billy's choice, David's eyes widened, and he tried again to dissuade the man and be rid of him.

"That's a hundred and fifty pounds. Are you sure?"

After a hot and stale belch, and a curled fist pressed to his chest, Billy gave a nonchalant nod as he spoke.

"Oops, 'scuse me. A hundred and fifty quid. Yeah, no problem, mate. If I like it, I'll 'ave another one, eh. Better give me another beer, too."

Uncertain about Billy's ability to pay, David's hand hovered over the key for a moment before entering the order. As he pushed the icons for the salmon and caviar, the whine of a squeaky wheel announced Larry's arrival.

Responding to Larry's "wheel," Billy turned and called out, "Hey, Larry! 'Ow are ya, mate?"

Larry nudged his cart up against the waste bins and spoke as he walked toward Billy.

"Not so good, Billy. Got me a bit of a cold."

With a dirty elbow on the bar and a foot on the rung of a barstool, Larry made a quizzical face at Billy.

"What you doin here, Billy? Ain't no burger and chips at this place."

Billy winked and nodded, and his smile combined to distort his face.

"I'm gettin a bit of a boost for Prague. Know what I mean, eh?"

"Ah, ya dirty bastard. You'll catch somethin awful one of these days."

"Not me. Always wrap it proper, I do."

David, back from delivering a bagel and lox to a customer at the other end of the bar, saw his nemesis.

"Larry, you're not supposed to stop at the bar and chat with customers. You've the…"

"Ah well," Larry said, nodding toward Billy. "He's not really a customer."

"What do you mean?"

"Me and Larry go way back, don't we, mate?" Billy interjected.

"That's right. So he's a mate, not a customer, see?"

Inclining his head at Larry's cart, Billy said, "I hear you've still got the squeaky wheel, eh?"

"Yep. Better to be seen and heard."

Larry and Billy laughed together at some shared joke, which David could not help but think was at his expense.

Wanting to gain control of the situation, he gestured to the waste station.

"Well, friend or not, you get the bins emptied, eh?"

Larry smiled, nodded, and stepped away from the bar.

"See ya at the dogs sometime, eh, Billy."

Then he walked off to the waste station.

"He's a good man, that Larry," Billy said with affection. "Salt of the earth."

A low ding sounded on the computer screen. Billy's food was ready. David collected it from the pass-through hatch. As he set it on the bar, he turned toward Billy.

"This should do the trick."

Billy, three beers down, and on a fourth that David had slipped onto the bar, whispered back, "Well, to tell you the truth, Dave, I have a backup plan. You see, to get your money's worth from the whores, you gotta keep it up, 'cause soon as you lose the steel, them girls are done with you. So, I got me a couple of little blue pills. So with the fish and the pills, I'm gonna be goin at for hours."

Unable to resist a dig, David grunted.

"So you have to pay for it then?"

Billy bristled and motioned with his fork as he spoke.

"Look here, I don't *have* to pay for it, Davey boy. I *choose* to pay for it. I get plenty o shags and bjs from the little bitches here, but they ain't too keen on doin some of the things I like. Well, most of them aren't. Anyway," he said, as he lowered the fork and stabbed a piece of salmon. "Variety is the spice of life, right?"

Between forkfuls of salmon and caviar and swigs of beer, Billy commented on the food.

"Not bad, this stuff. Only ever had fish and chips before."

"What do you do for a living then, Billy?"

"Me? Oh, a bit of this and that. You know. Whatever."

"You have a girlfriend?"

Billy choked on his food.

"Girlfriend? You gotta be kidding. I just shag 'em and leave 'em. Had lots, got me lots of kids, too, but I don't need them. Well, I gotta go. What's the damage, Dave?"

Without flinching at the cost, Billy placed a pile of crumpled ten- and twenty-pound notes on the bar and left with a smile and light step.

David hadn't liked the man. And the fact that he and Larry were friends only affirmed the rightness of his dislike.

Then thoughts of Billy and Larry merged with images of Troy and produced a conclusion that the world would be a better place without likes of them. And, added his malicious subconscious, people like Jason West.

TWENTY-ONE

Sweat, light but persistent, had dogged David all morning. And the more he thought about it, the damper he became. Stress caused the perspiration, perspiration caused the stress, and round and round it went.

And Jason West had started it all. Then J-MO, the bitch gossip that destroyed lives, had reminded David of the gossips who had helped end his acting career. Then that wanker Mr. Taylor, nose in the air, full of criticisms and complaints. And the bloody white trash lout, Billy, bragging about his sexual perversions and his illegitimate kids. And of course, Larry. No surprise that he was a friend of Billy's. Never mind Troy.

"To hell with them all," David muttered to himself as he stepped off the bus and crossed the road to the sidewalk outside the Bell. Today was Wednesday, which meant dinner-and-movie night with Jenny. It had been a fixture in his life since his acting career had ended.

Outside, on the Bell's small patio, John, the bartender, collected empty glasses, straightened chairs, and wiped off tabletops with a cloth that looked dirtier than the tables. Seeing David approach, he called out to him.

"Hey, David!"

"Hi, John. Busy today?"

"No, dead quiet. You coming in for a quick one?"

Without stopping, David answered with a smile.

"Tempting, but my sister, Jenny, is coming for dinner tonight, and I've got to get some food, tidy up a bit, and start cooking."

"You should come tonight. We're having a two-for-one curry night. Save you the bother of shopping and cooking."

"Good idea, John," David said over his shoulder. "But she's a bit of a homebody, and we're going to watch a movie. See you tomorrow for the quiz."

"OK. Cheers."

Jenny, David thought with sadness, was more than a homebody. Shy and bookish in her youth, and disinclined toward physical activities, she had excelled academically. Her straight "A" record in high school had gained her easy access to university, where she studied and graduated with distinction in science and physics.

Both he and Jenny had attended Manchester University, lived at home, and commuted to school, but David, unlike Jenny, often stayed over at other student flats, or with girlfriends.

They had been quite close during their childhood, and despite the predictable drift that occurs as siblings pursue their own lives and careers, David's disease had brought them closer again.

Jenny, like his parents, had helped David through the physical difficulties of his disease, but Jenny had been the one to help him manage the emotional and psychological problems. Now thirty-three, single, and still shy and bookish, Jenny worked in research for Ridgetop, a global expert in veterinary parasitology.

Thoughts of his sister's introverted and cautious life brought up an unexpected surge of bile from his stomach to his throat, and reminded him that their sibling bond extended beyond normal family experiences.

His illness and depression and her empathy and compassion had forged a deep, yet healthy co-dependency between them. They both needed help—Jenny to give, David to receive. However, that wasn't what caused the bile to rise in David's throat now. He and his sister *had another* bond. One that he hadn't thought about for a long time.

Jenny, three years younger than David, had been in first year university when he was in his fourth and last year. Shy and trusting by nature, she had accepted an invitation to a house party hosted by fourth-year students. Several other first-year students were going, as well.

Alcohol, cannabis, and other drugs had been abundant as the senior students sought to coerce the younger students to do crazy and stupid things, including—if possible—sex.

David, aware and not innocent of the party's intentions, had arrived late in the evening and engaged in the revelry until he recognized one of the girls as a friend of Jenny's.

After a frantic search, he discovered his sister semiconscious and facedown on a bed with an older man standing over her. The man, a former university student who still lived in the house, had his pants down and was poised to enter Jenny's upturned and naked bottom.

Incensed, David had battered the man mercilessly until others had to pull him away. With a broken arm, fractured cheek, and no front teeth, the man had initially pressed charges, until Jenny's lawyer threatened a counter charge of attempted rape.

Jenny, drugged during the ordeal, had recalled little of the actual event. She only spoke of what had happened one time, when she had held David's hand and said a simple thank you. That gratitude, which conveyed immense emotion, had cemented their bond.

Swallowing the bile, David wondered how much of that incident contributed to Jenny's "quiet" life. More importantly, as his budding persona took shape, he wondered where that man was now.

Unaware he had stopped in the street, and startled by an elderly passerby who asked him if he was alright, David shook his dark thoughts away, continued to the store, and considered what to buy for dinner.

Jenny had three favorite meals: lamb, chicken, and pasta. They had had chicken last week, and lamb the week before. That left pasta for today. After gathering the, sauce, ground beef, peppers, zucchini, onions, garlic, and a crusty loaf, David hurried home to clean up and start cooking. Jenny, due at five p.m., would bring wine, beer, dessert, and the movie.

Cursing the plastic bags that cut into his wrist, he inserted the key to unlock the outer door to the house. He jumped and cursed again when Robbie suddenly spoke behind him.

"Hi, David. What are you making for Jenny tonight?"

"Jesus, Robbie, don't sneak up on me like that."

"Sorry, I didn't mean to. Anyway, what's for dinner?" he asked as he held the door for David.

Inside, David handed him the key to the inner door to his flat. With the door open, David took the key back and winked.

"I don't know what's for *your* dinner, Robbie, but I'm making pasta and meat sauce for me and Jenny."

"That's one of Jenny's favorites, right?"

"Yes. Where's your mom?"

"Upstairs, I think. I'm just home from school, and I haven't been up yet. Can I come in?"

"No. I mean, yes. But go see if your mom's home and ask if you can come first."

"What if she's not home yet?"

"Then leave a note, so she won't worry."

David listened as Robbie shouted for his mom as he ran up the stairs and put his own key in the door lock to the flat upstairs.

Two minutes later, Robbie's footsteps pounded back down the stairs and stopped outside David's door.

Inside his flat, David moved to the door and waited for Robbie's "secret" signal.

Knock, pause, knock, knock, pause, knock.

On cue, David opened the door.

"Home?"

"No."

"You left a note?"

"Yes, but there was one for me, too," Robbie answered as he handed a scrap of paper to David.

Before David could read the note, Robbie continued.

"See, it says she will be late, and that I should check in with you when I get home. Can I stay with you till Mom gets home?"

"Alright," David said with a smile, as he thought of the hundred and one questions Robbie would ask while he made dinner. "But I'm going to shower and change first. You head back upstairs and do some homework or something, and come back in twenty minutes, OK?"

Robbie pushed away the happy grin that had formed dimples in his cheeks, adopted his best deep voice, and quoted one of his favorite movie lines.

"I'll be back."

With Robbie gone, David sniffed himself, shed all his clothes, and put them directly in the washing machine. Naked, he headed to the bathroom, opened the small window, turned on the fan to blow air out, and arranged his special soaps and shampoo before turning on the shower.

When he was finished, he smiled again at the thought of Robbie's intense curiosity, shut off the water, dried, and went into the bedroom to dress.

Then Robbie's distinctive knock sounded again, and when David answered the door, instead of coming in, Robbie tossed a soccer ball in his hands excitedly.

"Is it OK if I go to the park with Nico and Michael? I'll be back in an hour, and you could tell Mom where I am when she comes home."

"You mean Nico and Michael from over on Ascot Street?"

"Yeah, you know them, don't you?"

"Yes, alright," David agreed as he remembered the two scruffy brothers and their soccer-crazy father who spent too much time and money in the Bell. "But you be back by five," David warned as he checked his watch.

Mindful that Jenny would also arrive at that time, he hurried inside to chop vegetables and start cooking the ground beef.

As the knife fell and the meat sizzled, David's mind wandered to the list he had made in the pub, and how he should deal with the root cause of all his stress: Jason West.

TWENTY-TWO

Restless, David paced. The digital clock "ticked" to 6:26 a.m. Shadow, unaware of his master's angst, sprawled and purred in deep REM sleep on the sofa.

The day before, Friday, had begun as usual at three a.m. Despite a frustrating shift at the airport, several beers at the Bell, and a late night watching movies which had taken David to 1:30 a.m. on Saturday morning, sleep had eluded him. At least, not the kind that rejuvenated.

Instead, hounded by recurrent fantasies to deal with the source of his restlessness, Jason West, David's sleep had been sporadic. More tired than when he'd lain down, David fingered the rumpled, single A4-sized piece of paper that hung between his thumb and forefinger.

It was a homemade advertising flier, or had been, until he had ripped it down on his way out of the pub, where it had been thumbtacked to the life-stained corkboard in the entranceway to the Bell.

Written in black marker, the flier announced that Around Again would have a "one-day-only, 50 percent discount" on a "great selection of used clothing for all ages and needs." Around Again was a secondhand shop on Tudor Court in Feltham, according to the advertisement.

David didn't really need any clothes. Not used ones, anyway; he had enough of those. But he *did* have an idea; an idea that frightened and exhilarated him. One that nudged him into a decision that, at eight a.m., he would take an hour-long walk to the used clothing store.

~

Wary of waking Clair and Robbie, David thought he had managed a soundless exit from his flat. He should have known better. Robbie, always alert and observant—or nosy and hyper, depending on whom you listened to—leaned from his bedroom window above the common entrance and called down.

"Hey, David. You going to Bedfont Park? Can I come?"

"No. Not today, Robbie."

"Please? Mom will be sleeping for ages, and I got nothing to do. I won't bother you."

Bedfont Park was David's sanctuary from the world, and although Robbie had accompanied himself and Clair there a few times during the summer, he had never taken Robbie in the early morning—or by himself.

"Sorry, Robbie. It's you know, private time. I'll see you when I get back. And let your mom sleep."

"Oh, OK," Robbie answered, disappointment clear in his voice. "But I'm gonna wait right here for you."

Lying to Robbie didn't feel right. Uncomfortable, David gave the kid a smile and left quickly. But as he stepped off the curb and crossed the road, he realized that if he followed through on his idea, he would be lying a whole lot more. And not just to Robbie.

After pacing his flat earlier, the chance to stretch his legs felt good. The air, as ever, was damp, but crisp. Tudor Court, the location of Around Again, lay on Castle Way, about halfway between Feltham Rugby Club and Hanworth Villa Football Club.

He had watched rugby and football games at both clubs in the past, and had a good idea where he would find the shop. An hour after leaving Robbie hanging from his bedroom window, he paused in front of the entrance.

The shop, housed in a unit of what had once been a distribution warehouse for light industrial products, had a single glass door to the left of a large floor-to-roof window. Grime, declining in thickness from bottom to top, covered both door and window, and obscured the inexpertly arranged mannequins and displays. Several large orange Bristol boards, covered with black marker noting discounts, limited-time offers, and poorly sketched images of clothing, confirmed the one-day sale.

As he approached, an erect and tall elderly woman smiled as she held the single door ajar for David to enter the shop. Mingled with the woman's heavy perfume, the musty aroma of "used everything" wafted into his nostrils and triggered memories of past visits to used clothing shops.

Back in high school, Ms. Cook, the young and vivacious drama teacher, would organize trips to secondhand shops to replenish the underfunded drama department's supply of clothing and props. The visits also usually included impromptu direction from Ms. Cook to create and act out a short scene based on any ten articles of clothing or props they could find in two minutes.

"Come on then, dear," whispered the woman who held the door. "Are you going in, or staying out?"

Lost in his recollection of Ms. Cook, David had stopped just inside. He took the heavy door from the woman and held it as she stepped past him.

As he turned to enter the shop, a gruff, unshaven man with mismatched shoes and a large, well-used duffel bag faced David. Impatient, he reformed and shortened the old lady's question.

"In or out?"

Without a reply, David stepped aside and held the door for the man.

"Right then," the man said as he brushed past and out into the world.

The door banged behind David like a cell door. Inside, bright industrial lights, holdovers from the building's previous use, provided glare instead of warmth. Dust, light but active, swirled above the clothes. Accessories, arranged by size, gender, and function on long runs of tubular steel frames with metal and plastic hangers, formed intimidating lines.

Steel shelves, gray, dented, and scuffed, held dress shoes, work boots, sport shoes, and a large collection of rubber Wellington boots. Hats and scarfs, without order or category, hung on treelike stands improvised from long metal rods with spaced hooks fixed in plastic buckets with cement.

Tables, piled high, hoarded, rather than displayed, things that would not fit onto racks, shelves or "trees." Still reminiscing about the class trips with Ms. Cook, David ambled between the rows of used clothing and associated items.

After perusing the wares and dodging two robust women pushing small carts loaded with clothes, he paused. Shoes up or hat down, he mused as he scanned the shop for a place to begin. He could tackle the list in his head from either end, so long as each item conformed to his need for anonymity.

He needed forgettable, plain, and nondescript. Grays, blacks, and dark blues would suit, with no odd designs or unusual accessories, such as oversized buckles or weirdly shaped buttons. Also, David cautioned himself, the costume, as he had begun to think of his soon-to-be-made outfit, must be weather appropriate.

"You look a bit lost, luv," a smart, middle-aged woman shouted out. She wore a blue apron with the words *Around Again* printed in white letters cinched tight across her chest. "Do you need some help?"

"No, thanks. I'm just taking my time."

"Alright then, but give me a wave if you need anything."

David began with "hat down." Within ten minutes, he had an ensemble of clothes draped over the handle of his shopping cart. The shoes took the longest to find. There were plenty of size eight and a half, black, lace-up pairs, but he wanted comfortable ones. He settled on a pair of lightly worn Rockport Derby shoes and added them to the cart.

At the checkout, the same woman who had offered help commented on David's selection as she punched the prices into the cash register.

"If you don't mind me saying, luv, these lot are a bit drab. There are some smart anoraks and a few good leather coats by the back. And these dark sweaters and pants won't get you noticed."

The cash register added David's purchases and dinged as it displayed the total. He passed two twenty-pound notes to the lady and spoke with a somber voice and downcast eyes.

"They're for a funeral. I don't want to be flash."

"Oh, I'm sorry, luv. I didn't mean to…"

"That's OK."

Four used plastic bags from Tesco held David's purchases as he left the shop and set off for the one-hour walk home. During the trek, he noticed a man enter and exit the front gardens of houses.

David slowed and watched the man push an A4-sized, black-and-white single sheet of paper into the mail slot of each house.

With unremarkable plain, dark clothing, the man entered and exited unchallenged and unnoticed. David noted the man's confidence and carefree posture, and the idea in his head added another detail and pulled him further along the path from concept to reality.

It was 10:30 when he approached the front door to his flat. Withdrawing his key, he looked up for signs of Robbie. Relieved the kid wasn't waiting as he had promised, because Robbie would surely notice, and ask about the bags, David moved quickly, crossed the hallway, and entered his flat.

Above David, Robbie, who had stood on his bed to the side of the window out of sight, pressed a small spiral-bound notebook on his knee. Under the heading "David," he noted "Back at 10:30" in neat blue ink from a well-chewed plastic pen. Beside the 10:30, this time using a different chewed pen with red ink, Robbie wrote, "Four plastic bags???"

TWENTY-THREE

Mission Impossible III. *Ethan Hunt and his team infiltrate the Vatican and need to gain access to a surveillance room. Crouched on his knees, Ethan uses his lock-picking skills to open the high-security door.*

Robbie and his mom had rented *MI III* a few months earlier, and while he didn't exactly recall if Ethan used hairpins, Robbie was certain lock picking was real, and that with enough practice, anyone could do it. And all he needed, according to the YouTube video, was two hairpins. Then he could finally discover David's secret. Well, Robbie thought, two hairpins, practice, patience, and a lot of luck.

He decided on six hairpins, because Robbie believed in being prepared. He laid each of them side by side on his desk in front of the computer screen. On screen, a paused video titled "How to Pick a Lock with Hairpins," waited to be un-paused. Two standard "pin and tumbler locks," each screwed to separate pieces of wood, lay next to the hairpins.

The hairpins had come from his mom's hair supplies basket. They had been easy and quick to obtain. The locks had been more difficult to get, and took longer. One, old and a bit stiff, had come from a busted door the school janitor had replaced. The other, a new lock "found" by his friend, Nico, for a pound, had come from a nearby building site.

Robbie, who had watched the five-minute video thirty-three times, held a hairpin in one hand and restarted the video. As instructed, he bent the first hairpin open until the ends were about ninety degrees apart. Next, using his teeth, he removed the bit of rubber from the straight end on the hairpin.

Then he inserted about a centimeter of the now-exposed metal end in the mouth of the older lock and applied upward pressure to create a slight bend in the metal. Next, Robbie bent the other half of the hairpin back on itself to make a kind of handle. This hairpin, as per the video, was now a lock pick. The second hairpin, after bending the folded U end into a three-centimeter right angle, became the lever to apply—when inserted in the lock—pressure and rotational force on the lock mechanism.

Following the instructions, Robbie inserted the lever in the lower side of the keyhole and applied rotational pressure to the barrel of the lock. With the lock mechanism under pressure, he inserted the pick above the lever and began to feel for the first pin of the lock and tumbler system.

With constant pressure on the barrel, each pin had to be picked at and forced upward, until the rotation of the barrel prevented the pin from falling back down. Eventually, with all the pins forced upward, the rotational pressure on the barrel would act like a key to open the lock.

At least, that was what happened for the thirty-fourth time in the video, as Robbie fiddled and struggled unsuccessfully for the first time with his hairpin tools and the newer lock.

The video played a forty-second time as it accompanied Robbie's thirteenth and successful attempt to open the lock. Amazed that he had actually done it, he reset the lock and tried again. This time he needed only seven attempts to open the lock, then four. After an hour and a half, with sweaty, numb fingers and tired eyes, Robbie, who could not do better than four attempts, took a break, munched a bag of salt and vinegar chips, and allowed himself some self-congratulations.

After a bathroom visit and a much-needed hand washing, he made a second set of hairpin tools and applied his new skills to the older lock. He expected the older lock, which had rust and grime on it, to be more difficult to open, but he only needed three tries before the lock yielded.

His success brought on a flood of fantasies as Robbie first imagined himself as a thief stealing jewels and money, so his mom wouldn't have to work anymore. Then, realizing that thieving was bad, he became a government agent recovering stolen documents critical to England's defense system.

Excited with his newly learned ability, Robbie gathered a soft facecloth from the bathroom. Then, just like in the movies, he laid his lock-picking tools on the cloth and carefully folded it over them. The cloth he placed in his own locked box in his closet.

As he did so, he suddenly wondered if his own secrets were that secure. What if his mom had learned how to pick locks? After chuckling at the image of his mom crouched like Ethan Hunt before the lock to his chest, Robbie became serious. He now had the ability to open David's box and discover his secrets. Now he had to decide if he should really do it. And if he did, what would he do with whatever he discovered?

TWENTY-FOUR

At seven a.m., sweat and odor, the unwanted companions that hounded and tormented David's existence, simmered on the verge of eruption as he fought to corral his excitement and apprehension. He was excited by the clothes for his disguise that lay tucked out of sight under his bed, yet apprehensive that he had taken a fateful step. To calm himself, he rolled an ice cube around his mouth and inhaled deeply.

Three hours later, the black, knee-length overcoat, dark blue trousers, black lace-up shoes, gray scarf, and a brownish hat that was a cross between a flat cap and a beanie gave David the desired blandness he was after. A blandness that seemed to make him disappear as he passed in front of the brick and stone frontages of the Victorian-era houses on Lauderdale Road in West London. Clear, black-rimmed glasses, a last-minute prop added from a box of costume accessories he kept in a closet, completed the disguise.

A lingering dampness, a light drizzle, and weak light courtesy of dirty white clouds matched his muted, dull clothing. In his leather-gloved hands, David carried a thick stack of fliers taken from the entrance to Tesco Express, the nearby grocery store. The colorful flier listed daily, weekly, and "one-time-only" special offers available for a limited time, or until the next flier came off the printer.

Cars, lined bumper to bumper on both sides of the narrow street, made the sidewalk claustrophobic as David, head down, stepped over uneven flagstones and dodged open-topped wheelie bins already emptied by the early morning garbage collection.

He had pushed the first flier through a letterbox at 9:45 at the far end of the street on the opposite side of the road to Jason West's flat. By ten a.m., he had passed Jason's flat, crossed the road, and started his delivery run on Jason's side of the road.

Ten or more people, a mix of old, young, male, and female, white and brown, had shared the sidewalk with him. Focused on the need to navigate obstacles, listen to earphones, or gaze at cell phones, nobody took any notice of the drab man delivering fliers no one really wanted. And nobody said good morning, either.

Finding out where Jason lived had been unexpectedly easy, if a little convoluted. First, after a quick internet search, David had called Jason's agent, the one from the airport. Pretending to be a producer from Scottish TV seeking a lead for a detective drama, David had asked the agent to provide some background on Jason's suitability for the part.

While the agent had talked, David had listened and made a mental note of the man's voice. After a few minutes, David hung up. He had what he needed. A few days later, David called the agent's office a few times until the receptionist, or assistant, who had introduced herself as Julie, advised that the agent was away for the day. A half hour later, David called again and mimicked the agent's voice and tone.

"Julie, what's West's postcode? Somebody wants to send him a personal gift for god's sake, and I need the address now."

After a pause and a few keyboard clicks, Julie responded.

"W9 1JA."

"Right, and what's the street again?"

"Lauderdale Road, 83 A."

Simple as that, David had hung up.

Lauderdale Road in Maida Vale made sense. Not far north of the West End, and only twenty minutes from Piccadilly Circus. It was also close to the BBC's main London recording studios, as well as the area of Little Venice. Maida Vale had long been a favored locale for working actors. Not exclusive, but regarded as "medium cool" by the websites that concerned themselves with such things.

Number 83 Lauderdale Road, like most large Victorian-era houses, had been converted into multiple flats. The upper floor and attic, once the refuge of the lower servant classes rarely seen by the house owners, had become a chic studio apartment. The second and third floors were spacious one-bedroom flats with "unique features and character," while the ground floor, Jason's flat, boasted a formal dining room, a large kitchen, a drawing room, and a reading room with double-patio doors that opened onto a private treed garden. The Victorians were fond of porches, and two white columns stood guard in front of the main front door.

David approached Jason West's home, and with fliers clearly visible in his left hand, pushed open the solid black wooden front door with his right. Through the door, he stopped in the entrance hall. What had been the house's original grand entrance now had four additional black doors, each with a stylish brass letter symmetrically placed in the center below an oblong-shaped, double-paned window. Each door provided individual access to the building's four flats.

Three doors, B, C, and D, stood to the right. Door A stood to the left. Three letterboxes, B, C, and D, hung together on a wall, and each held a sticker with gold lettering, with the same blunt message "No Soliciting—No Fliers."

Despite the message, David stuffed a flier in each mailbox, then turned to door A.

Up against it, he peered through the head-height window into a roughly eight-by-ten-foot entrance hall. Another black door, with the number 83 preceding the letter A, stood to the left. A mailbox with the same sticker and different letter hung on a wall beside the door. A three-seat wooden bench, an umbrella stand, and a plain doormat completed the room.

A firm push to overcome the self-closing mechanism, opened the outer door, and David stepped into the private entrance. With his back to the outer door, he studied door 83 A: solid wood with a spy hole and two locks. David, not a locksmith, but a flat resident, had two locks on his own door. One a dead bolt, the other a self-activating latch.

The latch locked itself behind you when you went out, or in. The dead bolt needed either a key turn from the outside when you left, or a turn with a handle from the inside if you "locked up" for the night. Both could be opened from the inside, of course.

At floor level, about four feet from the door, a small single-pane rectangle window caught his eye. Curious, David crouched down. On his knees, he looked through the dust-covered glass into Jason West's flat onto a cream-colored wall and the chrome legs of a table. Unknown to David, the window was an eccentric leftover from the Gothic revival era, when stained glass was popular with the Victorians. Now the stained glass was gone, but the window remained.

Crouched on all fours, inside Jason's private entranceway, David contemplated the small window. He guessed it was about twelve by eighteen inches, and about four feet from the front door. Too small to fit through, and besides, his ideal plan for Jason's death required entry to and exit from the flat without leaving a trace. This would preclude smashing the glass. Or would it?

A memory about the use of sugar glass, made from sugar, corn syrup, and water as a prop for breaking windowpanes in plays and movies, merged with thoughts of a conversation about using tape to hold glass in place while it breaks. With an idea forming in his mind, David pressed a flier against the window and tore the paper to make a template of the glass.

Pleased with his success, and flush with an idea of how to gain undetected entry into West's flat, he stuffed the makeshift template in his overcoat pocket and exited the small entrance.

As the outer street door closed behind David, the inaudible and dimmed flashing of the motion-activated camera hidden in the false ceiling of the main entrance stopped recording.

TWENTY-FIVE

The pasta sauce was ready but Jenny was late. So was Robbie. Jenny had called, but Robbie couldn't. During the half hour that Jenny had said she would be late, David went in search of Robbie.

He found him in the park, tucked under a bush holding the end of a long stick up against his cheek, his left eye "sighted" down the length of the stick. A plastic water bottle, with the bottom cut off, had been tied midway down the stick. Robbie had his right eye focused on the opening and out through the neck of the bottle.

Engrossed, he didn't realize David's presence until he spoke to him.

"Any sign of them yet?"

"No, sir," Robbie replied without moving.

"Well, you've stood watch long enough. Time to eat."

"What if they come while I'm eating?"

David, familiar with Robbie's playacting and fantasies, wanted to extend the scene a little longer, but Jenny would be arriving soon.

"Where are your friends? I thought you were playing together."

Pulling his cheek from the stick, Robbie eased himself from his prone position under the bush and sighed.

"We did for a while, but they wanted to go to the new building site over on Tatton Road and see what was lying around. But I didn't want to go, because I saw a woman by the trees. I think she was a spy or a scout. I watched her through my scope for ages. She's gone now, but I'm keeping watch for intruders."

"Good choice, Robbie, but you should have come home like we agreed. It's twenty-five past five already."

Upright, Robbie brushed himself off.

"I'm sorry, David. I, you know, found this stick and then the bottle, and…"

"It's alright. Come on, let's go."

When David and Robbie arrived back at the flat, Jenny and Clair stood talking outside the front door. Clair, with her straight-legged faded blue jeans stretched out at the knees, rumpled sweater, worn running shoes, gray anorak, and a beat-up shoulder bag clutched in a ring-laden hand, nodded to Jenny as she spoke.

"See, I told you they were off playing together!"

In contrast, Jenny, who had likely come straight from work, wore black "sensible shoes," plain dark pants, a white shirt, an unbuttoned, dark waist-length coat, and held a smart black zipper-style document bag.

As David approached them, with Robbie a few steps behind with his "rifle" over his shoulder, Jenny quipped in mock annoyance, loud enough for David to hear, "So much for my dinner, then."

It wasn't just the clothes that marked the women as drastically different from each other. Clair had short, dyed reddish hair, multiple earrings in each ear, high, prominent cheekbones, a pert nose, and a thin, almost shapeless figure which hid taut muscles and what David hoped was smooth, blemish-free skin.

Jenny, unadorned with jewelry, had shoulder-length brown hair, pudgy cheeks, and a wide nose above a full body, with noticeable breasts and wide hips. Yes, they were different in many respects, but equal in that David loved them both.

While Robbie hugged his mom and explained what had happened, David unconsciously made mooneyes at Clair.

When Jenny coughed, David recovered.

Clair, who had blushed, turned away, opened the door to her flat, and called lightly, "Have a good dinner, you two, and keep the noise down!"

David smiled. He always kept the noise down because he used headphones when he watched movies, especially when he couldn't sleep because of his shift work.

~

"Dinner's almost ready," David said to Jenny as he moved toward his own front door and inserted the key. "Just have to boil the water."

While the water heated, he set two places at the small square table that straddled an invisible line between the kitchen and the living room.

Jenny, happy to let her brother set the table, moved around the living room and straightened the two cushions on the sofa. Then she closed the curtains, folded a newspaper, and generally squared and tidied things that didn't really need attention.

Like him, she needed things neat and organized. Both of them had a slight tendency toward OCD, which meant that they each had their own definition of tidy and organized.

Done with the living room, Jenny made for the bathroom. Halfway down the short hallway, she paused at the door to David's bedroom. Jutting out from under the bed, a plastic bag with clothes spilling from the open top caught her eye.

"Wine or beer?" David called from the kitchen, as Jenny moved closer to the bags.

"Wine, please. I'll be right there."

She lifted the clothes, rummaged a little, and wondered what David wanted with them.

"Come on, Jenny!" David called. "Dinner is ready."

In the kitchen, he handed her a glass of wine.

"What's the movie tonight?" he asked with excitement.

"I brought *Pleasantville*. It's been ages since we've watched it, and I thought we could do with a good, uplifting kinda story."

"Great," David answered with a broad smile. He thought Jenny's choice was typical of her optimistic outlook on life. "That'll be fun."

Warmed and assured by her brother's smile, Jenny sipped her wine.

"Say, David, you seem pretty cheerful. What's going on?"

He had his back to her as he tipped the pasta and water into the strainer over the sink.

"Nothing. Just glad you're here, that's all."

"Have you and Clair…?"

"No, no. I…"

"I'm sorry, David. I didn't mean to pry."

A grimace crossed his face.

"You're not. It's just that, well, I have to take things slow. You know that."

Jenny did know. Few romantic, or even platonic friendships, had survived David's condition. Moving to her brother beside the sink, she placed her arm around him and pulled him close. Words weren't needed as strength, comfort, support, and love flowed from one sibling to the other.

"How's it going?" Jenny asked, referring to David's condition. "Any changes? Are you managing alright?"

The last of the water had drained from the pasta, and with a flourish, he transferred the steaming penne noodles to a warmed bowl. Then he added meat sauce and placed the bowl on the table. Pushing aside thoughts of Jason West and the miserable weeks since he'd seen him, David grinned.

"Yes, all good. Just the occasional flare-up if I get overtired or stressed, but everything is going pretty well."

"I'm so glad. It's good to see you happy. Listen, I was going to tell you later, but there is a new soap product on the market. It's called Hydrox Face Wash."

David sat and nodded for Jenny to do the same. Then he reached for the serving forks and loaded pasta onto his plate.

"I know about it. I got an email alert from my online support group on Monday. Two women in the group have tried it and said it works pretty well. I'm going to get some on the weekend."

"And you're sure you're OK, David?"

"Yes. Absolutely. Come on, let's eat."

He hummed as he passed a plate of pasta to Jenny, topped off her wine, and sprinkled Parmesan cheese.

"Hey," she continued. "It's the clothes, isn't it? That's what you're so happy about."

"Clothes? What clothes?" David blurted, caught off guard.

"The ones in the bedroom. The bags of old clothes. They were half out of the bag, and I went in to tidy them. Have you gotten a part, David? That would be so wonderful."

Using a mouthful of pasta to stall, he thought about the clothes. He was sure he had tucked them well under the bed, out of sight.

"Oh, those. No, no part in a play or anything like that. I found the bags by the road and they seemed alright, so I brought them in. I thought I would drop them in one of those donation boxes. No need for them to go to waste."

"That's thoughtful of you, David. Well, if it's not Clair and you haven't landed a part in a play or something, then why are you so cheerful?"

He wanted to tell his sister that after years of apprehension and fear about his condition, of hiding in a seafood bar, of failed relationships and friendships, of living life through movies, of being impotent, of being a victim, he finally had a purpose.

A purpose that would exorcize his anger, redress his injustices, and enable him to be the actor that he should be. And that purpose was the destruction of Jason West.

Instead, around a mouthful of bread, David channeled happy thoughts into his eyes.

"I'm not sure, really. I just feel pretty good about things, that's all."

"Well, whatever it is, I hope it keeps on."

"Yes," David replied. "Me, too."

Twenty-Six

Jason West, the narcissistic, conceited, and scheming little bastard, had done well for himself, David grudgingly acknowledged. But as he placed a latex-gloved hand on the single pane of the twelve-by-eighteen-inch rectangle window, four feet from the front door of West's trendy ground-floor flat, he had a pleasing thought: *Your success can't save you now.*

West, according to his official website, was "on location in Germany to audition for a proposed adaptation of Philip Kerr's novel, *Berlin Noir: The Pale Criminal.*" The website hadn't provided exact dates, but a fan blog, hosted by that strange breed of humans who identify and obsess with public figures, posted hourly updates on the minutiae of West's life. Just before eight p.m., when David left his flat, the most recent blog entry included a photo of West outside a chic Munich restaurant.

By 9:20 p.m., after a one-hour train and tube ride from Feltham via Waterloo to Maida Vale station, David had walked confidently along Lauderdale Road. Besides intermittent vehicle traffic, only a dog walker, three youths, and a middle-aged couple shared the path with him.

Dressed in the same drab clothes as when he had delivered the fliers during his earlier "rehearsal run," David focused his mind on playing the part he had fashioned for himself. He hadn't hesitated when opening the outer door, stepping in, and turning left. Then he had opened the second door and entered Jason West's private entrance hall.

With his left hand pressed against the window, David chuckled to himself as he imagined a scene from the 1959 film adaptation of *The Bat*. In the movie, the murderer used a small blade to cut a hole from a glass-paned door, which he then unlocked and opened by reaching inside.

David, who knew from research and stage talk that cutting perfect holes in glass windows with sharp objects was all Hollywood lore, wished it was so easy.

Instead of a sharp knife, a diamond ring, or the circular glass cutter of moviemaking, he took a steel claw hammer with a thick wad of towel over the blunt end from a black holdall. With his right hand, after two practice swings, he hit the window hard.

As expected, the glass broke. Instead of a loud tinkling of falling glass, however, a dull thud accompanied the hammer's blow. Instead of falling, the glass stuck to the Gorilla Tape David had used to cover the entire pane.

The technique required as small a window as possible, with the glass completely covered in tape, and one firm hit with a hammer, followed by firm pushes with the palm of the hand. This was all according the website that had provided David with the information.

As instructed, he had pushed until the glass bent inward. Then, after switching the hammer for a knife, he cut gaps between the tape and the glass until he was able to tear a hole large enough for his hand and arm.

With an extendable claw used by garbage collectors, David had easily reached the door lock. Then he flicked the dead bolt and the self-locking latch. A more difficult part required him to push the door from outside with his foot as he leaned in to flick the self-latch open.

Moments later, he successfully entered the flat.

With his back against the door, he paused to listen to the low hum of approval from the audience he knew watched his every move from the darkness.

Satisfied, David stepped left, knelt beside the broken window, opened his black bag, and gently withdrew a towel swaddled in Bubble Wrap.

He eased a grimy twelve-by-eighteen glass rectangle out and laid it on the floor. Working quickly, he laid the towel and Bubble Wrap in front of the partial broken window and tapped and pulled the remaining glass from the frame. After removing it, he scraped out the old putty and cleaned up the debris.

The replacement glass, cut to size from the paper template he had made on his first visit, fit the window perfectly. Within five minutes, he had secured the window in place with fresh putty.

David then entered the flat's living room, and from around the baseboard behind a sofa, he used a small brush and a piece of paper to gather dust, hair, and other household debris which had accumulated in hard-to-reach places.

Returning to the new window, he held the paper to the bottom edge and lightly blew the household debris onto the wet window putty. When he was satisfied that the putty appeared old, he blew the remaining dust and dirt on the putty, holding the sides and top of the window. Together with the grime that he had applied a few days earlier to the glass facing outside, he was confident he had obscured the newness of the glass.

With the glass in place and the door locked, David paused. Instead of the usual closed-off spaces of Victorian design, the interior had been modernized into an open-plan layout. Weak light from the street reflected off the glass and stainless steel in the kitchen area to the left, creating a shadow beyond a sofa, several chairs, and a table in the living room area directly ahead. To the right, he found the cache of Scotch bottles he had expected.

About twenty of them, most consumed between a half and a third, stood with their labels outward, toward the back of a well-polished table. Six heavy lead crystal glasses stood guard in front of the bottles, along with napkins and two empty silver bowls. A small ice bucket, with the tongs lying on top of the lid, completed the arrangement.

David studied the labels. All were single malt, none less than ten years old, and two, almost empty, had been casked twenty-five years earlier. Caol Ila, and Ardbeg from Islay, were the prominent ones. The same two West had asked for at the airport. Positioned around the room, on side tables, walls, and the mantle above the gas fireplace, there were awards, photos, and playbills, all proclaiming Jason West's success.

They seemed to mock David a failure. A failure David blamed on West, and people *like* him.

Fighting an urge to smash it all, David entered the kitchen, opened the freezer drawer at the bottom of the fridge, and took out a full tray of ice cubes. Over the sink, he pried out two cubes and set the tray on the draining board.

Manipulating the audience's anticipation, he moved slightly to allow the light from the street to illuminate his actions. Assured that he had their attention, he opened his holdall bag and withdrew a small stainless steel hot/cold thermos. Then he unscrewed the top and tipped out two ice cubes made with cold-pressed peanut oil onto the ice cube tray, nudging them into the two empty spaces.

Under the faucet, as cold water dripped on the two replacement ice cubes, David recalled West's rudeness when ordering food at the airport, and how he had preferred his Scotch:

"And put it over ice, but only two ice cubes… And I'll take a bagel and smoked salmon. But the bagel has to be peanut-free."

"You have a peanut allergy, sir?"

"Yes, otherwise I wouldn't be asking for peanut-free, would I?"

Done with the water, David returned the tray to the freezer. Next, he walked down the hallway past the front door and entered West's bathroom. After a quick search, he found two EpiPens. One in the drawer beside the sink, and one in the medicine cabinet.

One at a time, following instructions on the package, David formed a fist around the auto-injector, with the black tip facing down. Then he pulled off the safety cap and arranged the black tip against the triple-folded towel he had placed on his thigh. After a firm push, the auto-injector released the spring-loaded needle and the lifesaving epinephrine seeped into the towel.

After recapping the EpiPens, he placed them back in the drawer and the cabinet. He found and emptied two more. One in a bedside table, and one in a kitchen drawer. After an internal debate, he returned to the bathroom and pocketed one.

David expected that West would have traveled with an EpiPen, but he was certain that the actor would be more likely to pour a drink before unpacking, then reach for the EpiPens in the kitchen, bathroom, or bedroom before rummaging through his luggage.

David stood by the front door intending to take a self-satisfied last look at the life and times of Jason West, and also to inhale the admiration of his audience.

Instead, panic ripped through him like wildfire. To the left of the front door, obscured slightly by several coats hung on a freestanding rack, a red light pulsed. Pulling the coats aside, David's heart banged as he read the digital message scrolling across the small screen of the alarm system: "Alarm Activated: Response Dispatched."

Confused, because he hadn't heard an alarm, and afraid because he had lingered in West's flat, David quickly pulled the door closed and ran out through the private entranceway to the main front door.

Gasps of disbelief filled his ears as the audience sensed his imminent capture.

Expecting sirens and flashing lights at any moment, he managed to check himself at the door and peer up and down the street. All was quiet, save for regular traffic and pedestrians, so David forced himself to walk to the street and across the road.

As his foot hit the pavement, a white car with "Security Response" stenciled in black letters on the side eased to a quiet stop in front of West's flat. Two black-clad men, large flashlights in hand, exited the car and approached the main front door to West's building. As they passed out of sight, David, trembling and soaked in perspiration, walked on.

Two streets away, tense and overcome with emotion, he stopped.

Loud, enthusiastic clapping and shouts of "well done" had replaced the gasps of disbelief from the audience. Humbled and grateful, David bowed low and drank in the adulation.

When the lights faded and the curtain fell, David acknowledged that he had been lucky. That he had been spared the consequences of a beginner's mistake. Then his delusional subconscious altered the narrative to portray him as a gifted actor who had "simply adjusted and adapted to the unexpected."

No, David assured himself, it hadn't been luck that he had eluded the security guards summoned by West's silent alarm system. It had been his superior acting abilities, and the rightness of his actions.

Secure in his delusions, he returned home to bask in his success.

TWENTY-SEVEN

"What's the hurry, Robbie? It's only half past seven. You've an hour before you need to leave for school."

Stuffing his lunch in his school bag, Robbie, avoided his mom's eyes as he told his lie.

"Oh, Shadow has been a bit, you know, fussy, and David, well, he thought he needed a bit more play time. So I thought I would go early and play longer. Is that OK, Mom?"

Clair, pleased that her son's connection with Shadow supported his acceptance of David, helped Robbie shoulder his school bag and then reminded him about David's flat.

"Yes, that's fine. But be sure to lock the door and bring the key back before you go to school, OK?"

"OK, Mom," Robbie tossed over his shoulder as he tore through the front door and pounded down the stairs.

Once inside David's flat, he fought to stay calm and patient as Shadow purred and rubbed to communicate his demand for attention. Fifteen minutes later, which was about the amount of time he usually played with the cat, it capriciously "dismissed" Robbie and curled itself on the sofa.

With Shadow satisfied and settled, Robbie unzipped the small pocket on the front of his school bag and reverently withdrew the soft cloth that contained his homemade lock picks. With unconscious stealth, he crept to David's bedroom, closed the door behind him, and dragged the laundry basket to the center of the room. Holding his breath, he tossed the clothes on the bed, reached in the basket, lifted the wooden box out, and placed it on the floor.

A rapid exhale followed, as Robbie studied the shiny brass lock on the front of the box. Doubt swept over him. Doubt that he could actually open the lock, but also dread about what the box might contain. Hot, despite the fact that David rarely turned the heating on, Robbie steeled himself, unrolled the cloth, and took out the pick and lever.

Playing the video in his head, Robbie inserted first the lever, then the pick. With pressure on the lever, he wiggled the pick up and down in search of the first pin of the lock and tumbler system. Immediately, distinct clicks sounded as three pins released and lifted upward. The remaining pins took a little longer, but in less than five minutes, the barrel rolled and the lock clicked open.

Excitement trumped doubt, and Robbie lifted the lid. Inside, he was surprised to find a plain black binder similar—but thicker—to the ones he himself used. Impatient, he withdrew it, immediately opened the cover, and flipped through the pages.

Trawling through the binder, Robbie was first impressed and then awed that David was an actor. Then he became angry at the details of David's disease, the need for therapy, and the loss of his acting career. Toward the end, as he learned more of David's struggles, empathy displaced anger, until finally; all he felt was admiration and respect for David.

The onslaught of emotions, which he didn't fully understand, quickly drained Robbie. Aware that he would have to study the information more thoroughly, he brought his camera from his school bag and photographed every page. With the photographs taken, he returned everything to its place, then reached down to the floor to collect his tools and the cloth.

In his peripheral vision, a plastic Tesco grocery bag under the end of David's bed caught his attention.

Intrigued, he pulled the bag and a second one out and looked inside. In a few moments, the bag's contents lay on the bed: a black coat, a pair of blue trousers, black shoes, a scarf, and a plain brownish hat. Certain he had never seen David in these clothes, and disturbed as to why they would be under the bed rather than in the closet or drawer, Robbie clicked away with his camera. Done, he rebagged the clothes, pushed the bags back under the bed, and exited the bedroom.

A quick glance at his watch told him that he had to be going, but as he made his way to open the front door, Shadow meowed loudly from the bathroom. Like most cats, Shadow was reluctant to use a dirty litter box, and scooping it was one of Robbie's main jobs. Distracted by his snooping, he had forgotten, but now he rushed to the bathroom.

The cat, with reproachful eyes, waited while Robbie scooped the damp litter in the garbage can and tossed the dry turds into the toilet and flushed. As the water swirled, Robbie noticed a yellow and red plastic cylinder positioned upright on the window ledge beside the prickly cactus plant.

Picking up the cylinder, he read the word EpiPen through the plastic cover. They weren't common at his school, but he had seen some kids with them, and recalled that they needed them for asthma, or if they ate something like nuts.

Robbie had solved the secret of David's box, which really wasn't much of a secret—more just personal stuff, and he felt guilty because it kinda showed how David had worked hard to overcome a lot of difficulties with his disease.

But now, with hidden clothes, an EpiPen that he had never heard David or his mom talk about, and a weird entry on the last page of the scrapbook about being a prince, Robbie felt more uncertainty than he had before he opened the box.

In fact, it seemed like David had a ton more secrets. And that made Robbie more worried for his mom than ever.

TWENTY-EIGHT

Everything about killing West had exhausted David. The clothes, the reconnaissance, making the replacement windowpane, the cold-pressed peanut oil ice cubes, breaking into West's flat. Not to mention the security guards and the excruciating wait for the bastard to take one last drink. No matter how many showers he took or the number of times he changed clothes, David still sweat and stank.

Adding to his real-world stress, David's subconscious repeatedly relived and embellished his acting performance, and emphasized his ability to break into the flat, set the trap, and leave without a trace.

This, his inner self boasted, had been *real* acting. Layered between reality and delusion, he created in his mind an imagined scene of West's last moments.

How his skin had swelled, reddened, and itched. The tightness in his chest, the constriction of his throat, and his weeping eyes and runny nose. Then desperation, as West scrambled for an EpiPen, clawed off the protective top, and stabbed himself in the thigh. His confusion as the symptoms worsened.

How his desperation then changed to panic, as he stumbled from room to room to grab and apply another empty EpiPen. Then a final hope, as West ripped open his luggage for the EpiPen he traveled with. Too late, his heart racing, his throat swollen to a close, his face distorted and bloated, West had expired without fanfare, witness, or audience.

Six days David waited: three before West returned from Germany, and three after. Then, West's agent sent Julie, the woman David had tricked into providing West's address, to the flat with a spare key to find out why West hadn't answered calls.

To David's delight and sense of justice, Julie, in an interview with *Celebrity Magazine*, had revealed that the smell from West's flat had been unbearable.

When West "officially" died, David's sweating eased.

Equally perceptive of himself as he was of others, David realized West's death had changed him. It wasn't a single, dramatic alteration, but a gradual, incremental sensation that he possessed new abilities: a self-awareness mixed with power and a growing belief that he had a right—almost a duty—to judge those worthy of life, and more importantly, those condemned to death.

Fueled by resentment, bitterness, and injustice, he embraced his burgeoning psychosis, unaware that a neurological gateway to a hybrid sociopathic and psychopathic psychology had cracked open in his mind.

~

On the flat-screen HD TV suspended above his head, the update on West's murder, relegated to a footnote on the 24/7 Sky News channel, hadn't changed much during the last week.

The Specialist Crime and Operations section of London's Metropolitan Police still had no idea exactly how or why up-and-coming actor Jason West had been murdered, if media reports could be believed.

But David didn't believe the media. He suspected the police knew *exactly* how West had died, but that they didn't know *why*.

David did. And he wouldn't be sharing that knowledge with anyone.

All had gone well, except for a brief scare when early news reports indicated the police had video recordings of the main entrance to West's flat, and had interviewed two security guards who had responded to an alarm. The anxiety ended when later reports revealed the older video recording device only had a forty-eight-hour recording time, and that the security guards had actually seen nothing.

The reports and declining media interest, aided by his subconscious, reinforced David's delusional infallibility. As he tuned out the looped narrative, a woman's voice, loud and rude, assaulted his ear and replaced the staid drone of the TV anchor.

Thirty feet away, a phone pressed to her ear with her shoulder, J-MO weaved an erratic path between commuters as she hurried toward David's bar. Words, some soft, most harsh, streamed from her mouth as she dug phones, a notepad, and pens from her bag and arranged them on the bar.

Mouthing "coffee" between grunts and sharp rebukes, she eased herself onto a barstool.

As David placed the requested coffee on the bar, J-MO dropped her left shoulder, deftly caught the phone in her left hand, pressed the screen icon to end the call, and placed the phone on the bar beside the three other phones.

"Ms. Ogden," David began with some concern, despite his distaste for the woman and her profession. "What happened?"

"Oh, this?" J-MO asked proudly as she gestured to the puffy blue blemishes around her right eye. "Some little lesbo bitch took a cheap shot at me a few days ago. She's got a part in *Coronation Street*, but that might be all over now."

"Why?"

"Because I told the truth about her and the woman she was sleeping with. Apparently, she was surprised when her family and her boyfriend disowned her."

"That's terrible."

"Yes, I know. Cheating on her boyfriend with a woman. Imagine how he feels. He's handsome, too."

"I mean, terrible for *her*."

"For her? What about me? Not to mention, her poor dad, who is devastated that his little girl likes other girls. And what about the rest of her family? Her gran, the poor old thing, is…"

J-MO's self-serving rant continued, but David was thinking instead of listening.

"…and if I say so myself, it's a bloody good job that I'm good at what I do."

Tirade over, J-MO pushed her chin in the air and stared expectantly at David.

"What," David asked, with quiet menace clear in his voice, "do you actually produce or achieve?"

Eager to spread the gospel according to J-MO, and missing the edge in the question, she responded even more self-righteously than usual.

"I produce *truth*. I expose lies that hide the truth. Without me, people would never know the truth behind the gloss, and the facade that hides the reality of entertainment, politics, and business."

"What about the people you hurt, though? The lives you destroy?"

"I don't hurt them, David. They hurt *themselves* through their actions, their deceit, and their lies. I simply turn the light on them."

"Don't they have a right to privacy?"

"Not if what they are doing is wrong."

"But who decides what's right and wrong?"

"Don't be silly. If someone's husband is shagging another woman, or a politician is criticizing some policy or other while doing the very thing himself, they deserve to be exposed."

Creases spread across David's forehead, and half-clenched fists complemented his frustration and budding anger.

"There could be reasons why they are acting that way. Reasons you wouldn't know anything about. Besides," he continued, oblivious to his own growing hypocrisy, "morality isn't fixed, or up to one person to decide."

"Exactly, David," J-MO said, beaming with wide-eyed enthusiasm or deliberate ignorance. "*I* don't judge. I just provide information."

Thankfully, she then informed him she was late due to the "bloody traffic," gulped her coffee, and left before the discussion deteriorated even further.

Glad to be rid of her, the thought that had seeded after her previous visit grew a little stronger as David, empowered by his disposal of Jason West, conjured a wishful image of J-MO choking to death on her own words.

TWENTY-NINE

Reverend David Tate, of St. Mary's on the northern edge of Bedfont Green, near the junction of the A315 Staines Road and Hatton Road, held a half-hour Healing & Prayers Communion every Tuesday at 7:30 p.m.

Mrs. Grace Chapman, a lifelong petitioner for the healing power of Communion for the world at large, hadn't missed a Tuesday in many years. Although slowed by age, arthritis, and the need for a wheeled walker with a seat, Grace Chapman insisted on her weekly pilgrimage.

"Are you sure you don't need a hand, Mrs. Chapman?" Reverend Tate asked her with some concern. "Mr. Wills, our groundskeeper, will be happy to see you across the green."

Halfway down the metal ramp to the pavement, she paused.

"I can manage, Reverend. If God doesn't want me to get home, then it's His will. And who are we to mess with His will?"

"I'm sure God does indeed want you to get home, Mrs. Chapman, but there's no harm in getting a little help from…"

At the bottom of ramp, she decided to make things clear.

"I'll be fine. I've done this a thousand times before, and I don't need 'old Mr. Wills' to help me!"

The reverend smiled. He wished more of his parishioners were as stoic and independent as Mrs. Chapman. *And as generous with their donations*, he thought, before quickly chastising himself.

He watched his faithful practitioner reach the gate and said a prayer for her safe arrival home.

Grace Chapman was eighty-four years old, a former head nurse at the nearby Ealing Hospital since its opening in 1979, until her retirement at sixty-five in 1999, and the widow of Sidney Chapman, a lifelong bus driver, deceased in 2008.

Now she paused at the start of the path across the green. Eyes heavenward, she considered the dark sky above her. The color of strong tea, she decided, tinged with wan November light. It certainly threatened rain. Wind, light but steady, pushed the clouds back and forth and bowed and jostled the thinner branches of the trees.

Grace could have taken a taxi. With her own pension, a survivor's pension from her husband, and having never carried the financial burden of children, she could have afforded a taxi both ways if she had wanted.

Resolute, like many people of her generation, Grace pushed her four-wheeled walker down the curb and crossed the narrow road in front of St. Mary's. Up the far-side curb and onto the asphalt path that wound about 250 meters through the trees to Staines Road,

Grace thought she would stop in at Singh's and get some bacon for tomorrow's breakfast.

Too bad, she thought to herself, *that the nice girl Clair wouldn't be there at night.*

Apprehensive about the rain, Grace set off a bit too quickly. Out of breath and uncomfortable with pain from her arthritic hips, she slowed as she approached a bench set a few feet off the path.

With another glance at the sky, which had darkened a little more, she told herself that she only needed a two-minute rest. With careful steps across the narrow strip of grass, she sat heavily on the end of the bench and set her walker beside her. Slumped forward, chin on her chest, she breathed slow and steady.

Behind one of the several oak trees that dotted Bedfont Green, Troy fingered the axe handle with his right hand. Originally four feet long, he had shortened the handle to two feet, four inches—two inches less than the distance from his armpit to the top of his trouser belt.

Wrapping his fingers around the smooth hickory, he tugged the axe handle free from the Velcro strap that secured it under his left arm.

His father, Charlie, known as "mad Charlie" on account of his habit of talking to himself and urinating on cats, had at some point in his unremarkable life, owned the original wood-splitting axe. Then it had passed to Troy when Charlie, intoxicated and in dire need of a piss, had chased a cat in the road and ended up under a bus.

With the axe handle in hand under his coat, Troy now stepped from behind the tree. Watching for other people, he walked slowly to the rear of the park bench. As he approached, he thought of how stupid old people were. He had seen the old lady with a wad of five-pound notes in her hand a few times at the store. And just a few days ago, he had overheard Clair, the skinny chick with the nice ass, telling the woman to keep the money out of sight and only bring out what she needed.

Troy's first instinct had been to rob the old woman in her house, but when he followed her home, he discovered she lived in a bungalow unit with a warden and an alarm cord in every room.

Today marked the third Tuesday he had waited for her. The dark sky and absence of people on the path or the green convinced Troy that luck was finally on his side. Robbing people, always weaker and older than himself, had provided him with a steady source of income for minimum work. And he saw no reason to change.

The way he saw it, the strong took from the weak; simple as that. His usual method was to push a person from behind, kneel on them, and take whatever he needed from a bag or pocket. If his victim tried to turn around and look at him, he would simply tap them with his axe handle. Not too hard, though. He had no desire to kill anyone. He used just enough force to encourage the person to look away. It always worked.

Two steps from the back of the bench, a police siren wailed. Troy froze. His hand tightened on the axe handle.

Grace's head came up at the sound and swiveled left and right. Troy withdrew the axe. Distorted by the wind, the siren's wail swirled, faded, then ended.

Stimulated by the sound, the old woman sat upright. A low sigh accompanied a slight stretch, and her hands, tucked in the pockets of her coat, withdrew and held a handkerchief to her face.

Opportunity presented, Troy stepped forward, grabbed the handle of the walker with his left hand, and dragged it behind the bench. After flipping open the lid that covered the small storage compartment underneath the handle bar, he snatched Mrs. Chapman's plain brown handbag.

Grace, her back to Troy, but attempting to turn to the left, called out, "What are you doing? Give me my walker!"

Bag in hand, Troy stepped right to avoid Grace's eyes.

As she turned right, he moved left.

"What do you want? Give my walker now, or I'll call the police!"

"Shut it, you old hag. I've got what I want. You shouldn't have all this money with you, anyway. What good is it to you?"

Twisting left and right, but unable to turn far enough around, Grace answered him in a condescending tone.

"What good is it to *me*? I've worked all my life for my money. What have *you* done, eh?"

Troy, the handbag contents emptied on the ground and a clutch of paper money in his hand, tossed the bag over her head and purred, "I take what I need. Work is for losers."

"Go away, you swine. Leave me alone."

She cowered at the sound of grunts and crunching metal behind her.

"Fuck you, Grandma," Troy shouted as Grace's walker, with the frame bent and twisted and two wheels snapped off, landed in a heap beside the bench.

"Let's see you get home with this now."

Despite her stoic resilience, Grace's tears fell and mixed with the rain that had begun to fall.

THIRTY

His step light and assured, David walked with uncharacteristic confidence through the airport terminal. His faint smile suggested a combination of cheerfulness, excitement, and even a little arousal.

This almost euphoric sensation had grown and deepened since the death of Jason West. Not immediately, though. The first few days, while he waited for the discovery of West's body, had strained David's nerves.

Then there had been a few anxious moments about the CCTV camera in the lobby and the security guards. However, finally convinced that no evidence, direct, indirect, circumstantial, or otherwise, existed to connect him to West's murder, the self-assured warmth he felt now flooded through him.

Determined to have a good Monday and a good week, David had changed into his newest and cleanest uniform, greeted Nancy and Paul warmly, and set to work with enthusiasm. Even Larry, who squeaked by at seven a.m. took his sweet time to sweep and tidy, trying to get a rise out of David, could not derail his upbeat mood.

At 7:30 that morning, Alice, an account executive for Hewlett Packard and a frequent flier, breezed into the bar. She was one of David's more regular and welcome customers.

For six months, on roughly two Mondays each month, Alice had brightened David's morning while in transit from New York to some UK or European destination. With cheerful eyes, a crisp, purposeful voice, and impeccable manners, she always ordered the fresh fruit salad and the yogurt and granola with a black coffee.

Mid-forties, trim, confident, and attractive enough to turn the heads of male and female customers alike, Alice inclined her head now as she spoke.

"Hi, David. How are you today?"

"Hi, Alice. Great, thank you. A good flight?"

"Oh, yes. Always good with British Airways. Can I have…"

"Fresh fruit salad, yogurt and granola, and a black coffee," David answered, finishing Alice's sentence.

She smiled and withdrew an iPhone 8 from an elegant leather Lo & Sons Seville handbag, which she placed gently on the bar. Then she threw David a "I know I work too much" expression, tapped some buttons, and read her texts.

Pushing his own buttons on the screen to order Alice's food, he thought about Alice and the almost unconscious process whereby he had learned so much about this professional woman from the NoHo neighborhood wedged between New York's better known and more populous Greenwich and East Villages.

Her name, title, profession, company, office location, business phone number, and email addresses had been easy. Like many other business people's compulsion with networking, she had simply given him the information when he had asked, in accordance with head office instructions to "identify and keep frequent travelers coming back."

Alice had dropped her business card in a supposedly confidential locked box for the chance to earn free meals.

David emptied the box every few days and sent the cards to head office for the inevitable "marketing follow-up," together with a note on the customers he thought were most worthy of winning a free meal. He liked Alice, and had tagged her as worthy. And she had received a winner email the following week. The win had actually been the catalyst for their first real conversation.

After about twelve stops for breakfast at Sea Food World, with each visit taking an average of fifteen minutes, David had enjoyed almost three hours of conversation with Alice. Despite being fragmented, disjointed, and occasionally shallow, he had learned a great deal about her over time.

Things like her hometown, when she graduated from university, her single status, her interest in the environment and space travel. Her opinions on Trump, Obama, Brexit, sports, and all manner of innocent, personal details.

Alice smiled at David when he placed her black coffee on the bar, prompting an erotic and lustful fantasy to temporarily dislodge his professionalism.

Warmed by her presence, his Monday couldn't have had a better beginning.

After she left, more "good" customers came and went, and by eleven a.m., his mood was so good that he considered staying longer just to help with the lunch-time rush.

At 11:05, with his back to the concourse as he placed clean glasses on the shelf behind the bar, David shuddered as an unmistakable shrill voice punctured his euphoria.

"No, I didn't, and I don't bloody care what he says, or what anyone of them says."

Firm heel clicks replaced the voice as the other participant in the conversation spoke on the phone.

David, a frown replacing his smile, turned as J-MO spat an expletive into the phone, ended the call, and slumped onto a barstool. A long, low sigh, tainted by stale cigarettes and alcohol, wafted from her glossed lips and into his nose.

"My god, David," J-MO complained as she settled her phone collection on the bar. "Can you believe some people? No one wants to take responsibility for anything these days."

Angry and irritated at the sight and sound of her, he struggled to project the required customer service image as he forced a terse welcome through his compressed lips.

"Ms. Ogden."

Flustered, she didn't catch the edge in the greeting and picked up one of the four phones, scrolling in search of a contact. Focused on typing a text, she didn't look up as she spoke.

"Just a coffee."

Thankful that "just a coffee" suggested J-MO's visit would be short, David hurriedly provided the caffeine and stepped away to attend to other customers.

From the other end of the bar, he watched her face and body contort as she jabbed at the keyboard on her phone.

Nancy, who David knew followed J-MO's blogs, nudged past and motioned toward her.

"Your 'friend' got her fingers burned yesterday."

"What do you mean?"

"Apparently, she ran a story about some French politician who had a Muslim woman hidden in a flat in Paris, who he was, you know, using for sex."

"I think I remember that."

"What? You said you never follow social media stuff, and you detest that J-MO woman!"

"I mean, I remember her telling me a while ago that she was going to Paris to expose some politician who had a Muslim woman or something. What do you mean, 'she got her fingers burned'?"

"That's just it. Turns out that the guy did have a Muslim woman stashed in a flat in Paris. But he wasn't using her for sex. Apparently, the woman is almost seventy years old, and he was sheltering her until she could get some papers or documents or something."

"Well, what's wrong with that? I mean, it seems he was helping her, right?"

"I don't know, but the politician's wife and kids read about J-MO's accusations in the media and all hell broke loose. It's a mess for him and his family."

Confusion and indignation furrowed David's face.

"But the sex thing isn't true, right?"

"Oh, David," Nancy replied. "It doesn't matter if it's true or not. When J-MO posts a story, everyone gets on board. The man is denying it, but everyone wants to believe the gossip, and society tends to see the worst in people."

Nancy's story only reinforced David's already disdainful and growing anger toward J-MO. Forced to return to her orbit to access the ordering terminal, he tried to avoid eye contact, but she still wanted to gripe.

"Oh, David, there you are. People are so stupid. I can't believe what they believe."

Anger rising, and unable to resist retorting, he decided to test her.

"You mean the French politician thing?"

"Yes, exactly."

"You were wrong about him."

"Wrong? I don't bloody well think so," she answered in a shrill voice.

"But I thought the woman was old and he was giving her a place to live…"

"Oh, David, don't be like the rest of the sheep out there. He wasn't protecting anyone. I bet there was a younger woman originally, and he switched her for the old hag and made up the story."

"What about evidence? I mean, can you prove it?"

"Believe me, David. He had a woman in the flat for sex."

"But what about his wife and children?"

After a long sigh, and a condescending look, J-MO spoke in a soft tone of voice.

"You still don't get it. It's all about the story, and showing the dirty linen of the stars, and people who think they are better than everyone else."

"But what about the truth?" he asked, louder than he had intended.

"Truth, David, just like beauty, is in the eye of the beholder. I just tell it the way I see it. It's not about the person it's about my readers. After all," she finished with a flourish. "It's Just My Opinion."

"And what about *your* dirty laundry, Ms. Ogden?" David suddenly asked.

Palms up in the universal expression of nothing to hide, she continued.

"Me? I'm an open book. Nothing here except what you see."

Deciding he needed to know how far J-MO would go, he asked a hypothetical question.

"What if you discovered that a person had a disease? Say, something not contagious or dangerous, but something that caused embarrassment and was a constant battle to cope with. Maybe something that could even lead to depression. Perhaps a fashion model with weird hair growth, or an athlete with some kind of muscle problem, or something really private that didn't affect anyone else. Would you still tell the world about it?"

"My god, David," J-MO exclaimed as her face lit up with misinterpreted comprehension. "You've finally got a story for me! *Of course* I would tell the world. Now out with it, and if it's really good, I'm sure we can reach an agreement."

"What about the person, though? What about their privacy? What if it would hurt or embarrass them?"

"Like I said, it's not about the person; it's about my readers. Now tell me what you know."

J-MO, convinced that he was holding out for more money, badgered David until the last possible moment before she had to run to catch her flight. Even then, she promised she would be back to pry it out of him.

As she barged through the crowded concourse, a disturbing thought from several weeks earlier jolted David. What if J-MO got Jason West to tell the story of Wanda? How long would it be until someone "outed" him and the world learned that David Edwards, former upcoming Shakespearian actor, worked in an airport sushi bar because he stank of fish?

Fury, raw and vicious, twisted his features until he chuckled to himself as he realized that West could never tell J-MO the story now.

Relieved, David relaxed for a few moments, until paranoia pricked his fears. How many people had West told that story to? How many people had been at the party when it happened? Millions of people followed J-MO's blog and website. What if someone decided to recount the story and did one of those "where are they now?" things?

That would be exactly the kind of thing J-MO would love to reveal. The kind of thing her "readers" would eat up. And she wouldn't care about David. Hadn't she just told him that it wasn't about the person, but the story?

He began to imagine the headline: *Shakespeare's Fish Discovered at Airport.*

At this, his fury returned to fuel and justify his thoughts. J-MO, who destroyed lives and reputations for personal gain and entertainment, was not a good person. Moreover, she had become a threat to David.

"Let's see just how open a book you really are, J-MO," he mumbled under his breath.

THIRTY-ONE

"Hi, David," Jenny spluttered as she pushed open the unlocked door to David's flat. Then she plonked a grocery bag on the floor, kicked off her shoes and wriggled her arms out of her jacket. "Sorry I'm late."

David, his back to the door as he mixed and tossed a salad on the kitchen counter, called back, "Hi, Jenny. That's alright. Work again?"

"Yes. Sometimes I wonder why everything is urgent and nothing seems to be done in regular time anymore."

Crossing the small space from front door to kitchen, Jenny pecked her brother's cheek and hugged him.

"Smells good. Chicken?"

"Yes. And salad with bread. You brought white?"

"Yes, and some Foster's."

"Dessert?"

"I'm not telling," Jenny said, grinning. "It's a surprise."

"Fine," David returned with his own grin. "Then I'm not telling *you* what movie we're watching."

She smiled and moved away, gathering plates, cutlery, and glasses to set the small two-person table. With the salad tossed, David opened the oven and pushed and poked some sauce-covered chicken around in a dish.

"Another ten minutes, Jenny," he announced. "How about a drink?"

"Yes, please," she replied. As usual, she had set about straightening papers, cushions, and various items that didn't really need to be straightened.

As he poured the wine and popped the tab on a beer can, he watched his sister with warmth and gratitude. She had always been there for him. Always supportive, positive, and selfless.

"You look very happy today," Jenny noted as she responded to the look of affection in his eyes. "What's going on?"

"Oh, nothing really. Just glad it's Wednesday, that and you're here."

"Well, if this is the effect I have on you, I should come twice a week for dinner. That way at least I'll get two healthy meals a week! Now, tell me what's really made you so chipper."

"Oh, I don't know. Things are just going well at the moment. Clair is good, too. Even after my um, relapse, she has been great and…"

"So, you two are what—an official item now?"

"Not exactly, but I'm hopeful, you know."

The oven timer dinged to signal the ignominious end of the chicken.

"You get the salad and bread," David said. "While I get the chicken."

Seated at the table, he spoke between mouthfuls.

"You heard from Mom and Dad recently?"

"Yes. They've been busy with volunteer work. Mom at the information kiosk at the hospital, and Dad started doing cleanup work with a local group for Sinderland Brook."

"I didn't know Dad was into the volunteer stuff. When did that happen?"

"About a month or two ago. When was the last time you spoke to them?"

David's face tightened a little when he remembered that the last time he'd spoken to his father, it had been a few days before the Jason West incident at the airport. Since then, and up until now, he hadn't been very conversational.

Jenny sensed her brother's discomfort and spoke softly.

"I'm sorry, David, I didn't mean to imply any-thing."

"It's OK," he answered quietly. "It *has* been a while. I spoke with Dad a few days before, you know, the Jason West thing. I haven't felt much like talking since then. Well, except for the last few days, that is."

Uncertain about her next comment, Jenny pressed her lips together and reached for David's hands before she spoke again.

"I wasn't sure if I should mention this, but as you brought it up, did you hear that Jason West is dead?"

Inside, David wanted to yell that *yes*, he did know that the bastard West was dead. He wanted to tell his sister that *he* had killed West, and that the man had suffered the painful death he deserved.

That was also the reason why David felt so damn good. But because Jenny had always been able to read

194

the truth in his eyes, he bowed his head toward the table.

"Yeah, I heard it on the news. Can't say I'm sorry, though."

Jenny, who was pro-life, anti-capital punishment, pro-rehabilitation, anti-war, and all about forgiveness, predictably rose to David's comment.

"Oh, David. You can't believe that. I know he was mean to you and that he hurt you, but his life was cut brutally short. And from the news reports, he really died a horrible death."

David should have known better and kept his feelings about West's death to himself. His sister was almost in tears, for someone she hardly knew, someone who had hurt him and contributed to the ending his career. It really seemed her empathy had no bounds.

David was the opposite. He had a strong sense of judgment and disdain for people who didn't contribute to society, or actively *abused* society. These convictions had been growing inside him since West's death and the presence of parasitic people like J-MO. He couldn't hold back his anger any longer.

"Well, I'm *not* sorry. West was a bastard. He loved putting people down, joking at other people's expense, and spreading rumors. He wasn't a nice person, Jenny. He deserved to die, to protect other people from getting hurt."

"Maybe he was all those things, David, but being unpleasant doesn't make you a bad person. And even if he was as bad as you say, did he really deserve to be murdered so young, and in such a horrible way?"

"Come on, Jenny. You know what he did to me. Who knows how many other people he humiliated? Look, at the airport, he reveled in retelling that humiliating story about me. How many times do you think he had retold it since it happened? And how many other victims of his malice are there, suffering in silence?"

"I agree that he was mean-spirited, and I know he hurt you deeply, and yes, he probably has done the same to others. But honestly, David, should he really have been murdered for being a joker with bad taste?"

"He was more than a joker, Jenny," David replied heatedly, his voice rising with anger. "He was *poison*. And he's not the only one out there, either."

Startled by her brother's outburst, Jenny turned to him in concern.

"What do you mean?"

"Nothing," he muttered at first, but then encouraged by his own rhetoric, he continued speaking.

"What I mean is, people like West, who spend their time putting others down, causing misery and pain. What do they actually produce? What is their contribution to society? Why should they get away with their shit?"

"You don't really believe that do you, David?" Jenny asked softly, more moisture collecting in her eyes.

Now he realized that he had gone too far and revealed too much—especially to his sister.

"Oh, Jesus. No, Jenny. I'm sorry, really. I just got a bit wound up about West. You know, even after all the years, it still hurts, and when I saw him at the airport, it all came back to me. I got bitter and twisted again for a while, but it's over now. I've met with Rachel, and she's helping me work it out."

"It's alright," Jenny replied, wiping the back of a hand across her face. "You just had me worried for a minute. You can't go back to all that hate you had before."

She was right. He couldn't return to the hate. Now he had to *exorcize* the hate. And that's exactly what he intended to do.

THIRTY-TWO

Annoyed that on impulse, he had used his own computer to search for the details of Jason West's agent, David decided to use the more anonymous public library services to search for J-MO. The Bedfont, Feltham, and Hounslow libraries, all within walking distance, provided free internet access, as well as use of computers.

Initially, with less than a meter between the public access computer terminals, David had felt nervous that someone might see and remember the websites and the subject of his internet searches. But after a few minutes, as he observed other library patrons glued to their respective screens, he doubted they were even aware of his—or each other's—presence, let alone what they might be looking at.

Assured of his anonymity, David realized that J-MO had been both right and wrong. She was indeed an open book. She had profiles and contributions on the UK top social media sites, such as Facebook, Twitter, Instagram, and Google+. In addition, she could be found on LinkedIn, Tumblr, and Pinterest.

Everything a person could want to know was available, from her shoe size, favorite food, preferred sports team, music tastes, and even some obviously romanticized details of her first love, at the age of fifteen. It was all wrapped in positive, action-oriented syrupy words that oozed condescending self-importance. Repulsed by the propaganda, David clenched his teeth as he sought the only piece of information he really wanted: J-MO's home address.

On Facebook, home was listed as being "in one of London's trendiest areas," and LinkedIn only provided a P.O. box for correspondence. While her tweets often mentioned taking the morning and evening trains from various stations, David could only narrow her home location to a broad area in South West London.

Hours of trawling J-MO sites, news articles, white pages, business directories, and even other writers' comments about her produced no home address. Several email addresses and telephone numbers were available, but still no brick-and-mortar address.

Resigned that he would somehow have to follow her home, David absently toyed with J-MO's profile photograph on LinkedIn. Stylish in black and white, it showed her working at a computer in a brightly lit studio-type office, in which the view from the window was maybe two or three stories above ground.

At first, he imagined killing her where she sat by strangling her from behind as she typed some poison on her blog. Drifting in and out of frustration and fantasy, David downloaded the photograph and opened it with Microsoft Office Picture Manager software.

Using the software, he zoomed in and out. As he magnified the photograph, the view from the window behind J-MO expanded. Then a memory tweaked in his mind. Excited, David fiddled with the image until he recognized one of London's lesser-known landmarks, the "skinny house," unmistakable in its profile.

Located on the corner of South Terrace and Thurloe Square in Knightsbridge, the house narrowed at one end to just seven feet, and claimed to be London's thinnest house.

David had seen the house before, more or less on the walking route from South Kensington station to the Victoria and Albert Museum. David and his girlfriend at the time, Joanne, had stopped to look at the building before crossing Thurloe Square Gardens to the museum. Like many people, they had stood before the house and done a double take at its narrowness.

With Thurloe Square in Knightsbridge to focus on, David researched through J-MO's posts and tweets and discovered numerous comments about restaurants and bars in the area. Armed with this information, all he needed next was to find an apartment building in Knightsbridge with a view of the skinny house.

Using Google Maps and Street View around Thurloe Square, David found a long row of four-story Victorian-era buildings that would likely provide a view similar to the one in the photograph.

Next, using property agents' websites, he viewed photographs of current listings for a variety of flats, from studios to three bedrooms. While nothing matched exactly, the general tone, shape, and height were consistent with the view from J-MO's profile photograph. Satisfied he had the home located within a block or two, David turned to her schedule.

This proved easier, but still problematic. She did not have a regular schedule. Summoned by phone, email, and social media posts, J-MO had once boasted, "'I go where and when the story is. I don't keep regular hours. One day I might be in Berlin, the next in Rome, and another in some unheard-of place in South Wales.'"

Her style was to tease her audience with an announcement on one of her social media sites, that she would "Soon be traveling to 'X.'" With that tidbit, readers and followers would generate thousands of speculative posts and comments on why she was suddenly hightailing it to "X."

En route, J-MO would feed the frenzy with tweets and posts of her progress to the destination, but never reveal exactly who she would be meeting, or why. Many times, the destination city was no more than a meeting point. Then, when she "had the goods," she would tweet that she was on her way home and that "revelation, truth, and Just My Opinion would be coming soon."

David interpreted this to mean that she would only reveal all after she had gotten home and written or edited whatever soul-destroying article she believed passed as journalism.

Unbeknownst or unconsidered by J-MO, however, the habit of teasing her audience with "location" updates provided an almost real-time account of when she would be away from her home and office. Now that David knew roughly where she lived, and the approximate days and times she would be on her way home, all he had to do was wait and observe.

But before that, he needed to make a visit to Thurloe Square and figure out a way to silence J-MO once and for all.

Thirty-Three

Preoccupation with J-MO had put David on a high. The expectancy of acting in a new role and contributing to the development of the play, the narrative, and of course, the final act, soothed and calmed his emotions. In turn, his body synchronized with his serenity of purpose, causing a significant decline in his sweat and overall smell.

Then the letter arrived.

The plain white office envelope wasn't addressed directly to David, but the letter may as well have been. Below the corporate Sea Food World logo, after a brief preamble from management about the importance of cleanliness, professionalism, and personal hygiene, an italicized excerpt from a customer detailed the complaint. Indicators of the exact location had been blanked out with xxxxxx.

I am a frequent patron of SFW. In general, I am quite satisfied with the service, and the selection and quality of the menu. However, in the interest of concern for your business, I must point out that there is a problem with the SFW location in xxxxxxx.

To be direct, the bar area often has a faint yet distinct odor of decayed fish. I understand of course that SFW is a purveyor of seafood, but the smell is one of dead—rather than fresh—seafood.

At first, I thought the odor might be associated with the waste bins. However, I can say that most of the time, they seem to be appropriately maintained and serviced.

After careful attention, I localized the smell to the actual bar area, and in some instances, to the proximity of some servers.

Whilst I have no desire to cast accusations against individuals or cause jeopardy to anyone's livelihood, I would request SFW's investigation into this matter.

In the spirit of openness, I must mention that I do possess a well-developed sense of smell. However, I am sure that in the interest of customer satisfaction, SFW would want to address this situation forthwith.

Sincerely,
Xxxxxxxxx

The head office letter ended with the reminder of corporate policies about personal hygiene, a call to action for rigorous adherence by all employees to those policies, and a commitment to support any individual who might need more personalized assistance. A final note referenced a subsection of the employment contract that dealt with personal hygiene and wellness.

Fortunately, the letter had arrived with a collection of other correspondence concerning food stocking policies, refrigeration issues, price adjustments, and other everyday business. Thankfully, it had also arrived during David's shift, and he had been the one to open it.

Contained in an envelope marked, "To Be Posted on Bulletin Board," he had opened it with good intentions.

After reading the contents, however, all his good intentions, calmness, and serenity fled from David like air from a burst balloon. Unfettered rage spewed forth instead. Bitterness followed, and anger conquered all. He crushed the letter, and as moisture pooled and beaded all over his body, he had to run to the staff room.

However, unlike other incidents, David's recovery time had shortened considerably. By the following morning, his animosity remained, but the sweat had retreated. The calmness returned when he added Mr. Taylor to his growing list of people whose existence he questioned. Now the man had become a threat to his own well-being.

The letter incident had been a week ago. Now, as David stood behind the bar, Taylor appeared on the concourse and David felt an urge to smash him in the face. But he would *not* smash Taylor. Instead, he would be a model of service and cordiality, because today, David wanted something, something that he needed to advance his plan.

"Good morning, Mr. Taylor," David said pleasantly as he placed an immaculate glass, napkin, and bottle of water on the bar. "What may I get you today?"

A smirk, slight and condescending, stretched Taylor's compressed lips as he eyed the place setting.

"Just the usual."

"Certainly."

David punched in the order, stocked the fridge with juices and imported beers, and observed the man in front of him. Despite his dislike of Taylor, he had to acknowledge and admire the man's appearance. He was immaculate.

Over the past months, David had learned much about Taylor, despite his dislike for him. He knew that as a regional sales manager for Proctor and Gamble's line of men's care and grooming products, he never promoted a product that he hadn't personally used, or one that he did not believe in. His first name, gleaned from his business card, was Arthur. He also had a sensitive nose, fastidious eating habits, didn't smoke, and as evidenced by his letter of complaint, was a mean, petty, and dangerous man at heart.

But what David needed to know was where the bastard lived. An earlier internet search had revealed Taylor was the third most common surname in England. There were more than 450,000 people named Taylor in England, and thousands in London and surrounding areas. Taylor's business card, which David had prompted him to place in the free draw box, only listed a corporate address.

Casual questions about his home life, commute to the airport, what sports he liked, his favorite local restaurant, and his proximity to various London events over the past few months had yielded little information beyond a few generalities or mixed messages.

For example, Taylor's commute to the airport could take between one and two hours, depending on where he came from, or which route he took. Taylor also said that he had many favorite restaurants, but none that he would call "local."

When the bell chimed, David retrieved food from the pass-through hatch and set the plate in front of Taylor, who simply nodded.

Now or never, David thought to himself.

"Mm, Mr. Taylor, I wonder if I could ask you a personal question?"

Surprised by the request, Taylor acquiesced with a slight nod.

"Last night, at my local pub, I was taking part in the quiz night competition when…"

"Really," Taylor interjected with a smirk.

"Yes. One of the questions at the quiz, or the health section of it, asked what hyperosmia is, which no one knew the answer to until…"

"Yes, you are right," Taylor answered, keen to display his perceptive superiority. "My ability to smell things, especially things that smell bad, is caused by hyperosmia. I'm surprised that a pub quiz night would include something as uncommon as hyperosmia."

"It was a bonus question, and they are usually difficult."

"Well, now you know," Taylor said as he dismissed David and returned to his breakfast.

David hesitated, until Taylor, aware of his stare, spoke again.

"Is there something else?"

"Yes, if you don't mind. I was wondering how a person manages with such a problem when they live in a city like London, which is full of smells and odors and all…"

"The way to manage, as you put it," Taylor announced, as though talking to a five-year-old, "is to live away from the odor of humanity and its activities."

David sensed he was getting close to what he needed and remained silent.

Taylor continued.

"I live in Bolney, Haywards Heath. I chose the place because, as you probably don't know, there is a prevailing coastal wind and lots of fresh air."

"Oh, well that makes sense, then. I bet you can't wait to get home from work each day."

"Actually," Taylor replied, falling into his superior tone again. "I work mostly from home. Except for Wednesdays, when I travel to meetings with my employees. Even then, I'm home by nine p.m. Now, if you don't mind, I'll have my bill."

THIRTY-FOUR

The route to discover J-MO's flat included train changes at Vauxhall and Victoria stations. At Victoria, David entered the washroom as a middle-aged man wearing worn, dirty running shoes, baggy gray pants, a black anorak with a blue Chelsea supporter's scarf, and a black backpack.

Ten minutes later, he emerged in dark blue jeans and black lace-up brogues, a little scuffed, but improved with black polish and a soft cloth. He also wore blue Oxford-cloth button-down shirt and a black, three-quarter length London Fog-style raincoat. A costume, as David thought of it, that he had acquired from a visit to another used clothing store. The backpack and his other clothes, he placed in a nearby LuggageHero storage facility which had spread all over London since terrorist attacks forced the removal of twenty-four-hour lockers at train stations.

He was ready for the rehearsal.

In what he hoped was a young, hip appearance, more in keeping with the trendy area of J-MO's flat, David walked from the South Kensington tube station to the thin end of the "skinny house" on the corner of South Terrace and Thurloe Square in Knightsbridge.

From the wedge end of the building, he strode the street and admired the white pillars and black iron railings that fronted the separate street-level entrances to the three-story apartments.

Outside number 8, he paused and studied the photograph he had downloaded from J-MO's profile photograph on LinkedIn. Imagining himself in her studio-type office or room, he "looked" out of the aboveground window. From street level, David compared the imagined window view with the top of the trees and the green area of the Thurloe Square Gardens on the other side of the road.

His gut said he was right. J-MO's lair was in the building, but he didn't know which flat. Thirty of them overlooked the garden. Still outside number 8, he stepped between the two white pillars that flanked the stone step and scanned the door and side panels for any indication of who lived there.

He didn't expect J-MO to announce where she lived, but perhaps by elimination, he could narrow down the options.

Of the thirty flats, only two—Mr. F. Fowler at number 4, and J. Ross at number 14—felt secure or important enough to tell the world where they lived. The flats also had one thing in common: a SECOM security service sticker close to the doorbell.

Thoughts of the security system and his almost fatal mistake at West's flat made David nervous. Conscious that despite his trendy attire, he had loitered up and down the street for more than ten minutes, he crossed the road and followed the line of the black iron fence that surrounded Thurloe Square Gardens.

From his previous research, he had recalled that the garden and adjacent streets were named after John Thurloe, an adviser of Oliver Cromwell, who had owned the land in the seventeenth century. The communal garden was now reserved for use by local residents, which presumably, thought David, included J-MO.

Halfway along the four-foot-high fence, banked by dense trees and foliage, David halted at a gate. It was locked. A white sheet of type-written paper, neatly aligned in a transparent plastic wallet, hung from the gate on a plastic zip tie.

"Take no notice of that, mate," a man with a hoarse voice said behind David.

Startled, David turned to find a short, roughly dressed, unshaven man smiling at him through toothless gums.

"Pardon?"

"That sign. Don't take any notice. The toffy-nosed bastards who live in the posh flats round here might think they own the bloody place, but there is a spot further down by the post box where you can easily hop the fence without being seen."

"Oh, er, thanks," David mumbled to the back of the man, who had begun to walk away.

Left alone, David studied the sign. Large, bold printed green letters at the top the page announced *Thurloe Square Gardens 1840.* Under the heading, an image of a leafy tree with a circle around it symbolized the gardens' forest-like landscape.

Below the tree, thirteen rules concerning behavior, access, and authorized use ended with a final instruction to "Report any serious infringement in writing" to the address provided.

Around him, the bustle of a busy London street hummed and droned. Cars sped and slowed, pedestrians walked, and the city lived. Unimportant to the milieu, David took the photograph out again, turned it different ways, and glanced up at the building again.

After a few moments, he concluded that if J-MO did live in the building opposite the gardens, which, as he looked at the angle of the photo, he was certain she did, he would somehow have to gain access.

With obvious CCTV cameras, which he assumed were monitored somewhere close by, and certain that undetected entry and exit would be difficult if not impossible, David accepted that he needed another way to get to her.

Frustrated, he followed the fence and peeked through the railings and foliage at the gardens. Inside, the few people he could see either held one-sided conversations on cell phones, occupied benches while staring into nothingness, or seemed to stroll the gravel pathways without purpose.

David also noticed dark places beneath the trees, shadow-filled recesses between hedges and widely spaced lampposts. He checked his watch. It was only 5:30 p.m., and long, dense shadows had already formed under the trees and along the pathway. Imagining the darkness at night, a thought crystallized in his mind and an idea materialized.

He wiped a light sheen of excited perspiration from the top of his cheeks as he realized that he didn't need

J-MO's exact address. Furthermore, he had no need to enter her home. All he needed was something that J-MO wanted more than anything else. Something that she could not resist.

He simply needed a story and a phone number. A tale she couldn't resist, and *her* phone number. The story he could fabricate. The phone number might be even easier.

About a month earlier, David recalled that J-MO, frustrated with him because he had no story to tell, had slid a card across the bar and commented that it had her private number.

As he stood before the park now, at the spot where the man had said one could easily hop over unseen, he remembered the card, and that he had placed it in the pocket of his waistcoat.

His habit at the end of each shift was always to empty his pockets when he changed from work to street clothes.

Sometimes he placed his pocket contents on his locker shelf. Sometimes he emptied them at the bar and tossed stuff in the garbage. He couldn't recall what he had done with the card from J-MO, but he did remember their conversation. J-MO, as usual, had been pushing him to provide her with overheard gossip.

"Anything, David. Anything on anyone you recognize or might be a bigwig in a company or a political party. Drunk, on drugs, with a pretty girl, or boy. Something like that."

"Like I said, Ms. Ogden, I really am too busy to notice what people are doing. I don't think it's…"

"Oh, I know what it is. You're worried people might know you called me. Don't worry, though. I am very, very discreet, and never reveal my sources."

"No, it's not that. I just don't think people's private lives…"

J-MO, not listening and convinced of her assessment of David's character, and everyone else's, then reached in her bag, withdrew her card, and slid it across the bar.

"This," she preened, as though bestowing an honour on him, "is my private cell number. Call me on this when you have something."

Offended by J-MO's arrogant assumption of his corruptibility, but savvy enough not to offend her, David recalled placing it in the small pocket of his waistcoat.

If that card was in his locker, David thought with a broad and malevolent smile, *then he had found a way to get J-MO exactly where he wanted her.*

The journey to discover her lair, or rehearsal as David's subconscious had portrayed it, was over. Not only had he located his prey, but he had also influenced the development of the story and how he, as the protagonist, would lure his prey into his trap.

Content with his performance, he inclined his head to acknowledge the polite clapping from the small group of the director's friends granted permission to watch the rehearsal. Secure and confident of his role, David "exited the stage" in his mind as he left Thurloe Square Gardens.

214

THIRTY-FIVE

Plenty of seats, no lineup at the bar, and a low murmur of conversation against a backdrop of fruit machines usually characterized eight o'clock on a typical Thursday night in the Bell. However, when David and Clair entered at five after eight to have a drink before the quiz began at nine, seats were few, a roar had replaced the murmur, and the fruit machines were silent.

Gossip, speculation, and rumor had tripled the usual number of Thursday quiz night patrons, and the tone of the conversations conveyed anger and frustration.

Edging their way through the crowd to the bar, David and Clair nodded to friends and acquaintances and waited for Gary to serve them.

Tracy, a regular at the Bell and a nosy, if well-meaning community busybody, nudged Clair from behind as she spoke.

"You know old Mrs. Chapman, don't you? Doesn't she come in your store?"

Clair, forced to turn by the nudge, nodded in reply.

"Hi, Tracy. Yes. She comes in almost every day. I can't…"

"No one can," Tracy said, interrupting her. "It's a bloody disgrace."

"How could…?"

"I'll *tell* you how. As I told everyone else in here, it's the drugs. That's what gets them doing it. They just don't care what they do or who they hurt. No one's safe anymore."

Drinks obtained, David turned from the bar and handed a vodka and orange to Clair.

"Oh, hi, Tracy," he mumbled as he contained his dislike of the woman, and gossips in general. "Can't chat, got to get a seat for the quiz. Come on, Clair."

Discussion about the robbery of Mrs. Chapman dominated the air as David and Clair weaved their way to the alcove by the window where the quiz team of Don, Bill, Debbie, and Steve usually sat.

"We saved you seats," said Don, the self-proclaimed leader and organizer of the team.

"Bloody packed in here tonight," Bill observed as David and Clair wedged themselves into the bench seat beside Debbie.

"Everyone is right pissed about the attack on the old lady. Can't believe what some fuckers will do."

"You know the old lady, right?" Debbie asked Clair.

"Yeah. Mrs. Chapman. Nice old lady. Complains a bit, but harmless and alright compared to some of 'em."

"Who do you two think did it, then?" Bill asked.

David eased off his coat and tucked his and Clair's on the window ledge behind them.

"Too many to choose from, Bill. You know what it's like round here late at night. Yobs pissed up, shouting and knocking things over."

"Yeah, I know, but this was in broad daylight."

"Well," David said, between slurps of beer. "Not *exactly* broad daylight. It was past eight, and pissing rain."

Bill swallowed a mouthful of his own beer before making his point.

"Daylight, nighttime—doesn't matter for these tossers. There's no police anywhere these days to stop 'em, no matter what time of day it is."

The assault on Mrs. Chapman dominated the conversation until, at five minutes to nine, Eric, the resident Quiz Master, called the competitors to order. After announcing the five teams, reminding non-participants not to call out answers, and wishing everyone luck, the quiz began.

Twenty-five questions into the requisite fifty questions that constituted the Thursday night Bell quiz, Eric called a fifteen-minute pause to enable competitors a chance to "use the facilities and replenish drinks."

Clair and Debbie, at the bar to get drinks, sensed a change in the atmosphere before they saw and heard the reason. As they and several others at the bar turned toward the front door, and the source of the disturbance, David and Debbie's boyfriend, Steve, stepped from the hallway that led to the bathrooms.

Four males entered the Bell. The first, Troy, well known and disliked by many, shouted over his shoulder at the three who trailed behind him.

"Come on, lads. My shout, innit."

Troy and his followers, each with a hand down the front of their sweatpants in the style of chavs, flanked their leader as he approached the bar.

"Yeah, sorted, Troy," a skinny kid replied, who might have been eighteen, but looked twelve.

"Let's 'ave a propa drink then, bruv," grunted another acolyte.

Together they crab-walked with a cocky swagger toward the bar, forcing people aside. A few customers down from Clair and Debbie, Troy signaled the bartender Gary as he shouted, "Four Strongbow, four Red Bull, and four vodka shots for me and m' bruvs."

Gary, sensitive to his patrons' discomfort, leaned in toward Troy and said quietly, "Just one round Troy, alright?"

Gary and Troy had schooled together and had been close once. Gary himself had been a chav for a while, until he met a girl and grew up.

Troy's followers downed the vodka shot and chased it with a Red Bull as quickly as Troy passed the glasses and cans to them. After Troy downed his, with overdone drama, he passed the pints of cider to his disciples. That done, he turned to Gary with a sense of bravado.

"What's the damage, Gary?"

"Eighteen fifty."

Troy, his face smug with nonchalance, dug in the pocket of his sweatpants. A tight roll of five-pound notes came out with his hand. He peeled four off the roll, passed them to Gary, and then stepped away from the bar.

"Keep the change, mate."

Uncaring about the murmur of irritated resentment that bounced off his back, Troy led his group across the pub to stand in front of the dartboard that was not in use during quiz nights.

David, who like everyone else, had witnessed Troy's crassness, reached Clair at the bar and took his drink from her.

"Did you see that?" she asked.

"Yes. Typical. Doesn't give a shit about anyone else. Just barges in front of everyone. Gary only lets him in because they used to be friends way back."

Clair, her face creased with disdain, nodded toward Troy.

"I don't mean that. I mean the money."

"What money?"

She pointed directly at Troy as she spoke.

"He had a roll of fivers."

"Yeah, so what? Probably sold some stuff he nicked, or got his dole money."

"I don't think so. I think that money is Mrs. Chapman's."

"What?" asked Debbie who had been listening to their conversation.

Steering Clair back toward their table by the window, David whispered in her ear, "What? I mean, how do you know?"

"I told you before, David. Mrs. Chapman always had a wad of five-pound notes with her when she came in the shop. I must have told her a hundred times not to bring that much money out."

David looked at Troy.

"I don't know, Clair. Five-pound notes are not that unusual."

"Yeah, but a wad of fivers after Mrs. Chapman gets robbed? I'm telling you, David. It's *her* money."

Debbie, who had listened with growing interest, added her opinion as she too stared in Troy's direction.

"Well it's just the sort of thing that bastard would do. He has been done before for threatening people. Everyone knows he'd nick anything that wasn't nailed down."

Troy, holding court with his crew, who were laughing at something he said, caught the glances of David, Debbie, and Clair. Fixing on Clair, he pushed his tongue through his lips and mimicked what he would like to do to her. Encouraged by his acolytes, Troy reached for his groin and signaled even more intent.

Clair, not one to let an insult pass, and already convinced that Troy had attacked Mrs. Chapman, responded to the tongue with a clearly mouthed "fuck you."

"You wish, bitch," he mouthed back as he took several steps toward her.

Clair and David stood as Troy reached the table.

"What do you want?" spat David before Clair could speak.

"Aye, protectin the little woman, are ya?"

Clair, up on the balls of her feet with her fists clenched, spoke for herself.

"I don't need protection from a coward like you."

People close by quietened at the exchange. As the quiet rippled outward, tension built.

"I ain't no coward. If you weren't such a slag, I'd slap you straight."

"That's enough," David said as he edged from behind the table.

Troy's crew crossed floor and stood behind their leader.

Clair grasped David's arm to hold him back.

"Don't worry, David. Troy only picks on old ladies."

Flushed red and chin thrust forward, she challenged and accused Troy. "Isn't that right?"

"Don't take non ov dat shit," chimed a spotty-faced kid behind Troy as he bounced on the balls of his feet and sensed a fight.

Caught between the need to show leadership and some other thought, Troy hesitated.

"What's the matter, Troy?" Clair asked. "I'm not old and weak enough for you, like Mrs. Chapman?"

"What you talkin 'bout," Troy stammered, caught off guard by the direct accusation. "You crazy, somfin?"

"I saw that roll of five-pound notes. Mrs. Chapman always had a wad of fivers in her bag. Is that where you got your money from?"

"You don't know nuffin," Troy shouted. "You better watch your mouth, accusin me of stuff I never did."

"Or what? You going to get me on the green one night, too?"

The pub, silent save for the rustle of people jockeying for a better view, waited for his response.

"Come on, Troy," bleated another of his boys. "Enuff of this shit. Let's go. Bitch is crazy."

Adopting a superior attitude and trying to save face, Troy smirked as he spoke and turned to leave.

"Yeah, noffin going on here. Just some skinny chick running her mouth."

"Yes, go on. Get outta here," spat Clair to Troy's back.

At the door, he looked back at her with a cold, malevolent smile.

"Jesus, Clair, that was a bit much," David said as they resumed their seats.

"What do you mean?" she asked, trembling a little. "We all know it was him."

"No, we don't. I mean, yes, Troy is an asshole and exactly the kind of shit that would rob an old lady, but we don't have any proof, Clair."

"The money, David. Where else would he get money like that? It's too much of a coincidence. It *has* to be him."

"Maybe it was, maybe it wasn't, but you can just go around accusing people, Clair."

"I know he did it. I can tell by his stupid face."

"He's trouble."

"I'm not scared of him, David. He's just a bully, and I got over bullies a long time ago."

As Eric the Quiz Master called order to restart, David had a sense of foreboding that Troy might become a problem only he could solve.

Thirty-Six

Something wasn't right. Robbie didn't know what, but things were weird. Not just things, but David, as well. He knew David was a good person. All that stuff in his scrapbook about his acting, losing his job because of his disease, how he managed and never said anything about how hard it must be. David *must* be a good person.

That was the problem, though. Robbie "knew" David was good, but what was going on? Propped up on his bed, his forehead creased with concentration, Robbie tried to make sense of the latest photographs and notes he had made about him.

More clothes. This time, hanging in the closet. Jeans, a blue shirt, a long, black raincoat, and a pair of shoes. To Robbie, the clothes hung like they were matched with each other, a kind of uniform, or like he had seen on TV commercials for young men. It didn't make sense.

David never wore anything like that.

Then there was the paper in the kitchen drawer. Thickish paper, with the word *weatherproof* visible when Robbie had rotated the paper to the light. And one piece of paper, about five inches long, had been in the garbage. The words *"the worst gosips"* were written on it, but the word *gosips*, which Robbie figured was supposed to be "gossips" had been spelled wrong. This was, thought Robbie, why it was in the garbage.

Even weirder than that were the little metal letters and the small hammer. When he played with them, Robbie discovered that if you held a letter on a piece of paper and hit the back with the hammer, the letter appeared on the paper. Knowing what the stuff was for didn't help Robbie understand why David needed it, as he couldn't find anything in the flat with the letters stamped on.

But what really didn't make sense was the last entry in the notebook Robbie had found in David's locked box. *I am The Prince,* was crazy. When Robbie searched Google, the first result was for a *LazyTown* children's cartoon music video for a song called "I Am a Prince." Then yucky stuff about sex and someone being the "prince of pain."

After that, things about Prince Philip and The Prince of Egypt. After fiddling around with the words, Robbie discovered a book called *The Prince*. But that made even less sense than the cartoon because it was about five hundred years old and about politics.

The more Robbie thought, the stranger and weirder it all was. Whatever David was doing, it couldn't be good.

THIRTY-SEVEN

I'm off to the slopes, but not to ski. Someone's hiding money in this Toblerone land. Back tonight to reveal all.

J-MO's not-so-cryptic social media tease had begun at eleven a.m. on Saturday morning. For several weekends, David had monitored her feed in the hopes of finding such an opportunity. While she was busy digging for dirt in Switzerland, he reviewed and cemented his plans.

At five p.m., J-MO updated her followers:

I will be back with the TRUTH in time to make your night.

David decided it was time to leave his flat.

Above him, recessed in his bedroom, Robbie checked his watch and reached for his notebook.

As with his previous reconnaissance visit, David used a train station washroom to change his clothes and appearance. This time, though, he chose dark blue jeans, black brogues, an Oxford shirt, and a black, three-quarter-length London Fog-style raincoat.

He had added a ribbed navy-blue beanie hat, black-rimmed glasses, and a dark, hipster goatee beard. His final accessory, and the key to luring J-MO where he wanted her, was a worn leather briefcase which he tucked under his left arm.

With his "traveling clothes" placed in another LuggageHero facility , David strolled out of the South Kensington station and made his way to Fernandez & Wells coffee shop on Exhibition Road, one block away from Thurloe Square Gardens.

At 6:15 p.m., the trendy and popular coffee shop brimmed with patrons. Besides great coffee and the usual fare, it also provided charcuterie and select wines.

Squeezed onto a stool by the window, David sipped his non-fat latte and critically observed the supporting cast around him. He thought he recognized a few actors from his training years at the London Academy of Music and Dramatic Art. Overall, he was impressed with their character portrayals and costumes—and especially their ability to completely ignore him, the leading actor.

Halfway through his latte, David responded to the vibration in his pocket and checked his disposable prepaid cell phone.

J-MO's Twitter feed appeared across the screen.

Just off plane from Zurich. Guess who has "millions" stashed away from the taxman in Zurich's oldest bank?

More followed:

My blog at nine tonight—you won't BELIEVE it!!

Setting his latte aside, David placed a transparent ziplock bag on the table and smoothed out the creases. Through the plastic, he admired the black-inked printed words on each five-by-two-inch piece of all-weather writing paper.

GOSSIPING AND LYING GO HAND IN HAND

WHAT YOU DON'T SEE WITH YOUR EYES, DON'T WITNESS WITH YOUR MOUTH

GREAT MINDS DISCUSS IDEAS. AVERAGE MINDS DISCUSS EVENTS. SMALL MINDS DISCUSS PEOPLE.

THE WORST COWARDS ARE GOSSIPS

ENTER RUMOR, PAINTED FULL OF TONGUES

HIS FORWARD VOICE IS TO SPEAK WELL OF HIS FRIEND. HIS BACKWARD VOICE IS TO UTTER FOUL SPEECHES AND TO DETRACT.

The words were lifted from a famous movie, a first lady, a Jewish proverb, and Shakespeare's *Henry IV* and *The Tempest*.

David smiled at the thought that these would soon be the last words to pass J-MO's lips.

At 6:45, he left the coffee shop and stopped in a quiet doorway. By now, he figured, J-MO would be clear of the airport and on her way home, likely in a taxi.

As David had witnessed in many movies, the objective required that the victim came to meet their killer willingly, and with the impression that they controlled the location and timing. The challenge was to manipulate the victim to select the location the killer had already chosen.

After a deep breath, he consulted the business card J-MO had given him and dialed her private number. With his plan prepared, he waited for her to answer.

On the fifth ring, her shrill voice answered, a little thick with drink.

"This is J-MO. Who wants me?"

"Hi, Miss Ogden."

"Bloody hell. *Miss Ogden.* No, no, J-MO, please!"

"Well, er, J-MO, I…"

"Hold on a minute."

The sound of ice clinking into a glass and a gurgling of liquid was followed by a shout.

"Bloody hell, watch it! You're making me spill."

"Miss Ogden, are you alright?"

"What? Yes, just a useless bloody driver. I don't know why I keep using this limo service."

"Right, well, I have…"

"Just a minute. You called me Miss Ogden. Are you Don from the airport fish place?"

"David. From Sea Food World. You gave me your card and…"

"David, yes, that's it. My god, what a trip I've had. You won't believe what I found out."

"Zurich. I know."

"What?"

"Your Twitter account. I'm a follower, so I…"

"Oh, yes, of course you are. Well, wait until nine tonight, and the story I'm about to reveal. It will…"

"That's why I'm calling."

"About Zurich?" she asked, concern tempering her enthusiasm. "What do you mean?"

"No, not about Zurich. About a story. A really big one. You said to call you if I, you know, heard anything."

J-MO, interest piqued, became instantly professional.

"Yes, I did. OK, David. Right, go on then, I'm all ears."

"I have a briefcase."

"A briefcase?" She sounded impatient. "Well, OK, but what's in it?"

David kept one eye on his audience, who followed the exchange with intense interest, as he reeled J-MO in.

"I don't know. It's locked."

"Locked. You mean you haven't opened it? Look, David, when I said you could call me with something, I didn't mean with lost property. It's not really what…"

"It's not lost."

"What do you mean?"

"I know who it belongs to."

More intrigued, J-MO took the bait.

"Alright, David. Who does it belong to?"

"Do the initials D.D. M.P. mean anything to you?"

After a moment, between traffic sounds, J-MO spoke with both a tone of excitement and scepticism in her voice.

"Well, if M.P. is in capitals and separate from the D. D., then yes, I'm guessing you have the briefcase of a Member of Parliament. But I don't recall any D.D."

"I do," David said. "D.D. is Daniel Durvis."

"Durvis? You mean the one doing the Brexit thing?"

"Yes. His official title is the Secretary of State for Exiting the European Union."

"You're fucking kidding me, David," J-MO blurted, forgoing any pretence at refinement. "How the hell did you get that?"

"That doesn't matter. What matters is whether you want it, and how much will you pay for it."

To his horror, the line went silent.

"Are you there, Miss Ogden?"

"Look, we can't talk about this over the phone. We have to meet."

David smiled and tipped his head toward his audience as J-MO entered his trap.

"Alright, but it has to be now. I don't want to hold onto this any longer. If I get caught with it, I'm fucked."

"Now? How can we do that? I'm in a limo on my way home."

"Look, I'm meeting my girlfriend tonight at the Hard Rock Cafe in Mayfair at nine. You can meet me outside, at say, quarter to nine. But I want to know how much…"

"I can't meet you there. It's too public. Too many eyes. Let me think."

After a moment, J-MO took control of the situation.

"Do you know Kensington?"

"Well, it's not my usual haunt, but yes, I've been to the Victoria and Albert Museum."

"Alright, do you know the thin house?"

"Oh, yes, I've been past there years ago. Why?"

"Look, there is a garden on Thurloe Square. It's private."

"Private?"

"Yes, and you need a key. Anyway, do you know it?"

"Not really, but I'm sure I can find it. But if it's private…"

"I have a key. There's a gate about halfway down Thurloe Square. I'll meet you at the gate at eight. We can go in the gardens and talk there. It's dead quiet in there and no one will see us. The Hard Rock is only fifteen minutes away on the tube."

David pretended to think, playing his role.

"You didn't say how much."

"That depends what's in the briefcase. For all I know, it might be a ham and cheese sandwich."

He decided to play his ace card.

"I don't know. I really need money. Maybe I should call the *Daily Mail*…"

"A thousand."

"What, that's not much. Forget it, I'll…"

"I mean a thousand now. More, if it's worth it."

"How can I trust you?"

"How can I trust you, David?"

"Alright, eight o'clock at the gate. Where did you say it was again?"

~

Cars, bumper to bumper, lined both sides of the road. Streetlights, more decorative than functional, cast deep shadows on the pavement adjacent to the iron fence that contained the gardens. Irregular lights, some bright, some faint, seeped from the windows of the flats that lined the other side of the road.

Twenty feet from the gate, concealed in the darkness of a tree that overhung the fence, David waited.

At 8:02, light spilled from the open door to flat 28. J-MO, unmistakable in a brash fur coat, came out, checked traffic, crossed the street, and walked to the gate.

Tense and alert, yet primed for his performance, David pressed the briefcase under his arm and strode toward her.

A cigarette just lit, J-MO scanned the street. Not recognizing him, she looked past David.

Two steps away from her, he spoke.

"Hi, Ms. Ogden."

Startled, she stepped back and challenged him.

"What? Who the hell are you?"

"It's me, David."

Leery, she peered at him.

"What the hell? Are you in disguise or something?"

"Oh, this?" He chuckled, enjoying the moment. "Yes, kind of. Jane—that's my girlfriend—and me, we like to dress up as different people when we go on a date. It's like you meet someone new on the outside, but someone you will already like on the inside."

J-MO, her head shaking with bemusement, shrugged.

"Well, I've not heard of that before. Anyway," she said, pointing to the case under David's arm. "Is that it?"

"Yes."

"Let's have a look, then."

"Not here," David said as he looked left and right with feigned concern. "Let's get in the park, out of sight."

No fool, J-MO, hesitated and sought proof.

"Just a peek at the initials first."

He had expected and prepared for this. Using instructions from several websites, he had dipped the leather flap of the bag in water to dampen it. Then, using a hammer and an alphabet stamp set purchased from Artisan Leather Supplies, he had lightly tapped each letter into the leather. A touch of white paint, dulled with some dirt, highlighted the initials.

In the dim light, and eager to believe, J-MO accepted the forgery. Turning from David, she withdrew a key from her coat pocket, unlocked the gate, and held it while he walked ahead. The gate, on a spring-loaded hinge, clunked closed.

She passed him by two steps, turned, and pointed.

"Just ahead, there's a bench."

When they reached it, J-MO lit another cigarette and held out her hand to David.

"Right, let's have a look at it."

"What about my money?"

"Here," she snapped as she reached in her pocket, withdrew a tightly rolled bundle, and held it out to exchange for the briefcase.

As he took the money and handed the case over, David looked her in the eyes.

"What will you do with it?"

J-MO caressed the case, touched the initials, and prodded the lock as she answered.

"Depends what's in it, but at the least, his career as an M.P. is over. Can't be leaving his briefcase around and expect to keep his job, can he?"

"But it was a mistake," David replied, testing out his conviction that J-MO had no decency. "He had three or four bags with him, he was late, and his aide had harried him to get going to catch the flight. It could have happened to anyone."

"Yes, but it didn't, did it? You got your grubby hands on it, and now I have mine on it. What if there are, you know, state secrets in here, and you sold it to the Russians?"

"But you don't want to just return it?"

"Why the hell would I do that?"

"I don't know. Maybe a reward? Or just the right thing to do?"

"Then why the hell didn't *you* return it? No, you're just like everyone else. You want money for nothing. Anyway, the right thing is to open this up, see what's inside, and then expose the bastard for being so goddamn irresponsible."

"No second chance, then?"

"Not bloody likely."

"I thought as much."

J-MO tossed her cigarette to the ground, ground it out with her foot, and as she turned to leave, nodded at David as she spoke.

"Call me tomorrow after I've had a proper look, and we can go from there, OK?"

"Yes, OK."

The cosh, homemade with three sturdy socks layered one inside the other and half filled with Shadow's cat litter, arched upward, descended and thudded onto the back of J-MO's skull before she had even taken a second step.

David didn't catch her when she crumpled.

With his hands under her armpits, he dragged her limp body to the speckled shadow of a nearby tree. After retrieving the briefcase, he rolled her onto her back and withdrew the ziplock bag from his inside pocket. Struggling a little with his gloves, he unsealed the bag and tipped the weather-resistant papers onto J-MO's chest.

While one hand squeezed her jaw and forced her mouth open, David's other hand pushed the pieces of paper past her lips and teeth and into the back of her throat. Even unconscious, her body sensed danger and forced her torso to twitch, her throat to contract, and her head to wriggle from side to side.

When she was on the cusp of consciousness, he rolled J-MO onto her stomach, pulled her arms behind her back, and pinned them under his knees. Then, with both hands on the back of her head, he pressed her face into the damp grass and dirt.

Light, strong and hot and compressed in a tight beam, illuminated the taut leather of his gloved hands. Voices, scattered and tense, vied to convey approval. Gasps, some long, most short, punctuated the night.

Moved by his adoring audience, David tightened his grip and pressed harder. Up through his inner thighs and groin, J-MO's oxygen-depleted muscles tremored and spasmed, triggering in him an unexpected pleasure.

Finally meting out the judgment of the people, he roared in triumph. Consumed by the rapture of his performance, he peered into the darkness of the theatre, eager to accept the wild adulation of the crowd.

Suddenly a metallic clunk interrupted David's delusion. Voices, both male, mumbled and snickered as they rushed from the gate to the nearby bushes. Moments later, without any preamble, the unmistakable sounds of some sexual act extinguished the light and the sounds in David's mind, and the audience faded away.

The meaty slap of flesh on flesh brought him back to reality. Now damp and cold, he released J-MO's head, rolled off her back, and stood up. Eager to be off stage, but professional enough to complete the post-script, David spread misdirection.

Around the briefcase, which he left open, with public domain articles about the Secretary of State for Exiting the European Union on display, David tossed a handful of twenty-pound notes from the bundle J-MO had given him.

At the bench where he had stood with her, he dropped a cigarette butt he had picked up on the street outside the tube station.

On the train home, high with his accomplishment and mentally preening with the success of his performance, David's fingers fondly caressed J-MO's business card.

THIRTY-EIGHT

"Gossip Choked to Death with Words" was the headline on the front page of the UK's leading tabloid newspaper, The *Sun*.

The information about the pieces of paper with quotes about gossips stuffed down J-MO's throat had taken a week to leak from the police investigation.

Since then, the tabloid press had competed with each other to create the best headline. Efforts included "Gossip Can't Swallow Words—Choked to Death" and "Gossip Stuffed with Words—Chokes to Death." David's favorite was "Gossip Murdered—Words Can Kill."

The media headlines and the memory of J-MO's body vibrating as it fought for life swirled and bounced in David's mind. He remembered the pressure of his hand on her head. The soil, grass, and leaves around him, which were moist and pungent, filled his senses as he relived the moment over and over again.

Without any effort, David stepped outside of himself and viewed his role as executioner with pride. In the distortion of his recall and psychological justification, he imagined bowing to the applause and adoration of a grateful and spellbound audience.

Deeper into his fantasy, he embellished the selection, coordination, and arrangement of his "costume," taking credit for the supposed ideal disguise with which he had infiltrated J-MO's "exclusive" neighborhood.

More recognition and accolades followed for his contributions to the plot development, the choice of location, and finally for committing the "perfect" murder.

"Are you gonna get off, or do you want to go back home, mate?"

The bus driver's rude cockney voice broke the spell and brought David back to reality with a thud.

"Alright," he mumbled as he gathered himself and made his way off the bus.

Drizzle floated from dirty clouds and covered him in a sheen of moisture on his short walk from the bus stop to the entrance to Heathrow Airport. He hadn't wanted to go in today, but he needed the money, and he had also taken a lot of sick days recently.

As expected, Nancy cornered him the moment he stepped behind the bar. For the past week, she had talked incessantly about J-MO, her frequent visits to Sea Food World, and about how David "knew" her.

"Oh my god. I can't believe it. Did you see the papers today?"

Incrementally forced to abandon the satisfaction and security of his fantasy by the intrusion of real life, David reluctantly nodded.

"Yes, I read the papers on the bus."

"Well, what do you think?"

"Think about what?"

"Having those bits of paper with quotes about gossiping rammed down her throat? Bloody sadistic, if you ask me."

"I don't know," David replied, as he shuffled sideways to hide the involuntary twitch of his lips that expressed an inner self-satisfaction. "Seems kinda poetic to me."

"Poetic?"

"Yeah. You know, live by the sword, die by the sword sort of thing."

"Oh, well, I suppose so. But she wasn't *that* bad. I followed her blog, and she always had some dirt on somebody. And most of 'em deserved it, if you ask me."

Tempted, but unwilling to share his venomous opinion of J-MO, David shrugged as he spoke.

"Maybe. I mean, I didn't follow her stuff, so I don't really know."

"Well, I heard that the police think it's one of the people she exposed, or something to do with what she was working on."

"That makes sense. Guess we have nothing to worry about then, eh?"

A harrumph signaled Nancy's temporary retreat from the subject as she and David parted to attend to customers.

~

Flitting in and out of reality, David's day passed quickly. By 11:30 a.m., he was relaxed and ready to go home at noon. He had mentally changed his clothes, and was debating whether to stop at the Bell on the way home. He was thinking forward to being with Clair for quiz night, and a sense of contentment had settled over him.

At 11:45, his contentment shattered when "Billy the lout," as David now thought of him, announced his arrival at the bar with a loud belch, followed by an equally loud blue collar maxim, "Better in than out."

Too disgusted to speak, David simply glared at him.

Ignorant or indifferent, or both, Billy bared his discolored teeth as he spoke his greeting.

"What ya up to, Davey?"

With David struggling for words, Billy took the initiative.

"Cat got ya tongue? It's me, Billy."

Nancy was at the other end of the bar, too far away, and neither Ed nor Mike, the noon-to-eight bartenders, had arrived yet. Trapped, David pasted on a smile.

"Billy. What can I get you?"

"Bottle o Stella, your best Scotch, and some of that Russian wild salmon I had the last couple of times."

Heavy with sarcasm, David pricked at the man.

"Celebrating, are you?"

"Yeah, you could say that. See, m' had a good win at the dogs last night, and I decided to treat myself to a quick day out to Prague."

"You're only going for the day?"

"Just nineteen hours, really. A quick in and out. Well, not *that* quick an in and out, if you know what I mean, eh?" Billy boasted, alluding to his sexual stamina with Prague's prostitutes. "Yeah, got me a last-minute deal on LOT Airlines. Only a hundred and twenty quid round trip. Plus, dirt-cheap hotel 'cause it's off-season, and on top of that, the girls will be desperate for business. Gonna be a good time."

As he slurped beer, sipped Scotch, and swiveled in his chair to ogle any and every woman who passed by, David punched in the order for Russian salmon and contemplated him.

He didn't *like* Billy. Hadn't since day one. And now it seemed the man would become another regular that David would have to endure.

What, he asked himself, *is the point of Billy?* He was probably the exact kind of person who consumed the bile that J-MO had forced on to the world.

In fact, the more David thought about it, Billy and J-MO were not unlike each other, in that they were both parasites. Like Jason West had been, too. Except perhaps that they fed off each other, which parasites didn't usually do. J-MO had produced, and Billy consumed.

"You look deep in thought, mate," Billy said as he waved his empty bottle and glass at David. "Any chance of another round?"

"Yes, of course. Tell me, Billy, did you hear about the death of that gossip columnist?"

"You mean J-MO, right? A bloody tragedy, that. Best bloody news of 'em all. That's what the BBC should do. More of them 'exposas' things like she did, so we can 'ave the truth. Can't believe she's dead."

Unsurprised that Billy followed J-MO, David didn't acknowledge Billy's goodbye when his shift ended at noon. He was too engrossed in his violent thoughts.

THIRTY-NINE

David had control. His lead role in the judgment and execution of the societal undesirables of Jason West and J-MO, had changed him. His life hadn't been this good for years.

Reassured by his successes, he relished the validity of his interpretation and application of the Machiavellian principles. Freed from the stigma of his disease to retake "center stage," he prepared to play his next "award-winning part."

Purpose, decision, action, David thought to himself as he walked along Peacock Avenue on his way to Feltham Library. At two p.m., the bright but not warm sunlight that cast early afternoon shadows on the sidewalk matched his mood.

In sunlight, pride welled inside him as he congratulated himself on his professional approach to his upcoming lead role to visit justice on the repugnant Mr. Taylor.

In the shadows, lust and anger buffeted David's professionalism: lust to mete out the ultimate justice on Taylor, and anger at the other societal parasites, such as Billy the lout and the thug Troy, who increasingly blighted his life.

However, today, like all brilliant actors, he would research the scene, review the stage, analyse the plot, consider the costume, and most importantly, develop the character. And he would build on the success of his past performances with the upstart, Jason West, and the parasite, J-MO.

As his thoughts oscillated and tumbled, David made good time and arrived at the library just after 2:30. On the steps, he paused to recap what he needed: a chemical formula and a street address.

The need for a chemical formula had been inspired by Bashar al-Assad, Syria's embattled president, who had, unknowingly, decided how Taylor would die. More accurately, the BBC special report on the alleged use of chlorine gas by the Assad regime in Syria's Idlib Province had provided David with the idea.

The report had included experts, who discussed the gas, how to make it, how it smelled, and repeated warnings not to mix bleach and ammonia at home.

The chance link between the use of chlorine gas and Mr. Clean's bloody sensitive nose seemed prophetic to David. And the more he envisioned the symmetry of Taylor smelling the approach of his own death, the more it reinforced his belief in the rightness of the part he had to play.

Inside the library, after helpful staff provided a password and directed him to a computer terminal, David accessed the internet and tapped the Google icon.

He recalled Taylor's pompous statement:

I live in Bolney, Haywards Heath. I chose the place because, as you probably don't know, there is a prevailing coastal wind and lots of fresh air.

Then David began his search.

According to a 2011 census, Bolney Village in Haywards Heath, West Sussex, had a population of 1,366.

Next, he entered "Taylor/Bolney Village" into the phonebook.bt.com website, which dutifully reported that eleven people called Taylor lived in and around Bolney Village.

But only one resident had the initial *A*, and he lived at number eight and a half Top Street.

Using Google Maps, David noted that Bolney was fifty-two miles from Feltham. Travel time by car would take between one hour and three minutes to one hour and twenty-four minutes, depending on route taken, and traffic.

As he didn't own a car and didn't plan to rent one, David checked the Southern train service and noted that train and bus travel would take approximately one hour and forty minutes.

Back on Google Maps, this time using Street View, David "walked" around Taylor's house on Top Street, observed the front yard and driveway, and zoomed in on his front door and windows.

Switching to "earth view," he soared over Taylor's home. David could see a secluded and fully enclosed back garden with a wide lawn, a stone patio, and two outside brick sheds. More importantly, the backyard ended against a large open field, which by zooming out and left, appeared to him as though it could be accessed through some hedges about three hundred meters from the backyard.

Back on Google Maps, he entered Taylor's street address for more precise details on train and bus travel. From the train station at Hassocks, Google recommended bus 278 to Ryecroft Road, and from there, a ten-minute walk to Taylor's house.

With Street View on, David "walked" Ryecroft Road. About one hundred and fifty meters on the right, he noticed a wooded gate leading to a worn dirt track. It cut away from Ryecroft Road and ended at Cherry Lane, less than two hundred meters from Taylor's house, and about four hundred meters from the access point to the field that ran behind Taylor's garden.

After taking notes on the location, roads, and train times, he entered "chlorine gas" in the Google search engine.

An immediate option to skip to "chlorine gas formula" popped up. David clicked on it and a text box opened with the chemical formula Cl2, which didn't mean much to him. Below the text box, other options, such as "how can I make chlorine gas?" and "make chlorine gas at home" got to the point.

A few more clicks brought up the following warning: YOU CAN DIE FROM THIS. BE CAREFUL WHEN MAKING CHLORINE GAS.

David had now found what he wanted. Following the instructions on the screen, he made notes.

Materials: One large jar, one small bottle.

1:1 ratio (by volume) of: household ammonia and CHLORINE bleach—not chlorine free.

Put the bleach in the bottle and the ammonia in the jar. Cap both containers.

Take containers to target area.

Open both containers. Pour the contents from the bottle into the jar.

Make sure your jar doesn't overflow.

When complete, leave immediately.

Note: Household ammonia is not pure, but it's the best available. Not Clorox or Cascade. Must be household cleaning ammonia.

With the apparently simple method sketched out, David made further notes on the toxicity and characteristics of the gas.

Humans can smell chlorine gas at ranges from 0.1-0.3 ppm. At 1-3 ppm, mild mucus membrane irritation. At 5-15 ppm, there is moderate mucus membrane irritation. At 30 ppm and up, immediate chest pain, shortness of breath, and cough. At 40-60 ppm, fluid in lungs. Concentrations over 400 ppm prove fatal in over 30 minutes. With 1,000 ppm and above, dead in a few minutes.

Chlorine gas can be recognized by its pungent, irritating odor, which is like the odor of bleach. The strong smell may provide adequate warning to people that they are exposed.

Chlorine gas appears to be yellow-green in color, heavier than air, and will settle in low-lying areas.

The last note, **there is no antidote for chlorine poisoning**, David underlined twice.

Satisfied, he closed his notebook, erased his search history, closed his session, and left the library with purpose and determination.

FORTY

The soft cotton sleeve of his pajama top quickly absorbed the tears that fell from Robbie's eyes with a tap, tap, tap on the transparent plastic wallet that contained the printed photograph of the second set of clothes he had discovered in David's bedroom closet.

Still puzzled about the style of the clothes and the certainty that he had never seen David wear any of them, Robbie was troubled, especially about the long black raincoat.

A second photograph, this time of the EpiPen in David's bathroom, prompted another teardrop. Dabbing the tear away, Robbie added information, gleaned from the internet, about the use and application of EpiPens to the margins.

On a separate page, he wrote out his questions:

Why hide (old?) clothes under bed?

Why have an EpiPen he doesn't need?

Why have clothes (old/new?) in the closet that he never wears?

Turning the page, Robbie wrote with thick, deliberate strokes of red ink.

Why is David lying to Jenny?

Unable to answer, he made a score of red dots as he bounced his wrist and struck the paper with the nib of the pen. As the dots multiplied, Robbie replayed the one-sided conversation he had overheard between David and his sister when he had lingered by the front door after a visit with Shadow.

"Yes, I think that's a great idea. Mom and Dad will love it."

"Probably."

"No, you don't need to pay for it all. I'll pay half."

"Well, yes, that's true, but I'm still paying my share."

"I feel great."

"What? No. None of those. Really, Rachel has been great, and I feel much more in control."

"Yes."

"Ah, um, about tomorrow night."

"Well, I can't make it tomorrow."

"No, nothing's wrong."

"Actually, I have a date with Clair."

"The movies."

"Oh, I'm not sure. Clair is choosing."

"Dinner. Yes, then probably the Bell."

"Er, yes, you're right. This will be the second missed Wednesday, but…"

"Of course. Thanks. We will."

"Yes, next Wednesday for sure."

"Love you too, Jenny."

Robbie didn't want to believe it. But no matter how many times he analysed what David had said, there was no other conclusion. He had *lied* to Jenny. Worse, he had used his mom as part of the lie. Robbie knew this because after hearing David tell Jenny he had a date with his mom the next night, Robbie, pretending not to know, and had asked his mom what the plan was for Wednesday night.

When she had replied "nothing special," but perhaps they could play board games or go to the park and maybe get an ice cream, Robbie had struggled to keep his knowledge of David's lie a secret.

With the weight of his uncertainty and the self-imposed responsibility to "keep his mom safe," Robbie closed the page and reached for spiral binder number 7b from the front of his desk against the wall.

Turning the pages until he reached the current day, he ran his eye across the headings: Time, Action, Comment, Unusual, and then looked down to the last entry.

5:45 p.m. / David leaves, no Jenny / No date with Mom, has a backpack.

Beside the basic entries, Robbie now added:

Where is he going? What's in the backpack?

His mom's voice, soft and caring, suddenly sounded through Robbie's closed bedroom door.

"Five minutes, OK, Robbie?"

"OK, Mom."

He checked his watch. Nine p.m. After a moment's indecision, he set an alarm for midnight. He didn't know when David would be back, but instinct told him it would be late.

His mom would be in bed by eleven. He didn't like it, and he was scared, but David now had more secrets than ever. He had told lies to his sister, and had practically crept out of the flat with a backpack Robbie had never seen him with before.

In Robbie's mind, there was only one course of action: he had to find out what David had in the backpack, and maybe that would help figure out what he was doing.

~

Robbie didn't need the alarm. Unable to sleep, his mind wandered and created disturbing possibilities about David's true character and intentions. Ten minutes before midnight, Robbie turned off the alarm, held his breath, and listened.

At five past midnight, certain his mom was asleep, he took his camera, the front door key from the kitchen, and crept downstairs and into David's flat.

An hour later, tucked under the blankets of his own bed, Robbie scrolled through the photographs he had taken. First, an empty space in the closet where the long black raincoat and other clothes had been a few days ago. And there were no bags of clothes under the bed anymore, either.

Second, because Robbie had been more suspicious and thorough in his search, he reviewed a series of photographs of the garbage can, as well as some unusual contents: a torn piece of packaging label with the words *Complies to ADR Regulation* in thick black letters, and most curious of all, three pieces of cut black cotton. Two small circles and one larger circle.

The ADR Regulation, according to Robbie's Google search, was short for The European Agreement Concerning the International Carriage of Dangerous Goods by Road. What did David want with dangerous goods? The three circles, when Robbie drew and rearranged them, looked like two eyes and a mouth. It didn't take him long to imagine a burglar's mask.

Although confused and worried, no more tears fell from Robbie's eyes. Instead, his teeth ground with a determination to discover who David really was, and more importantly, how he was going to protect his mother from him.

FORTY-ONE

"Ah yeah, what the fuck then? Come on, yeah."

A shudder rippled through David.

"Aye, Davey mate. Give me and Dosser here a couple of Stella, yeah."

Most restaurants retained the right to refuse service. People could be turned away if they were without shirts, shoes, or pants; if they were drunk, or smoking; or if they were being rude, belligerent, obscene, or foul mouthed. Usually it required the person to display one or more of these traits in excess, so that the proprietor could be clear about the refusal to serve.

In the past, David had refused to serve obviously intoxicated people, and occasionally, a person whose eyes and furtive mannerisms screamed some kind of substance use. Unfortunately, proprietors had great difficulty in refusing service to a person like Billy, who displayed all, or many of these traits, in only small amounts and for short periods.

In other words, they were a scourge of British society, the louts.

David instinctively knew what made a lout, but he thought that the description of "a young man who behaves in an unpleasant or violent way as a result of excessive drinking," was a bit wanting.

Billy had graced Sea Food World several times now, always talking about his trips to Prague to "get some action."

The action, David knew, was prostitution. Now it seemed that his friend, Dosser, was about to get a personal tour from Billy.

"I'll show you around, don't worry."

"Better not be a bunch of old scaggs."

"No scaggs, I'm tellin ya, Dosser. The muff is f-in awesome."

Faded jeans, a rumpled black T-shirt, and a black windbreaker jacket hung on Dosser like dirty laundry tossed over a chair. A lumpy head, "shaved to the wood," teetered on a scrawny neck, whose massive Adam's apple moved up and down like a yo-yo with every movement of his body.

Ignorant of his own unkempt appearance, Dosser turned to Billy.

"Is it clean?"

"Yeah. Clean, tidy, trimmed, any way you want it."

As each man grabbed a bottle of Stella from the bar and gulped half the contents in one, David reflected on Billy again.

Over the summer and fall, he had, despite David's obvious disdain, revealed a lot about his life. By way of income, Billy did "*a bit of this and a bit of that, if you know what I mean.*"

David didn't know exactly what Billy meant, but he suspected it included petty theft, selling and delivering drugs, being a doorman or a lookout, gambling, and any other number of furtive activities that men like him thought were shortcuts to wealth, fame, and substance.

After ordering a second round of beers and two orders of the wild Russian salmon, Billy explained to Dosser why he came to Sea Food World before he went to Prague.

"Seafood, Dosser. That's why I come 'ere. It's good for the juices, you know, an afro-des-iac. You know what that is, eh, Dosser?"

"Er…"

"Keeps your pecker up and gives you stamina," Billy blurted out with a nod and a wink.

Tending other customers, Billy's self-important voice gnawed and pricked at David's thoughts. Keeping his pecker up had been a theme of Billy's desire for seafood, one David regretted that he had at first encouraged. Beside his preoccupation with seafood and erections, Billy's other passion centered on greyhound racing.

"Every Thursday and Saturday night, you can find me at Wimbledon Stadium for the dog races."

More information had flowed as Billy, true to his stereotype, assumed that everything he did, said, or was interested in should be shared and boasted about with anyone and everyone.

Often riding the buzz of alcohol, he had told David about his council subsidized flat in Putney, and how it was only a half-hour bus ride to Wimbledon Stadium.

"Best part is, the flat is near Putney Heath, near the Shell station and the church. Do you know it? Anyway, it's great after a night on the piss at the races. I get the last bus and walk over the heath to clear m' head a bit.

Friggin awesome at night. Damn shame that the old place is closing down in March."

Beer-laden conquests of high school girls Billy had gotten drunk and taken back to his flat for a toke and a bit of flesh had also punctuated much of his narrative.

"Amazing what these girls will do for some cider and a bit of dope. They might go to school, but they aren't that friggin smart."

Back in the present, Billy was now bossing Dosser.

"Get it down ya neck," he commanded as he signaled David with two fingers for more bottles.

As David popped the caps, Dosser turned to Billy.

"So, what are yer gonna do about that slag, Cheryl?"

"Fuck all, Dosser. Not my problem."

"But she's tellin everyone it's yours."

"Don't give a fuck. Think she's the first one I've poked and planted my seed in?"

"I heard her dad's got somethin to do with the police. Might be trouble.'

"Nah, Dosser. You don't get it. I know who her dad is. He'll be too worried about what people will think about him if people believe the kid is actually mine. Like I told Cheryl, 'you go get proof and then come talk to me.' But no way Daddy is gonna want that kind of proof. The dads and moms never want to know or accept what sluts their little girls are."

"Man, you're pretty cool about it. If I…"

"Hey, I fuck 'em, and they like it. Their problem if they can't, you know, take care of it. Guess my little fellas are good swimmers eh?"

"How many kids do you think you've got then?"

"Five I know about. Probably lots of little Billys walking around. Gotta be good for the world."

"Ever think about what happens to 'em?"

"Nope. But I've seen a few of the girls pushing strollers around with some schmuck in tow, who probably thinks it's his kid."

David listened intently. Images and thoughts of Clair and her single-parent struggle flashed side by side with Billy's vile words, chauvinistic opinions, and callous indifference. Clair had never mentioned Robbie's father, and thoughts that someone like Billy might be responsible for her situation shaped David's dislike into hatred.

"What's up with you?" Billy asked as he took in David's twisted expression.

"Oh, nothing, just tired, that's all. Would you like another beer?"

Billy, half off his seat, chugged the dregs from the bottle, and put money on the bar.

"Nah, we're off. Gotta plane to catch, and women to plow. Keep the change, mate. Looks like you need a beer yourself. Come on, Dosser."

Dosser, equally adept at chugging beer, followed Billy's lead, and the two of them swaggered away with an air of comradely anticipation.

David, his eyes fixed on Billy's back, smiled with his own dark sort of anticipation.

Time, he thought, *to make sure there wouldn't be any more little Billys running around.*

FORTY-TWO

Eager to get in "character," David hurried to Feltham train station, entered a stall in the public washrooms, and opened his backpack. Having already worn a combination of the clothes he'd used for the Jason West and J-MO parts for his previous reconnaissance of Taylor's home, he preened with anticipation as he smoothed a few winkles from his latest costume.

Purchased at another secondhand shop, the black shiny shoes, white shirt, blue and gray Royal Air Force tie, black trousers and jacket, wool overcoat, black leather gloves, and a Fedora-style gray hat with a black band transformed David into an "well-turned out" older gentleman.

With a small mirror hung on the back of the stall door, he used his makeup skills to add wrinkles to his eyes, cheeks, mouth, and neck.

Satisfied with his appearance, he withdrew a second smaller bag from the bottom of the backpack. Sitting on the toilet seat, he rechecked the contents. Duct tape, two jars, his cat litter cosh, a short crowbar, a flashlight, disposable painters' overalls and overshoe booties, a ski mask, a collapsible walking stick, a flask of tea, and two sandwiches.

After putting his own clothes in the backpack, David exited the washroom and walked from the station to leave the backpack at LuggageHero. With the smaller bag, he walked slowly, like an older man,back to the station and onto platform 3, to wait for the train to Hassocks station.

Ignored by other commuters, no one noticed his gloved hand pick up a cigarette butt from the platform, a discarded paper napkin from a seat on the train, and a crumpled receipt tossed away by an acne-covered youth engrossed in a video game on his phone.

Lulled by the rhythm of the train, David's thoughts drifted to his morning conversation with Taylor. He had arrived, as usual, at approximately 9:15, taken a seat on a barstool, and offered David a cold "good morning."

"Good morning. The usual, Mr. Taylor?"

"Yes, thank you."

"Any coffee today?"

"No. Just water, no ice."

David, confident that this would be Taylor's last visit to Sea Food World, had watched the other man's nostrils wriggle, and challenged him like he had wanted to do for so long.

"Something wrong, Mr. Taylor?"

"What do you mean?"

"Your nose. It's twitching."

Taylor stiffened at David's directness and raised his voice.

"Well, as you asked, I sometimes get a waft of something a little off when I'm here. Not always, but sometimes."

"How about today?" David pressed as he leaned in over the bar toward him.

Forced back by David's posture, Taylor reclined and stammered.

"No. No, not at all."

"Excellent," David replied with enthusiasm. "We don't want you thinking Sea Food World is unclean, do we?"

"I'm sure everything is fine," Taylor said. His confidence returned as he added, "If I could have my breakfast…"

~

Clunks, squealing wheels, and a dramatic lurch pulled David back to reality as the train halted at Hassocks station. With his collapsible walking stick snapped in place, he carefully left the train and walked a short distance to the bus stop for the number 278 that would take him to Ryecroft Road.

Accessing the details of the route like memorized lines for a play, David got off the bus at Ryecroft Road, exchanged nods with two people with dogs, and walked the well-worn trail to Cherry Street, down through a line of trees and into a fallow field. From there, he followed the tree and bush line to the rear of Taylor's house.

Hidden in shadow, David observed. Two houses stood to the left of Taylor's house. No light shone from the first, which was furthest away. In the second house, beside Taylor's, he noted, through a set of patio doors, the static heads of two people watching TV.

Assured of his solitude in the darkness of the damp evening, he stepped from the shadows to the gate of Taylor's back garden. Struggling in the dark, he reached through the metal bars of the gate. With his hand covering the flashlight lens, he angled his head and arm and grasped the three-cylinder-numbered lock that secured the simple latch system in place.

As he braced himself against the gate to break the lock off with the crowbar, David felt the metal plate of the lock mechanism attached to the gatepost shift a little. Changing plans, he used the crowbar to pry the entire latch plate from the rotted gatepost.

Inside the garden, confident he remained unnoticed and remembering his mistake with the CCTV at West's flat, David put on the homemade ski mask and crept to the back door of the house. Through the rectangle window in the door in the darkened room, a red/green dot of an alarm system pulsed a warning.

Not surprised and not concerned, he crossed the grass to one of the garden sheds. Entering through the unlocked door, he sat on some boxes in front of the small window facing the house, poured tea from his flask, munched a ham and cheese sandwich, and waited.

Forty-five minutes later, at 9:10, cramped and a little stiff, David stood and stretched. A faint odor of fish reached his nostrils, and his bladder signaled it needed relief. Outside, his urine stained the shed wall.

Then the crunch of tires, clunk of a car door, and the sudden blast of light from the open-plan kitchen and sitting room announced that Taylor had arrived home.

Back in the shed, David stepped into the disposable painters' overalls and pulled the booties over his shoes. He watched Taylor pour wine, put a vinyl record on, open a book, and sit on high wing-backed chair in front of a glowing gas fireplace. His back was to the window.

Assured Taylor was focused on his book, David stepped out of the shed and approached the window. Holding the flashlight close to the windowpane, he flicked on the light and played the beam left and right in the room over Taylor's head.

As intended, the light reflected off hung pictures and fixtures, and caught Taylor's attention. He looked up briefly, but then returned to his book.

A moment later, David repeated the light show and Taylor, more aware, turned to the window just after David had shut off the light. Uncertain now, Taylor peered at the window, shrugged, and then returned to his seat.

As soon as he sat down, David did it all again.

This time, annoyed, Taylor got up, rushed to the back door, pulled it open, and called out, "Who's there?"

He stepped through the door, onto the pea gravel stones that formed a little moat around his house.

"I said, who's there?"

Met with silence, he turned to re-enter the house. As he did, David, who had pressed himself to the shadows of the wall beside the door, lunged forward and struck Taylor on the back of the head with his litter-filled socks.

As Taylor fell, David pushed him into the house and closed the door. Kneeling beside the motionless body, David paused and listened. A gasp, faint yet distinct, came from an indiscernible distance. Fighting to maintain his professional composure, David ignored the brief outburst from the rapt audience that, according to his imagination, struggled to hold its collective breath as they followed his every move.

Leaving Taylor unconscious, David walked to the stairs, intent on checking the bedroom and bathroom for the best place to put him. But beside the stairs, to the right of the front door, he discovered a small bathroom. Pleased with the realization that the small bathroom would make his task much easier, he allowed himself to acknowledge another sound from the audience that conveyed their admiration for his effortless change of plan.

Once back in the kitchen, he grasped Taylor's arms and dragged him to the bathroom. After wrestling the limp body onto the toilet and binding him with duct tape to the base and tank, David placed a strip over Taylor's mouth. With Taylor secured, David returned quickly to the shed and brought his bag inside.

From the bag, he took two jars and placed them at Taylor's feet. Then, using cold water and several slaps, he revived Taylor until he became aware and afraid. Then he began to struggle.

Poised before Taylor, David whipped off his ski mask with a dramatic flair for the benefit of the audience, certain there would be no cameras in the bathroom.

Unable to speak, his eyes wide with dilated pupils, Taylor looked at David in confused recognition.

Through the duct tape, his muffled questions struggled for coherence.

Confident now, David held Taylor's stare with his own and raised a finger to his lips in a call for quiet.

Rigid with fear, Taylor stilled, but then flinched violently as David leaned toward him and pressed his armpit into his face. With no choice, Taylor inhaled through his nose.

"What do you think of my deodorant?" David asked lightly as he pulled back and stood before Taylor, waiting for his reply.

Taylor, his nose twitching and wriggling, coughed, gagged, and tossed his head from side to side.

"That's right, Taylor. It was *me* you could smell at the airport. Every time your nostrils flared or your eyes creased at the odor, it was me. Well, I'm sick of people like you judging me. Condemning me for something I can't control. People like you have ruined my life. And now it's my turn to ruin yours. Once and for all."

Frantic, Taylor twisted his head in search of an escape. His torso convulsed as he strained against the duct tape.

"It's no good," David said as he put the ski mask back on. "You have been condemned. And the audience, *my* audience, demands a just and appropriate punishment for your sins."

As he spoke, David took a towel from the rack and ran water over it until it was soaked. Misinterpreting David's actions, that he was about to be strangled or suffocated, Taylor began a frenzied struggle to free himself.

Ignoring Taylor, David wrung the towel out a little, then wrapped it around his nose and mouth. He cinched it at the back and knelt down in front of Taylor.

Confused, Taylor strained forward and watched David unscrew the lids of two glass jars. The smell of chlorine and ammonia immediately filled the small room. Taylor, familiar through his own fastidiousness with the dangers of mixing chemicals, writhed and screamed beneath the tape.

With little time to spare, David glanced at Taylor.

"Now, if only you could close that fucking nose of yours."

At arm's length, he poured the ammonia in the bleach. Holding his breath, he closed the bathroom door behind him, took the towel off his face, and pressed it up against the bottom of the door.

Rubbing his own eyes and couching, David listened to Taylor cough and gasp as the chlorine gas entered his respiratory system. According to David's research, sneezing and throat irritation would follow, as well as the probability of vomiting and a severe headache.

David also knew that exposure to chlorine gas didn't necessarily kill a person if they were quickly evacuated from the toxic area and treated. But Taylor would not be evacuated or treated. His death would be slow, painful, and certain.

After waiting and memorizing the sound of Taylor's struggles for future enjoyment, David returned to the script. Using the materials he'd collected from the station platform and the train carriage seat, he set about leaving a false trail for the hapless detectives that would, in his own mind, flounder in their efforts to solve yet another perfect crime.

The cigarette butt he placed in the backyard near the window; the used napkin went on top of the garbage can; and the crumpled receipt he left on the kitchen floor. Then David took a second wineglass and filled it and swilled it to spill some over rim and down to the base. He set the glass next to Taylor's to make a stain on the table. Then he removed the glass, washed it, and placed it back in the cupboard.

Enough to cause some confusion, David thought as he wiped his wet gloves on his overalls.

Before leaving, he unlocked the front door and paused by the bathroom door. Muted sounds of labored breathing and wheezing filtered through. Satisfied, David checked his watch: 10:02. He had two hours and twenty-three minutes to walk the 5.6 miles to Haywards Heath train station, instead of using the Hassocks station as he had on the way.

On the kitchen counter, David stopped and considered Taylor's keys. It would be easy to take the man's coat and a hat from the peg by the front door, and use his car to get away. Then again, CCTV cameras would be an issue, and the car route would be picked up at some point. Then he would have the problem of leaving the car somewhere.

Back to the script in his head, David ignored the keys, stepped out the back door, and moved quickly to the garden shed. Inside, he took off the disposable painters' overalls and booties. With his bag packed, he replaced the latch plate, rubbed some dirt on it, and retraced his steps to Ryecroft Road.

Once there, David began his long walk to Haywards Heath train station. Moving quickly, and keeping close to hedges and trees, he hid in shadows to avoid the cars and trucks that passed him. He met no other pedestrians, and reached the station at ten past midnight.

The train he needed left at 00:25 to St. Pancras station, London. Once he arrived at Pancras, he left the station, walked along a few alleyways and discarded the heavy woolen coat, black jacket, trilby hat, black gloves, and RAF tie. After slipping on the black windbreaker he had brought in the bag, he tossed the painters' overalls and booties in separate garbage cans and returned to the station.

From St. Pancras, he took a fifty-five-minute train ride to Heathrow. At the airport, he lingered over a coffee, then used the "pay as you go" passenger shower facilities to clean up and reduce his odor before going to the staff room to change into his work clothes.

Exhausted, exhilarated, and still damp from the shower, David found a seat away from Sea Food World and let the adulation of the audience sweep over him.

Flowers rained on the stage, programs fluttered, hands clapped, and voices called "bravo," "magnificent," and of course, "encore."

Immersed in his delusion, David stood, faced the floor-to-ceiling glass wall that looked out over the runway, and bowed low to the sparkling lights. Deep into a third bow, the faint squeak of a wheel calmed the crowd, extinguished the lights, and brought him back to reality.

FORTY-THREE

That greyhound dog racing existed summed up David's knowledge of the sport. He didn't know anyone who was interested in it, and he didn't know anyone who had ever been to a race. When he consulted the internet, he learned why.

In mid-1940s England, fifty million people a year watched skeletal dogs run around oval tracks chasing fake rabbits for less than sixteen seconds. By 2013, less than two million followed the dogs. Once a three-billion-pound industry, scandals involving dog doping, illegal betting, race rigging, and revelations about mass dog killings changed the public's perception, and the industry rapidly declined.

Wimbledon Greyhound Track, located on Plough Lane in South West London, opened in 1928, and was, according to what Billy had told David, only a "half-hour bus ride" from his flat in Putney.

On Saturday evening, the racetrack doors opened at 6:30 p.m. David arrived at seven, and confronted by thousands of people, immediately thought he had made a mistake, as he couldn't hope to find Billy in such a mass of people.

As it turned out, an hour later, moments before David intended to leave in frustration, Billy found David instead.

"Hey, mate. What you doin here? Didn't know you liked the dogs."

Billy had emerged from the crowd without warning and had caught David unprepared. But already happy from drink, and with a natural disposition to talk, Billy placed an arm around David's shoulder, pulled him close, and extended his greeting.

"The airport, mate. You're the seafood guy. It's me, Billy."

"Oh yes," David replied, feigning ignorance and trying not to tense under Billy's touch. "I didn't recognize you. So many people come and go at the airport."

"Yeah, it's really packed tonight. As soon as they announced it's going to close down, the place gets full. The punters should have been out before, then maybe they wouldn't close the place."

"Yeah," David, answered, recovered now. "I read about the closing to make way for some housing and a soccer stadium."

"A bloody disgrace. Been racing here since 1928, almost a hundred years. Now they want to close it down for another bloody soccer field. Anyway, good to see you. Who are you with?"

A boisterous group of men rushing to watch the next race brushed past David and Billy, forcing them to the side, and closer together.

Up close and uncomfortable, David stammered the lines he had rehearsed for just such a meeting.

"No one. My first time here. Thought I'd give it a try, before, you know, asking my girlfriend to come."

Enthusiastic at having a newbie, Billy grinned as he spoke.

"First time, eh? Well your luck's in tonight, mate. Me and Dosser will show you around. He's over getting the beers. Come on, follow me."

David's original intention for visiting the race had been to observe Billy from a distance to discover his habits, and also get an idea of how and where he might end the man's life.

While Billy led the way, David reminded himself that adaptation and improvisation were the corner-stones of good acting. And tonight, thrown in the deep end with an unexpected and unscripted role, he would dazzle his audience.

With a broad canvas on which to play his part, David followed Billy, confident that this sudden change would help him achieve his original goal.

With Billy's compulsion to brag, talk, and show off, as well as suggestions of collusion and insider knowledge of the dog racing world, David's "act" required little more than the ability to listen, nod, and convey wide-eyed belief at some of Billy's stories. And the more Billy drank, the more he revealed.

Unfortunately, Billy's anecdotes about illegal betting systems, drug use to fix races, and supplying old dogs as practice to train younger dogs to fight only served to reinforce David's decision to kill him.

Billy's general attitude toward life, women, society, and the rule of law was also a major problem.

By 10:30, a half hour before the official close, David nudged Billy as he leaned against a rail overlooking the racetrack.

He was lightheaded from the pace of Billy and Dosser's drinking, and conscious of his worsening odor. It was time to leave.

"I've got to get going, Billy."

"What?" Billy blurted as he came off the rail. "There's a half hour and the last race to go."

"I know, but I don't want to miss the train. I'm knackered. Thanks for a great night, and for showing me around."

"Aw, come on, man. Get the next train. Dosser's gone for another round. You might win on the last race. I've got a good tip."

"I'd like to, but the schedule changes at eleven, and then I'd have to wait ages for the next train."

"Fuck the train," Billy said as he placed an arm around David's shoulder. "You can crash at my place, no problem."

The flash of opportunity tempted David. Realizing what Billy had already told him about where he lived, he tested the sudden thought and cast a line.

"Might be a bit cramped with Dosser."

"He's not comin back to my place," Billy exclaimed in surprise. "He gets off the bus the stop before mine. Number 39, goes along Withycombe Road and drops me off at Telegraph Road. Up Telegraph, then I nip across the old Putney Heath, past the church and gas station, and I'm home. No bother."

The information Billy provided about his route home, and the fact that Dosser would accompany them part of the way, quenched David's sudden temptation. He didn't know the area well, but the mention of a late-night, drunken walk across Putney Heath suggested many opportunities.

Sticking to his story of fatigue, which was real, and the need to catch the train, David accepted Billy's cell phone number and agreed to get in touch for another night at the races.

"Be sure to ring me, Davey," Billy called out as David turned to go. "I'll be here every Saturday till they close the old place down. Damn shame it is."

Barely out of Billy's sight, David already had part of a plan formulated in his mind. He would go to Putney Heath tomorrow, early, and walk Telegraph Road from the bus stop to the church and gas station.

One of these Saturdays, and soon, David thought to himself, *would be Billy's last race.*

~

Home by 12:20, David showered and sobered up. Too impatient to wait to use the library computer, he logged on to the internet and accessed the Transport for London website, and clicked the "Plan a Journey" section.

After entering a request for information on a journey from Wimbledon Greyhound Stadium to Telegraph Road leaving at 11:45 p.m., the system took four seconds to provide the details. A seven-minute walk to Burntwood Lane; nine minutes on bus 44 to Wandsworth Town station; three minutes National Rail South West trains to Putney station; two minutes on bus 39 to Withycombe Road; and an eight-minute walk to Telegraph Road. Arrival time: 12:40 a.m.

David noted that Billy's trip home from the races was not as direct or as quick as he had claimed. Using Google Maps Street View, David took an overview of the area. With various clicks and zooms, he soon determined the likely route Billy would take to get from Telegraph Road to his flat near the gas station and the church he had mentioned.

The next morning, up at 6:30 and out at seven on a cold, overcast Sunday morning, David took the train and bus from Feltham to Telegraph Road. At eight a.m., he began his reconnaissance on the quiet paved path that connected Withycombe and Telegraph Road.

About three meters wide, paved and intermittently bordered on either side by trees or open grassland, the path ran for about two hundred meters until it ended at Telegraph Road with steel bollards to prevent cars from using the path.

After just ten meters, David passed Roehampton Cricket Club on the right, and then the Telegraph gastro-pub on the left. Across Wildcroft Road, and past the T-junction with Portsmouth Road on the left, Telegraph Road narrowed to more of a lane than a road.

Large, posh houses on the left looked out to open fields, another cricket club, and heathland. After three hundred meters, the houses on the left ended and trees lined both sides of the much-narrowed road.

Adjacent to the last house, an unmarked dirt path led into the trees. According to Google, it would cross Putney Heath for about four hundred meters, then turn right, and a hundred meters on, run up against the properties of the Holy Trinity Parish Church on Roehampton Street. The Shell gas station was on the other side of the church on Ponsonby Road, and Billy's flat was somewhere close by.

David followed the dirt path to the rear of the church, where he stopped and checked his watch. His walk, taken at a slow pace to mimic how he expected an inebriated Billy to walk, had taken eighteen minutes from the beginning of Telegraph Road to the church. That would place Billy on the path across the heath at about 12:50 a.m.

Traffic was busy on the heath on Sunday morning: six dog walkers, three joggers, two cyclists, and two couples walking had shared the dirt path with him. Fifteen people in about ten minutes. David doubted it would be so busy at one a.m. on a Sunday morning.

Backtracking across the heath, he searched for a place to conceal himself while he waited for Billy. With heather, gorse, coarse grasses, and plenty of trees lining the dirt paths, hiding places were abundant.

He selected the point where the dirt path on the heath turned right toward the church. A stand of trees occupied the crux of the turn, but before the trees, the path had no tree coverage for about twenty meters, which David hoped would enable him to see Billy's approach.

Satisfied with the where and when, David strolled the heath to figure out how Billy would die. By the end of his walk, as he passed a woman throwing a stick for her chubby cocker spaniel, he had already decided the manner of Billy's death.

FORTY-FOUR

On the Thursday morning, after he had discovered the hazardous materials label and the "burglar's mask circles," Robbie had been reluctant to tend to Shadow. His reluctance changed to confusion and some fear when he found the cat's water bowl empty and saw that David's bed had not been slept in.

That had been weeks ago.

Since then, David had been happy, but not particularly interested in Robbie. His mom had said the same. Not to him, but to her friend, Debbie, who had stopped by for a visit one day.

David's comings and goings, as recorded in Robbie's notebooks, had returned to normal now, and aside from some of the clothes being back in the closet, only one unusual observation had been noted.

Poised over his notebook, Robbie read the entry:

Greyhound Racing, 7-11.

The information had been on a scrap of paper in the garbage. He knew what greyhound dogs were because his friend Jimmy had explained about them when Robbie had asked if his dog was sick.

Jimmy's dog, skinny and skeletal, and always shivering, was "like that so it can run fast." Jimmy's dad didn't race the dog, but used it to chase and frighten rabbits on the common.

Using Google, Robbie discovered the Wimbledon Greyhound Track, and from the website, understood that 7-11 indicated the time dog races were held on Saturday nights. He hadn't discovered any other information about dog racing in David's flat, however, and had thought little about it.

Despite David's apparent return to normalcy, Robbie remained confused, worried, and even more vigilant.

FORTY-FIVE

Neil Crawford should have gone home hours earlier. Straight from work, just like he had promised himself and Jacky, his latest live-in girlfriend.

Jane was the problem. Had been for two months, since she had started as the new assistant accountant at the haulage firm where Neil worked as the truck maintenance manager.

Thirty-four years younger than Neil's fifty-eight, Jane's beauty, body, and personality reminded him of his former wife, Alison.

Alison had left twelve years earlier, when Neil, in response to a demand from her that he choose either her or the bottle, had calmly poured himself another drink as she packed her bags and left.

Jane, twenty-four, intelligent, attractive, and competent, unintentionally drew Neil like a Hollywood film director to a nubile actor.

Along with five colleagues, Jane, Andy, Gillian, Scott, and Paul, Neil left work shortly before six, in time to get a double round of "happy hour" priced drinks. With a quick start on empty stomachs, the midweek hump-day fatigue faded, laughter and banter ensued, and more drinks flowed.

At eight, Andy and Gillian left for home. At nine, Scott and Paul invited Jane to join them at Panacea, a trendy, "younger crowd" bar in Manchester's city center.

Neil, desperate to keep the night going, got a double round, which stalled his colleagues' departure for another half hour. At 9:45, alone and despondent for his past glory days, Neil had a shot for the road.

With a nod to the bartender, who later claimed Neil had "looked fine," Neil left the Moss Vale Pub for the last time.

~

Six miles away, Richard and Dianne, married for forty-two years, eased into the heated leather seats in their 2018 Ford Edge. Out of the chill winter evening, content with their lives and each other, Richard touched the audio controls of the dashboard screen. Seconds later, the *Petite Overture* opening of the *Nutcracker* seeped softly from the car's eight speakers.

An early Italian dinner at Giovanni's, followed by a performance of the *Nutcracker* at Manchester's Dancehouse Theatre, had made for a wonderful evening. Both Richard and Dianne looked forward to going home and enjoying a glass of wine and a warm fire.

Edging the car through Manchester's busy downtown center, Richard touched his wife's hand as he spoke.

"A beautiful performance."

"Yes, one of the best."

"The costumes and sets seemed much more vibrant this year, too."

"That," Dianne pointed out with kindness, "might be your new glasses."

"Ah, yes, I'd forgotten about them. Well, even if the glasses aren't responsible for how good the costumes looked, they certainly make night driving a lot easier."

Through the lights at the junction of the A56 and A5063, and onto Chester Road for the five-kilometer drive to Altrincham, Dianne spoke again.

"Do you remember when David and Jenny used to come to the *Nutcracker* with us?"

"Of course. You know that's part of why I enjoy going so much. They were good times."

"We hardly see them anymore. What, with David's shift work at the airport, and Jenny's obsession with her laboratory work."

"I know. I miss them too, Dianne. But they have lives to lead, and…"

"Will they ever find anyone, Richard? Someone to be happy with? I worry so much about them."

"I worry, too. At least they have each other, and they still have their Wednesday movie and dinner night. That's where they will be right now."

Music filled the silence between them, until Dianne, her heart heavy with worry, announced, "I'm going to call them when we get home."

"Good idea," Richard replied as he checked his surroundings and noted that his progress had, in one of those rare moments, synchronized with green traffic lights instead of red. Smiling, he continued, "You can tell them what I want for Christmas."

~

Neil, a wily drunk, rarely parked his car in the pub parking lot. As a rule, he chose side streets about two hundred meters—or one cigarette—away from whatever pub he would be drinking in.

Five steps from his car, after a last drag, he flicked the spent cigarette to the ground. Two more steps, and the car lights flickered and the door unlocked. Behind the wheel, he marveled for the umpteenth time about proximity key technology as he reached and pressed the start button.

It was as though the system had been designed for drunk drivers. Not that he was drunk, but the system had certainly minimized the chance of the "fumble and drop" of one's car keys in the street. The start button was the icing on the cake, as were the automatic headlights. On the other hand, the inability to disable the seatbelt ding was not what he called progress.

Then again, the GPS had been a godsend. Touching the screen for home, Neil paused while the computer calibrated. When the voice said, "proceed two hundred meters, then turn right on Lostock Road," he pressed the clutch, engaged first gear, and pulled away from the curb. The idea of checking over his shoulder for traffic didn't occur to him.

Of course, the GPS selected the quickest route, which naturally included well-traveled and well-policed main roads, but Neil had soon discovered that if he drove in the general "quiet side roads" direction, the auto-calibration system would adjust accordingly.

Besides, he really did know his way home. Sometimes he just might miss a turn here or there. So instead of following directions on to the highway, Neil steered his car onto Crofts Bank Road, which would take him toward Urmston, through Flixton, and on to Carrington Road, which would force the GPS to recalibrate and take him on the A6144.

From the A6144, Neil would take Manor Avenue to bypass the busy Chester Road throughway. Across the circle at the junction of Woodhouse Lane and Manor Avenue, and then the third left would put him on Clough Avenue, and home.

Nine minutes later, as he approached the circle at Woodhouse Lane, Neil decided on a last cigarette. Striking his lighter, as he later told the police, was his only memory of his drive home.

~

Chester Road, which ran from downtown Manchester out to Altrincham and on into the hinterland, where it joined the A56, included Cross Street, Washway Road, Manchester Road, and Dunham Road.

With green lights almost all the way, Richard and Dianne made good time. Relaxed and comfortable, Richard signaled a right turn as he prepared to exit Chester Road onto Woodhouse Lane.

"Home soon," he murmured to Dianne as he noticed her eyes drooping.

"Good. I might pass on the wine, though, and have a bath instead."

Richard, his mind already pouring himself a glass of wine, slowed as he approached the circle at Woodhouse and Manor. A quick check to the right, and then he eased the car into the circle.

Neither Richard nor Dianne had the time to see anything, or react. And they never would.

A bystander, waiting at the Woodhouse bus stop for the number 9 bus, told police that the car—Neil's—"just flew out of Manor Road without slowing down."

Later, the absence of any skid marks to indicate Neil had attempted to break, along with his three-times-over-the-limit blood alcohol results, left no room for doubt about who had caused the accident.

According to the investigator, the impact point, rather than the speed or velocity of the impact, had caused Richard's death. Neil's car had struck Richard's door at an angle which had put the corner of Neil's front end right into Richard's door.

The impact had pushed metal through the side airbag into Richard's chest and abdomen, causing massive and instant blood loss. Had the impact been square-on, reported the investigator, he would have likely survived with little more than a concussion.

Just bad luck.

For Dianne, it had been even worse. Unharmed by the collision, she had suffered a heart attack and died before help arrived.

FORTY-SIX

"That was delicious, David," Jenny complimented him as she eased herself back in her chair, scrunched a paper napkin into a ball, and swallowed a burp.

"Just some old thing I threw together at the last minute."

"Oh, really? Well, is was definitely your best yet. Now tell me the truth. Where did you get the recipe? From Clair?"

"Ha. No, not Clair. She's good at cooking, but mostly basic meat and potatoes. You have Jamie Oliver to thank for this one. I was looking up lamb, and a recipe for lamb shank came up. It seemed easy, so, you know, I thought I would try it. You really liked it, then?"

"Yes, of course. I want the recipe."

"What for? Since when do you cook?"

"Well," Jenny replied lightly as she got up and took her empty plate to the kitchen sink. "I might *one day*. You never know."

David brought his own plate over and touched Jenny's arm as she made to turn on the tap.

"Let's leave the dishes. I'll do them later. What movie did you bring?"

"OK, if you're sure. I don't mind doing them, really."

A fake stern look from her brother said he wouldn't take no for an answer, so Jenny relented.

"Don't laugh, but I was feeling a bit romantic and nostalgic, and well, I brought *Casablanca*."

"You know, that's a good choice. I mean, I know it's a romance, but it's also about loyalty, doing the right thing, and what's right for society, and the world."

"That's a bit deep, even for you, David. What's got you thinking like that?"

"I don't know. I think it's the news. I mean, look at what's happening in the world. A good old-fashioned hero doing the right thing is just what we need."

At 10:50 p.m., as Rick Blaine, played by Humphrey Bogart, and Capitan Louis Renault, played by Claude Rains, walked arm in arm along the fog-covered runway, Jenny and David both stifled thick emotional gulps.

"It doesn't matter how many times I watch this movie, I always feel wrung out at the end. And I don't mean in a bad way. I…"

"I know what you mean, Jenny. Me, too."

"I'll help you with the dishes now."

"That's alright. I'll do them while I wind down. You get off home."

As she gathered her bag and wriggled into her coat, Jenny paused and looked at David.

"Hey, guess where Mom and Dad are tonight?"

"Mmm, let's see," David said slowly, as though he needed time to think and evaluate. "The early performances of Christmas shows will be just beginning, so…"

"Oh, alright. It's that obvious, is it?"

"Of course. They will be at a performance of the *Nutcracker* somewhere in Manchester."

"Do you remember when we all used to go together?"

"Giovanni's for pasta, the theatre, and then home for hot chocolate while Mom and Dad had wine."

Tugging on her coat sleeves, Jenny sighed.

"We should really make an effort to go and see Mom and Dad more often, David. They're not getting any younger."

The soft tone of her cell phone prevented his reply, and he raised an eyebrow in question as to who might be calling his sister late on a Wednesday night.

"Who?" Jenny was asking into the phone. "Police? What's happened? Did you say there's been an accident?"

FORTY-SEVEN

"Jenny," David said as they stood together in the living room of their childhood home. "What did the lawyer say would happen to the bastard who killed Mom and Dad?"

On the verge of tears, and a long way from reconciliation with what had happened, she didn't trust herself to respond.

David, unable to stem the odor of fish brought on by his anger and stress, prodded her gently.

"Jenny?"

"I don't want to talk about it right now. I just can't."

"Didn't the lawyer say he'd get off with a couple of years in prison, and a two-year driving ban? I don't get it. It's not enough. Jenny, please, I need to understand."

She sighed and finally relented to his questioning.

"He said that under the Traffic Act, or something, the maximum penalty is fourteen years for killing someone while drunk."

"Even fourteen years is not enough, but why did he say two years?"

"He didn't *exactly* say that. What he did say was that statistics on drink-driving deaths show that a third of drivers get no prison sentence at all, a quarter get less than two years, and only about a fifth get more than five years. No one has ever gotten the maximum, fourteen-year sentence. He just wanted us to be prepared."

Anger which had percolated without an outlet for days suddenly exploded from David.

"Prepared? Fucking prepared? The bastard was piss drunk. He should be put in front of a car and run over. I'd be more than happy to drive the car, and I won't need to be drunk to do it!"

"David, calm down. It's the law; we can't change it. Besides, the lawyer was only guessing what might happen. Maybe the man *will* get sent to prison for a long time."

Trying to manage her own anger and stress, Jenny distracted herself by tidying and rearranging photos. A plastic bag by the sofa caught her attention. Curious, she opened it. Then tears flooded down her cheeks.

Turning to her brother, she withdrew two small wrapped gifts. One with her name on it, the other for David.

They embraced and wept together. Uncharacteristically, Jenny stifled her sobs first. She pulled away from David, and her forgiving nature finally broke.

"You're right. If he gets off with a few years and a ban, it's not acceptable. I don't care what the law is. He killed Mom and Dad, just so he could have another goddamn drink. He bloody deserves to rot in prison until he dies."

David's own tears stopped as Jenny spoke, and a new sense of calmness suppressed his anger and grief. Holding his sister's hands, he spoke with conviction.

"Don't worry, Jenny. He'll get what he deserves."

FORTY-EIGHT

Their sibling role reversal just happened. Jenny fell apart, and somehow it was David who picked up all the pieces and visited her flat on Wednesdays. And on Sundays, too. Supporting his sister through the death of their parents, combined with the need to return to work despite a week of compassionate leave, stunted his own grief.

Weeks after the funeral, with Jenny settled, but distant, David's rage usurped his loss, and anger hemorrhaged from his mind.

Driven by a relentless, subconscious demand for revenge, his conviction that the unworthy must be punished finally overwhelmed any vestiges of normalcy in his brain and permanently anchored itself in his psyche.

He was the best person to judge, sentence, and execute these worthless human beings, and he would rise to the task.

Alternating between compartmentalized emotions and a facade of professionalism, David went into work and carried on, business as usual.

This morning, as he brought an unwelcome customer's breakfast over, and tried to keep his darker thoughts in check.

On the table, there was a full-color photograph of several brown-skinned naked children, all with telltale bloated stomachs. Large flies crowded around their pain-filled eyes as they held empty bowls in their hands. In the background, dark-skinned men unloaded white bags from a truck with the words *United Nations* painted on the sides.

A man with a nicotine-stained index finger stabbed at the photograph and pushed it to one side to make room for the coffee cup and bagel-laden plate.

"Pretty good, eh?"

The man was Philip Thompson, a former UK commando and mercenary. He was now a freelance photographer.

David had disliked him since Thompson's first visit to Sea Food World, when David had accidentally seen photographs of an injured child dripping blood onto his dead mother.

Another time, Thompson had spread photographs of child prostitutes in Thailand on the bar and said they were "pretty good too."

That had been months ago. Since then, Thompson had passed through Heathrow and David's bar about three times a month, depending on which human tragedy the photographer was set to exploit.

"It's horrible," David said quietly as he set the dishes on the table.

"That's what I mean. It's *supposed* to be horrible. That way people will send money."

When Thompson had first mentioned that his photographs were taken in order to raise money, David had assumed he had meant for a charity, like Oxfam, or an organization like Save the Children.

While the photographs had distressed David, he had grudgingly accepted that Thompson's trade in human misery had a positive objective.

It wasn't until a few weeks later, when Thompson, fawning over a photograph of a mother holding the mutilated body of an infant, had commented out loud to himself that the picture would pay for a nice long holiday in the Mediterranean, that David had become suspicious.

Disturbed and concerned, he searched the internet for the company Thompson was working for. He found a series of six websites dedicated to providing "aid, relief, and hope" to "all peoples affected by war, famine, and natural disasters."

Each website featured photographs credited to P.T. David recognized several of them. The site asked for donations and claimed that 90 percent of them went to provide needed services.

Sceptical, given Thompson's comment about the Mediterranean, David clicked all through the website until he found a section in very small print called "Donation Disbursement."

In even smaller print, the text clarified that the 90 percent of contributions directed to needed services was in fact based on the amount of contributions left "after operating, administrative, travel, insurance, liability, advertising, and salary expenses."

David's extensive clicking and reading through the site did not provide any details of how much these "expenses" might be.

At the mention of money, David decided to test Thompson.

"Money for what?"

"What?"

"You said because it's horrible, people will send money. I just wondered what the money is for."

"Oh. Well, you know, the usual. Medical supplies, food, water, stuff like that. Basic stuff."

"Like Oxfam or UNICEF, you mean."

"Yes, like them."

"So, you sell your photographs to the charities, or what?"

"Why are you so interested?"

Quick-witted, David had a ready response.

"I just wondered how I could, you know, make a donation to help, that's all."

"That's easy," Thompson replied with a greasy smile. On autopilot, he pulled a business card from the breast pocket of his shirt and gave it to David.

"You can donate through any of these websites." Unable to swallow the propaganda in the face of a new donor, he blithely continued. "And 90 percent of your donation goes to help the people."

"Wow, that's so great that it's 90 percent."

"Yes, we're pretty proud of that. Much better than those mainstream charities that waste 30 or 40 percent on paperwork and paying themselves."

Incensed by Thompson's barefaced lies, David drew deep upon his acting skills to maintain the role of a gullible and sincere person bent on helping the less fortunate.

To be certain of the decision he had already come to, he asked Thompson one final question.

"Must be pretty hard living for you, though."

"Eh?"

"You know, working for charity, traveling, taking all those photographs and not getting much pay, I expect."

"Yeah," Thompson replied, opening his palms and spreading his arms. "It's a pretty meager life, but helping people is what's important to me."

"Not much time or money for holidays, then?"

"Not really. Might get to Brighton if I'm lucky."

Starting to appear a little uncomfortable, Thompson scooped his latest photographs into his bag and stood.

"Well, gotta run, David. See you next time."

David, his newly cemented psyche fully in control, held Thompson's eyes.

"Yes, until next time."

FORTY-NINE

Information on Neil Crawford had been easy to get. Local and national tabloids wasted no time on their investigation and fact-finding. Within a few days, the man's life had been laid bare.

Interviews with his ex-wife, Alison, several former live-in girlfriends, acquaintances, and work colleagues all portrayed him as a heavy drinker who regularly drove. All the while, none of them could offer any insight as to why they did nothing to prevent it.

Crawford's workplace, home address, and regular drinking haunts were all listed. In addition, information came to light that he was on bail, off work due to stress, and awaiting a trial date.

Tabloid interest lasted for several days, until another human tragedy claimed the headlines.

After a week of compassionate leave, and the demands of helping Jenny, David waited patiently until he could get an additional day off work to add to the weekend.

Time he would need for his next "rehearsal."

Leaving Feltham on a Friday afternoon, he arrived at the Manchester bus station at eight p.m. A half-hour cab ride later, in the living room of his childhood home,

David stood less than five hundred meters from Clough Avenue and the home of the man who had killed his parents.

The room had no longer possessed any warmth. Tidied and depersonalized to make it ready for the upcoming sale, David shuddered and looked out the window, remembering.

Between his home and Clough Avenue lay Woodheys Park, a twenty-acre area with a small pitch-and-putt golf course, a five-a-side soccer field, and a play area for younger children. Woodheys had been a popular destination for David and Jenny and most neighborhood kids when they were younger.

Sinderland Brook was at the south end of the park. Originally a natural catchment and drain for runoff until it was canalized in the 1970s, it had also been a favorite play area. Despite constant parental warnings and threats to "stay out of the water," David, Jenny, and others had spent much of their summer play getting wet.

He had walked on Clough Avenue many times while growing up. Either en route to Park Road Primary School, which lay in Newton Park on the other side of Chester Road, or to the bus stop, but he couldn't recall any childhood friends who lived on the avenue.

He did recall that it was lined on either side with smart, four-bedroom semidetached houses, with tidy front yards, and one or two cars in most driveways. It had actually been similar to his own street.

Restless and angry now, David decided to take the walk he had been thinking of for several weeks. He needed to rehearse.

With careful steps in the moonless night, he walked across Woodheys Park. From the darkness, the smell of teenagers smoking drifted onto the breeze. Their slurred and profane voices echoed from the shadows of the trees that bordered the path adjacent to the bubbling water of the brook.

Little had changed, David thought as he recalled his own adolescent rebellions. On the far side of the park, through the alleyway that connected it to Link Road, he turned right for the short walk to Clough Avenue.

At number 121, four houses down on the left, David stopped. The house, with its brick walls, slate roof, white wooden window frames, and a dark front door with glass at the top was unremarkable amongst the other semidetached homes.

With curtains closed, no lights, and no sound, the house appeared empty. Between 121 and the next semidetached home, a wooden fence divided the space between the two buildings. A black metal four-foot-high gate, hinged on a wooden post, guarded the car-width passageway from front to backyard.

A yard David knew reached back to provide access to the path beside Sinderland Brook.

Conspicuous, David walked away. Ten or so houses further, he stopped. Anger ripped through his gut. His parents' killer was only meters away, safe, secure, and probably hiding.

David had come to plan and rehearse, but a new intent grew hot within him. Compelled, he turned around and quickened his pace.

Back in front of house 121, with sweat on his brow, David glared at the front door and willed the occupant to show himself. But, without telepathic powers to compel him, nothing happened.

Unable to suppress his anger, though, David scanned the street. Hoping he was unwatched, he shuffled to the dark space between the houses, opened the latched metal gate, and pressed himself against the wall. Motionless, he listened and cataloged the sounds of the night in search of a telltale noise from the house. As he waited and listened, his anger tempered, and he reminded himself of the dangers of impulsive actions.

Poised to leave the shadows, David heard the sound of wood on wood, as a swollen or warped door pulled free from its frame and squeaked in protest. Seconds later, the sound repeated as the door squeezed closed. A brief pause, then muffled footsteps, a stumble, and a low profanity. It appeared that someone, after exiting the back door to the house, had gone into the backyard.

Fighting to control a rush of adrenaline that instantly reignited his anger, David hugged closer to the wall and crept to the back of the house.

Feeble evening light reflected off worn, moss-tinged paving stones that led directly from the back door of the house, across the lawn, and into the trees at the far end of the garden. Through the trees a flame flickered, a cough sounded, and the unmistakable smell of cigarette reached David's nostrils. Then a latch clicked twice; once to open, and once to close, as a gate allowed passage.

Confident the person had passed from the backyard to the path beside the brook, David jogged across the lawn and through the trees. After a brief pause, he stepped through the gate.

The smoker hadn't gone far. The intermittent red glow from the cigarette tip marked the person's slow progress along the pathway.

Using the gloom under the canopy of tree branches for cover, David followed the cigarette and its owner.

Illuminating the stubbled face that sucked at the filter, the cigarette burned bright one last time before it arched through the air toward the water of the brook. A flash of flame, and then another cigarette replaced the discarded one.

Unable to distinguish the identity of the smoker by the brief flash of the lighter, but with a growing certainty he was following the man he wanted to kill, David quickly closed the distance between them.

Cigarette smoke trailed the man as he ambled along the path, his black Wellington boots scuffing the gravel. The unbuttoned front of a heavy woolen coat was loose at his sides. The scent of alcohol, stale after consumption, had attached itself to the man's skin, hair, breath, and clothes and it hitched a ride on the blue-gray smoke of the cigarette.

Unhurried, David wrinkled his nose and grimaced as he slowly approached the man from behind.

A meter away, the man turned.

Startled, David stopped.

"A nice evening for a walk, eh?" the man slurred from a mouth obscured by a nicotine-stained hand held inches from his lips.

He paused for air before sucking on the cigarette, which was between his finger and thumb. In the brief, red-yellow light of the oxygen-fueled cigarette, he was unshaven with ashen skin. His face was blemished with liver spots. He smiled around his large teeth.

"Er, yes. I guess so. A bit cold, though."

"You from around here?"

"No, I live near London."

"What brings you up to Manchester, then?" asked the man around a raspy chuckle. "Surely not the weather?"

From the darkness, impatient fans in the audience murmured to one another. *What's he going to do now?*

Acknowledging the question internally, David drew himself upright and decided to improvise the scene, as became a preeminent actor of his caliber.

"Girlfriend. Her parents live over on the other side of Woodheys Park. Needed a bit of air."

"Ah, needed to get outta the house then, eh?"

"Yeah. Hey," David added, playing his part, "where does this path lead, anyway?"

"Goes for a couple of miles. Follows the brook. Very peaceful, especially a little further up, where the path butts beside the brook. You can really hear the water gurgle."

David studied the man. He was definitely Neil Crawford. More haggard than in the media photographs, but with the same puffy red eyes. His sparse, off-brown hair and visible ear and nose hair conveyed an unwanted image of a rumpled grandfather. He seemed friendly, worn, and completely harmless.

Momentarily confused and ashamed that Crawford had become humanized, David thought of his mother and father. Rage and intent welled up again, and his fist bunched and he took a menacing step toward the man who had killed his parents.

"Fuck you!" a group of youths suddenly bellowed with mock intensity, as they burst from the trees fifty or more feet behind David and Crawford.

Not wanting to be seen, David mumbled a quick goodbye, hurried ahead on the path, and hid behind some bushes. The drunken kids reached Crawford, tossed a few obscenities at him, and disappeared back into the trees that bordered Woodheys Park.

Minutes later, Crawford, another cigarette betraying his course, ambled round the bend and toward David.

When Crawford came level with David's hiding place, he stopped, withdrew a metal hip flask from an overcoat pocket, unscrewed the cap, tipped his head back, and lifted the flask to his lips. Done, Crawford lowered and rescrewed the cap.

David, out of sight in the shadows, imagined the alcohol burning Crawford's throat, dulling his brain and reflexes as it had done the night he'd killed his parents.

With a slight tilt to the left and right, Crawford continued his stroll. A few meters on, he turned abruptly left and onto a grassy verge that bordered the steep-sided bank that held the cold water of Sinderland Brook. A step from the edge, he stopped, lit another cigarette, and inhaled.

David, who had followed him, arrived a meter behind him. Before David could speak or act, Crawford spoke to him without turning around.

"This is my favorite place on the path. There's a weir about twenty meters downstream. The water flows over and makes that soft sound. It's so soothing. Can you hear it?"

While he talked, Crawford edged so close to the lip of the bank that a third of his feet extended over the edge. Still without turning, he drew a long drag from his cigarette, swayed slightly, and expelled a satisfied sigh.

"Why are you really here, David?"

Gasps escaped from the audience at David's discovery.

Unprepared and unscripted, he faltered and stepped back.

"What's the matter? I'm a drunk, not an idiot. I saw you outside my house, standing and watching. You're not the first. Since it happened, lots of people have come by to stare, shout obscenities, and throw things. I watched as you stood outside, then walked away, then came back, and slipped down the side of my house."

Stunned as he processed Crawford's unexpected challenge, David said nothing.

"I recognized you from the newspaper photos. You and your sister. Jenny's her name, right?"

"Shut up, you bastard. Don't you dare say her name."

"You know that I wanted you to follow me out here."

Sensing the audience holding its breath, David challenged him.

"Why? So you can say sorry? That's not good enough."

Crawford pulled more nicotine from the cigarette and spoke quietly as he exhaled.

"Yes, I want to tell you I'm sorry. That I wish it had never happened. That none of the pain I have caused all these years with my drinking had happened. My marriage fell apart. I haven't seen my brother and sister in ten years. I even missed my own father's funeral because I was on a bender. I know I'm sick and I need help."

Incensed by Crawford's self-pity, David stepped closer to him.

"Sick? You're not *sick*. You're a drunk. A selfish drunk, who doesn't give a fuck about anyone or anything except your next drink. Don't ask for pity and help. You're *not* the victim. You're the killer. You killed my parents. You plowed your car right into them and you didn't even know it!"

Approval and expectation vibrated through the audience as David laid bare the crime and the man's guilt.

"Look," Crawford said in a tired, resigned voice. "What do you want from me, David? What did you follow me for?"

"I came to plan your death," David hissed to Crawford's back.

"Then kill me," Crawford answered lightly. "Well, what are you waiting for, son? Now's your chance. Come on. You'll be doing me a favor."

David recoiled from Crawford's words. It wasn't supposed to be like this. David wanted, expected, and needed the man to fight for his life, so he could take it away.

"You want to die?"

"I deserve to, don't I? It would be better than living with what I've done."

Confused and uncertain by Crawford's claim that living would be worse than dying, David felt cheated out of his revenge.

Then Crawford's tone changed.

"What the matter, son? Can't do it? I thought so. Too weak, eh? More scared of being caught than living with not doing it, eh?"

"What did you just say?"

Crawford took the hip flask from his pocket, unscrewed the cap, and turned to David with a big smile.

"Nothing, kid. You want a drink?"

Instant and intense rage overpowered David in that moment, and he hurled himself at Crawford. The impact launched the man backward off the bank and into the brook's cold water.

David, his momentum almost taking him down the bank, managed to stop at the edge. In the dim light, he watched Crawford's head bob out of the water.

In silence, Crawford seemed to stare at David as water flooded his open-topped Wellington boots, soaked into his woolen coat, and sucked him under.

Still and silent, David listened for a long time before he turned away from the water. Underfoot, he felt an impression through the sole of his shoe. Lifting his foot, he saw the threaded metal cap from Crawford's flask. He bent down and pocketed it.

In need of acknowledgment, David searched the darkness. No gasps or chants reached his ears. No calls for more, no applause, and no light. Crawford had robbed him of a performance. Goaded into the unscripted, unrehearsed action, David felt the chill of a cheated following.

Spurned by his fans, and without his blanket of delusion, David realized he had been stupid. His impulsiveness, contrary to all he had learned about murder and how to get away with it, had left him vulnerable and exposed.

On a precipice of panic, his subconscious, adopting a soft, cockney-accented voice, finally broke through the haze and spoke directly to David.

"'If you're an actor, you're on your own. You cannot control the stage.'"

Smiling at the selective quote from one of his favorite actors, Michael Caine, David slowly regained his composure and vowed that his next performance would be his best.

FIFTY

Weeks after his brilliant and improvised acting in the justified killing of Neil Crawford, David's subconscious craved and demanded another performance. Willingly submitting to the demand, David decided to sentence Billy the lout.

To satisfy the expectations of his audience for variety and originality, David decided on a new tactic for Billy's demise. Murderers, according to popular opinion, wanted to be unseen, unheard, and ideally forgotten. If a witness did materialize, the killer wanted to be seen as bland and generic, without any distinction.

But high on success, flush with righteousness, and unknowingly flirting with the very invincibility that he had cautioned himself against, David had a different plan. Like the use of a wineglass at the murder of Mr. Taylor, and money with J-MO, David decided to use misdirection in Billy's death.

Groups and organizations opposed to dog racing had been easy to find on the internet. SaveAct Greyhounds UK, a nonprofit organization dedicated to the welfare of greyhound dogs, had met David's needs. A well-organized website posted details of public meetings and awareness-raising events, and he duly attended a commemorative event for euthanized racing dogs.

At the event, poignantly held across from the Wimbledon racetrack on a cold Tuesday evening, David acquired pamphlets, two button pins, a bumper sticker, and A4-sized poster designed for supporters to post in their cars, workplace bulletin boards, or home windows.

More importantly, it was where David found Billy's killer.

Reginald was his name. His dogs, two thin, shivering greyhounds, both rescued from dogfight events, had for no apparent reason, been renamed Laurel and Hardy. Eager to demonstrate his commitment to greyhound welfare and an end to racing, Reginald had loudly and colorfully expressed his opinion that owners and trainers of racing dogs were filth who should be jailed for how they treated and exploited dogs.

However, Reginald saved his real venom for the people who went to races to bet money that made the whole thing possible in the first place. For him, the issue was black and white: no punters at the track, no racing, no dogs needed.

Anyone who attended dog races was scum and didn't deserve to be called human beings. According to him, they should all be whipped, jailed, and kicked out of England. Reginald wasn't alone in his views; neither was he the loudest, but he had a distinctive accessory that set him apart from others.

He carried, more than actually used, a walking stick. The stick itself was the usual length and shape, but unlike most others, his sported alternating horizontal bands of red, blue, white, black, orange, and green fluorescent tape. A letter on each band set vertically along the stick proclaimed, "end the cruelty."

The colors, David learned, were the British standard racing jacket colors worn by dogs during a race.

Reginald lived in nearby Tooting, and according to his own claims, he came to the stadium every race to protest and spread the word about the cruelty of racing to punters. It had taken little effort to engage him and allow him to pin a "SaveAct Greyhound" button on David's coat.

Aside from the distinctive stick, a loud voice, and extreme views, Reginald, with his dark overcoat, flat cap, corduroy pants, and army-style boots, was unremarkable in appearance and stature.

This suited David just fine.

~

At eleven p.m., on the second Saturday after meeting Reginald, David stepped off the number 639 bus at the corner of Putney Heath Road and Wildcroft Road, thirty meters up from the Green Man pub. Then he paused and waited until the bus and the two other passengers who had gotten off moved away.

Alone in the bus shelter, David waited, dressed in a dark overcoat, flat hat, corduroy pants, and boots, all similar to Reginald's attire. Out of sight, he wriggled his left arm and with his right he reached under his overcoat to unhook the colorful walking stick, which he had fashioned a few days earlier.

Leaning on it, he looked along Wildcroft Road to the pub on the right. After five minutes, two men exited the front door, took four short steps to the pavement, and engaged in the easily recognizable routine of lighting up cigarettes.

When blue smoke surrounded the men, David set off toward them, loudly tapping the walking stick and coughing. As he approached, the men, who were unintentionally blocking the pavement, stepped back to allow him passage. As he passed, one of the men, mistaking the colors on the stick for a Pride statement, mumbled to the other, "Wonder where he puts that, eh?"

David didn't know if the real Reginald had actually gone to the racetrack to protest that night, and if he had, what time he might have left. All that mattered was that if Reginald *had* been at the track, an eleven p.m. appearance outside the Green Man pub would be credible. Likewise, if Reginald had *not* attended the track to conduct his usual protest, then where had he been? And why was he at the Green Man pub? Either way, David figured enough doubt would be seeded to obscure the truth.

Content and satisfied that he—or at least the stick—would be remembered, David ignored the homophobic remark, crossed the road, and entered a tree-canopied path. He headed on toward Putney Heath. According to his earlier calculations, he expected an inebriated Billy to be on the path across the heath at approximately 12:50 a.m.

For the next hour and a half, "Reginald" walked and swung his stick along the pathways on either side of the stand of trees David had previously identified as the place where he would observe Billy's approach.

Of the two dog walkers, one cyclist, a tipsy couple, and a very drunken man that passed him, the dog walkers and the couple were when interviewed by police, adamant that they had seen Reginald "lurking" or "hanging around" the night Billy was killed.

At 12:30, with nobody in sight, David left the pathway, crept into the trees, and positioned himself to have a clear view of the path leading from Telegraph Road.

In the silence beneath the tree branches, reflections on what he had become filled his mind: the rightness of it, the validation of his acting skills, the adrenaline, like being on stage. The audience and the readers of news reports clung to the story and followed the developing script that he had set in motion. It was as though he was a playwright, a director, *and* the leading man.

All the world really was his stage. And Billy was the loathsome abuser of women, a thief, a purveyor of drugs, and a parasite on society. The audience expected—even demanded—that he receive a just demise.

Buoyed by his imagination and delusion, David began to sweat, despite the cool night.

Odor, harsh and bitter, wafted into his nostrils and opened the door for injustice, resentment, and anger to enter David's mind. At the peak of his heightened emotion, Billy, swaying with the contentment of the drunk, appeared on the path about a fifty meters from David.

Dressed in jeans, boots, and the same racing jacket he always wore, Billy took one or two sideways steps for every three or four steps forward.

David's right hand tightened around the bottom end of the walking stick, and he tapped the heavier handle end in to the palm of his leather-gloved hand.

When Billy's erratic walk brought him in line with his position, David, without any hesitation, stepped from the shadows, raised the stick, and crashed it down on the left temple of Billy's head.

Billy flinched, blinked, and narrowed his eyes, as though seeking recognition.

Incredulous at the man's resilience, David crashed another blow on Billy's skull. He crumpled.

David dragged Billy feetfirst into the trees, laid him facedown at the base of a tree, pulled his arms behind his back, and settled down with one knee between his shoulder blades. The other he placed on the ground.

From his pocket, David took a dog leash, expanded the loop, slipped it over Billy head, and tugged it snug against his throat. With his right hand, he slapped Billy's cheek and whispered into his ear.

"Come on, Billy. Wake up. It's time for the race. Hurry, or you'll miss it."

A few more slaps, and then Billy roused, coughed, rolled his head side to side.

"What the fuck?"

"Hi, Billy. It's David. From the airport."

"Oh, what the hell happened?" he asked as he maneuvered to pull his arms from behind his back.

"Not so fast," David said as he rose up off his knees, placed his right foot on Billy's back, and wrapped the end of the leash around his right hand.

"What the…" was all Billy managed to get out before the leash tightened.

Then his hands sprang forward and his fingers grasped and clawed at the leash.

"Stop struggling, and I'll loosen it."

Overcome with fear, Billy struggled some more.

"Stop, Billy, not like this. You need to know why you are going to die."

David's words had the opposite effect. Fueled by the instinct to survive, Billy clawed at the leash that was crushing his throat.

Dispassionate, David simultaneously pressed his foot and pulled at the leash. The vibrations of Billy's upper-body struggle flowed through David's foot, while sensations like a fish biting at a hooked line flowed through the leash as Billy's fingers fumbled for relief.

In his mind, applause from an adulating audience boomed, light illuminated his face, and calls of "bravo, bravo" rung out.

Intoxicated with Billy's life struggle, David loosened then tightened the leash, and adjusted the pressure of his foot to the crescendo of sound that called for more.

At the peak of the crowd's frenzy, Billy's fingers loosened and his torso stilled.

The audience quietened, and the lights faded.

"No, no!" David shouted as he pulled at Billy's corpse. "We're not done yet. We must do an encore. They love me, they love me."

The gloom beneath trees and the cool of the night muted David's fantasy, and for an uncomprehending moment he fingered the now-limp leash until the screech of brakes wrenched him back to reality.

Through the trees, two figures on mountain bikes raced each other along the path. Unconcerned that he would be seen, David maneuvered Billy's body until it leaned, crouched on knees and elbows, against the trunk of the tree.

The leash, he stretched out and tied to a low branch, as though securing a dog.

Beside Billy's body, David dropped the SaveAct Greyhound button that Reginald had so eagerly pinned, with a firm thumbprint, to David's coat when they had met at the commemoration event. After retrieving the walking stick from the ground and hooking it back into the crook of his armpit under his coat, David took a last look at Billy.

A piece of paper poked out from the top of Billy's rear jeans pocket. David pulled it out and recognized it as the night's race program from the stadium. After a moment's indecision, he stuffed the program in his own pocket, stepped out from the trees, and began his long walk home.

FIFTY-ONE

Being a shop assistant in a small general store on Staines Road in Feltham, twenty kilometers west of London, had not featured in any of Clair's childhood dreams. However, as a single, twenty-nine-year-old woman with a twelve-year-old son, Clair's Monday to Friday shifts at Singh's variety shop had become her reality.

Bruised yet strengthened by life, she possessed a pragmatism that enabled her to get the best from what she had. She was also optimistic that her future would be better. The shop, busy with a steady stream of customers and deliveries since her arrival at ten a.m., had, as usual, quietened down by 2:45 p.m.

In the calm, Clair stocked shelves, while Danny, the seven a.m. to three p.m. assistant, tallied the cash register, wiped the counter and generally "dogged it" for the last minutes of his shift.

She didn't blame Danny.

His shift was one of the busiest, and being over-weight, pimpled, and a gentle "gamer" who slept little and ate poorly, he always faded toward the end.

With his elbow on the counter, Danny swallowed a yawn and checked his watch.

"It's almost three. I'm off, unless you need something."

The digital clock on the wall blinked 2:50 p.m., but Clair didn't challenge him.

"OK, I don't need anything. Get on home, and for god's sake, get some sleep."

"Thanks, Clair," Danny said affably as he dragged his bulk to the door. "See you Monday. Have a good weekend."

"You too."

As he left, she responded to a buzz from her cell phone and checked a text from David.

Hi. Errand done. On bus. C u soon.

Clair slouched a little. Her eyes moistened with disappointment and apprehension. The quiz night confrontation with Troy had strained their evening, and their parting at the foot of the stairs to her flat had been awkward.

She had later realized that his caution about accusing Troy of attacking Mrs. Chapman without proof was motivated by concern, and not a comment on her ability to look after herself.

Yet she had been stubborn, and their evening had ended on a sour note. Then the death of his parents and his need to support Jenny, plus other preoccupations, had definitely cooled their developing relationship.

Mobilizing her thumbs, Clair texted David back.

OK. Lk fwd to c u. Good day?

Me 2. C u soon.

Another errand, she thought to herself. He had a lot of errands lately, as well as several trips across

London. Most had been for voice-over work, according to him, but some had also involved acting auditions.

Robbie had told her that he'd seen clothes, makeup, and even a few wigs in David's flat, so she had been happy for his progress.

He never gave her any details, though, or even indicated how the auditions went. She had no idea if he was getting parts or not. Not only that, but he had seemed somehow distant lately, yet focused on something.

Then again, David had struggled immensely with the death of his parents and the investigation by the police. That was enough to distract anyone.

Alerted by the door chime, Clair looked up to see the door swing closed and a dark figure scurry to the far aisle. Unnerved, she peered in the parabolic mirror positioned in the corner above the front door.

In the distorted image, she watched the back of someone reach the end of the aisle and turn left out of sight.

She switched her view to a second mirror positioned at the far end of the shop, as the figure, its back still to the mirror, remained in front of the fresh produce section.

"Can I help you with something?" she called out.

In the distortion of the mirror, the figure reached into the fruit section display.

Nervous, and certain something wasn't right, Clair tried again, a bit louder.

"Excuse me! I said, can I help you?"

In response, the figure pulled its arm back and whipped it forward around the end of the display shelves.

A large honeydew melon flew from a gloved hand, and Clair, startled, watched it bounce and roll the length of the aisle until it bumped up against her counter.

Distracted by the melon, she did not see the figure until it appeared directly in front of her.

"Hello, bitch," Troy said, his mouth split wide with a cruel smile.

Startled, Clair stepped instinctively back against the cigarette cabinet before recovering her composure.

"You'll have to pay for that," she snapped.

"Oh, I intend to," Troy hissed as he placed a five-pound note on the counter.

"You're a bastard. That's Mrs. Chapman's money, isn't it?"

"Maybe it is, maybe it ain't," Troy replied as he bent down, picked up the melon, and placed it on the counter in front of Clair. "How would I know, anyway?"

"Because you're the asshole who stole it from her."

Troy simply nodded, then opened the left side of his coat and reached in with his right hand.

"That's what I've come to talk to you about, Clair. You gotta stop runnin your mouth off about what you think you know."

With more confidence than she felt, Clair jutted her chin forward.

"Or else, what? You're a coward. I'm not—"

With his custom-made axe handle gripped tight, Troy's right hand suddenly flew from under his jacket, arced up behind and over his shoulder, and descended toward her head.

The thick end of the axe handle, propelled with all Troy's strength, crashed through the outer skin and split the melon open. Juice and seeds burst upward and sprayed onto Clair's chest and face.

"Fuck me. Did you see that? Just imagine if that was someone's head…"

Still backed up again against the cigarette cabinet, Clair's eyes darted to the back of the shop. Unknown to Troy, Robbie, who had a PD day, was in the storeroom helping with inventory.

With smug assurance, Troy wiped the axe clean with a newspaper from the rack beside the counter, then tucked it back inside his jacket.

Relieved he had put the axe away, Clair used the back of her hand to brush melon debris from her face.

"You won't get away with this. It's all on camera, you idiot. I'm gonna call the police right now."

"Your kid," Troy said softly. "Robbie, right? His head would be about the size of that honeydew melon, eh?"

"You stay the hell away from him," she shouted at Troy's back as he sauntered toward the door. "Touch him, and I'll kill you."

At the door, Troy paused and turned.

"Just keep your fucking mouth shut, Clair."

Frightened, despite her bravado, she trembled uncontrollably. Moments later, she jumped when the door chime sounded.

A gasp of relief gushed from her chest as David walked in, a bunch of flowers in his hand.

"Surprise!"

After she told him what had transpired and they calmed each other down, David held Clair's hand with an ureadable expression on his face.

"Don't worry. I'll take care of Troy."

Unnoticed at the back of the store, Robbie, who had witnessed Troy's assault on his mom, silently stepped back into the store room. His tears dried as he held on to and believed David's promise to take care of the thug Troy.

FIFTY-TWO

"Good Afternoon!" a firm voice bellowed behind David.

Startled, he stammered as an elderly man marched past.

"Oh, yes, hello."

"Lovely view from here," the man added as he strode off the Wharf Road Bridge.

Indeed, it was lovely, David thought, as he looked east and west along Regent's Canal, which stretched thirteen miles from Grand Union Canal, all the way to the Limehouse Basin Lock on the River Thames. Across the bridge, on the right, he could see the canal open to his destination: Wenlock Basin.

Discovering that Thompson the photographer lived at Wenlock Basin had taken a lot of frustrating research, as well as an unpleasant confrontation. Two weeks earlier, certain that Thompson was operating a scam on the backs of suffering women and children, David had searched his websites for a business or home address.

Instead, he just found circles, dead ends, and loop backs, with the same—or very similar—reformatted and rewritten content populating Thompson's six websites.

The only phone number, which David called several times, always defaulted to a voice message.

It thanked the caller, explained that all personnel were busy coordinating services or away on assignment, and directed people to the websites for information on how to make a donation. It did *not* allow the caller to leave a message.

The website email, listed on all six sites, generated an automatic response that mirrored the voice message and stated that emails were only answered once, "to reduce cost and maximize effective use of donations."

Only two things were consistent: the call to action to make a small credit card donation, and the complete absence of a physical address for either Thompson or his organization.

Social media searches yielded similar results. Lots of photographs and stories about what services the donations *would* be used for, which areas of the world *could* receive aid, and what type of problem *might* be addressed.

The absence of any definitive statements of what had actually been done with the money—and where—infuriated David.

Any internet searches for professional photographers quickly led to Thompson, but then immediately defaulted to linked websites and looped social media. David did find photographs credited to Thompson in local and national newspapers, but they were all ten or more years old.

David began to obsess over his inability to connect Thompson to a physical address. His obsession led to fantasies about following Thompson, or planting a bug in his bag, or perhaps getting someone at the airline to check his booking details for an address.

But, unlike the movies, David could not follow the man, had no tracking device, and had no connections in any airlines.

Also, Thompson always paid cash, so even a wild thought of trying to use credit card information somehow would not work, even if David knew how to.

In the end, the solution had come, as it often did, while he watched a movie.

Jenny, a fan of romantic comedies, had brought the French cult movie *Amélie* over one Wednesday night. During the film, Amélie, who works in a coffee shop, pretends to accidentally trip and spills the cup she's carrying on one of her coworkers, Georgette, so that she rushes out to the bathroom.

In David's version, he would spill coffee on Thompson, and while he went to the bathroom to clean up, David would "watch" his bags and cameras. Of course, while doing so, he would look for information.

The plan didn't go so well in reality. When the hot coffee landed on Thompson's legs, just above the knees, he hardly flinched. Instead of jumping up and shouting, as David had expected, he merely stood slowly and ground his teeth. Then, with calm efficiency, he had dabbed at the coffee stains with his napkin.

Stunned by his calmness, David spluttered his apologies, and as he had planned, offered to watch Thompson's stuff while he went to the bathroom to clean up.

"No need," Thompson answered quietly. "Just bring me a damp cloth and I'll soak out some of the coffee."

Disappointed that he did not intend to use the bathroom, David hurriedly brought both a damp cloth and a dry one. As Thompson dried his jeans, he emptied his pockets. From the left one, he withdrew coins and paper money, and from his right pocket, a key.

It was silver, and attached to a small black key ring with the words *Wenlock Basin* written in script on the side.

Thompson cleaned himself quickly, then handed the cloths back to David.

As David took hold of the cloths, Thompson fixed him with a hard stare, and spoke in a cold, menacing tone.

"You should be more careful. Some people might take offence."

Unnerved by Thompson's comment, and certain that it had contained an implicit threat, David returned to the bar to rinse out the cloths.

A few moments later, when he turned, Thompson had disappeared. Unsure why he was trembling, David wrote *Wenlock Basin* on a napkin and put it in his pocket.

~

Pushing thoughts of Thompson's veiled threat aside, David checked his watch, still tense with an undefined fear. With five minutes until his appointment, he inched up onto his tiptoes and peeked over the brick wall that lined either side of the short, narrow canal bridge.

About a hundred meters from the bridge, on the right, there were eight colorful narrow boats moored stern in to a cobblestoned walkway lined with a high wooden fence and assorted green trees and bushes.

Just beyond the boats, the canal opened up to the Wenlock Basin; a dead-end offshoot originally used to serve the industries and businesses that once depended on the canal to transport their raw materials and finished goods.

Back on the flat of his feet, David crossed the bridge and stopped at 56a Wharf Road.

An unwelcoming eight-foot high, silver-gray metal door with a narrow slot for mail, a welded metal handle to push and pull the door, and a rough opening for a key, stood unyielding before him.

No sign identified the address as the Wenlock Basin Houseboat Company, but Mr. Bradley had been clear during their conversation.

"Wenlock Basin is a private residential mooring area, and the only land-side entrance is through a private gate at 56a Wharf Road. There is no bell, but I will meet you at 2:30 p.m. precisely."

At 2:29, by David's watch, the door opened. A middle-aged man, dressed like a bank clerk in a dark two-piece suit with a white shirt and blue tie, introduced himself.

"I'm Mr. Bradley. You must be Mr. Williams?"

"Yes," David replied with ease, as he adopted the part and name he had selected for his reconnaissance of Thompson's home.

"Very good," Bradley said as he gestured for David to enter through the doorway.

After he had stepped through, the door, propelled by a thick steel spring, swung back and closed with a solid thunk.

"We take security very seriously, Mr. Williams. Only residents have a key for the entrance door, and every key is numbered and assigned to only one person."

Bradley passed David and led the way down an incline to the walkway that David had seen from the bridge.

As they walked, Bradley talked.

"Wenlock Basin, Mr. Williams, is a very private residential mooring for well-maintained narrow boats and discerning residents. The basin was excavated by hand in 1826 to serve the growing City of London. In 1832, John Edwards Vaughan, the son of the original owner, extended Wenlock Basin to a total length of 360 yards. In the 1950s, after the decline of canal carrying, the basin became derelict and was partly filled. Then, in 1982, it was revitalized as a private residential mooring by the Wenlock Basin Houseboat Company."

As they passed the eight boats David had spied from the bridge and turned right to follow the pathway into the basin proper, he turned to the older man.

"How many boats are moored?"

"We have mooring for thirty-six boats. We have a very low turnover of residents. In fact, you are rather lucky that a boat is available for sale. It's been more than five years since someone sold their boat and mooring."

"You're right," David answered truthfully, as he admired the condition and vibrancy of the boats. "They look impeccable."

"Quite so."

Three-quarters of the way along the cobbled pathway, after passing about twenty narrow boats, Bradley stopped and pointed.

"This beautiful boat is *Mollie*. She's a forty-five-foot Cheshire narrow boat built six years ago. She has a spacious sitting room, a galley kitchen, and solar panels for free electricity. Shall we board her?"

"Oh, she *is* lovely," David said with enthusiasm. He had never been on a narrow boat, let alone thought about living on one, but the romance of a water-borne home was infectious.

He followed Bradley down the steps from the stern of the boat and entered the interior. Inside, he browsed and listened to the other man's narrative as he explored the four separate cabins and two berths, onboard shower, and wood-burner stove.

Surprised by the large, open-plan living room/kitchen with built-in shelving, LED lights, and the bedroom, with its double bed, storage, and built-in wood shelving, David silently lamented that his lifestyle could not afford such luxury.

Back on shore, Bradley, came to the point.

"Well, Mr. Williams, I doubt you will find a better narrow boat in London than the *Mollie*. What do you think?"

"Oh, I agree. She would be perfect for me."

"I should also mention that each residential mooring has separately metered shore power, water, and a telephone access point. There is secure cycle storage and low-level lighting from dusk until midnight. In addition, there is refuse collection, recycling, and a portable toilet disposal point. And as I mentioned, residents are the only key holders for the private, gated access on the southeastern side of Wharf Road Bridge."

"Excellent," David interjected, nodding as Bradley continued.

"Two communal barbecue areas at either end of the mooring, together with a number of benches and tables around the walkway, provide space for outdoor living when the weather permits. And for extra security and service, as the resident moorings manager, I live on site at the last boat."

David, thoughtful, looked around and nodded again.

"Yes, this is exactly the place I'm looking for. Quiet, secure, and well maintained."

Bradley preened as he sensed a sale.

"Although," David added, playing the part and creating a concerned wrinkle on his forehead, "the price *is* a little above my budget."

"I am sorry to hear that, Mr. Williams," Bradley replied, as he struggled to hide his irritation. "But I can assure you that at £92,000, *Mollie* is priced very fairly."

"Yes, you're probably right. I'm sure I would regret missing this opportunity for a few thousand pounds."

"What do you do, Mr. Williams?"

Having finally gotten to the point David wanted, he answered with a smile.

"Photography and writing. They are both my work and my passion. They also require quiet and privacy, which it seems I will get here. I also travel fairly often, so security is important to me, as well."

"Well, well, Mr. Williams, you will be in good company here at Wenlock Basin. You see, we already have a photographer in residence."

"Really? I might know him."

"His name is Mr. Thompson. He lives on the *Fox Hole*, just six boats down from your *Mollie*."

Having finally gained a physical address for Thompson, David, who had seen him at the airport yesterday morning as he waited for a flight to Africa, pressed for more information.

"I wonder if he is home. I would certainly value his opinion on the suitability of the Basin for our shared interest."

Bradley hesitated for a moment as he weighed resident privacy with the desire to influence his client's decision.

"I don't usually disturb residents, but I suppose as you are both in the same business, and will likely get to know one another, we could see if Mr. Thompson is at home. Come along."

David followed Bradley to the stern of the *Fox Hole*. While Bradley stepped onto the boat and gently tapped on the door, David studied it. Painted crisp white lines bordered the solid red and black colors of the main cabin and door. Flecks of paint, scuff marks on the deck, and frayed stern ropes suggested that maintenance was not Thompson's strong point.

The one distinguishing feature that set the *Fox Hole* apart from other boats was the black metal bars that covered each of the windows.

With no response to his knock, Bradley stepped from the boat to shore.

"I'm sorry. He appears to be out."

"That's too bad."

"Well, I'm not surprised, really. Mr. Thompson travels a lot."

"Ah, like myself, then."

"Indeed."

Bradley's lips compressed and his eyes narrowed slightly as he wrestled with his decision. Once he decided, he pointed back toward the bridge and the whitewashed building that seemed to stand guard on the west side of the canal.

"You might find him in the Narrow Boat pub. Mr. Thompson takes all of his meals there."

"Oh. Does the pub have good food, then?"

"Well, the food might not be the main attraction for Mr. Thompson, if you know what I mean."

"Really?"

Suddenly aware that he may have gone too far, Bradley backpedaled.

"What I mean is that the pub has cask ales, craft beers, and a good selection of wines."

Having gotten what he came for, David quickly ended the meeting and left Bradley at the metal gate on Wharf Street with a promise to contact him shortly with his decision.

Then he crossed the bridge and paused at the front door of the pub.

Buoyed by his ability to locate his prey, as well as the knowledge that the photographer might have a drinking problem, David entered the pub for an afternoon pint. It was time to figure out how he would kill Thompson, who might well be the pub's best customer.

FIFTY-THREE

Murder, death, and suicide rarely featured in the lives of eleven-year-old children. Unless it was *personal*. Unless you were *Robbie*.

Personal meant the death of the man who had killed David and Jenny's parents. And Robbie, increasingly suspicious of David's activities, became confused and uncertain of his feelings toward him.

He was also fearful for his mother's safety, and had devoured the internet news of Neil Crawford's death.

Initial reports that had cast suspicion on David had fed Robbie's imagination and further tarnished his opinion of his neighbor.

Later reports, indicating Crawford's suicide, tempered Robbie's doubt and stimulated his compassion for David and Jenny. But then Robbie fell victim to the "problem of the internet."

The problem—or benefit—depending on your viewpoint, was the prevalence of links and pop-ups. In the case of Crawford's death, the problem centered on the media characterization of his death as "suspicious." The use of the word was in keeping with the online mantra of *The Sun* news media site that Robbie had chosen to use.

The Sun newspaper, a staple supermarket tabloid, replete with salacious and sensational stories, made its way into Robbie's orbit via his mother, who brought a copy home from her work every day.

Conditioned unintentionally by his mom to search *The Sun's* online news site, Robbie had been subjected to the media's goal to drag readers ever deeper into their website to be exposed to increasing numbers of subtle advertisements.

In the case of Crawford and "suspicious," *The Sun* captured readers' attention with a pop-up link to "other suspicious deaths."

Robbie, intelligent, but not immune to the power of marketing, clicked on one of the links. It took him to several stories of suspicious deaths across the UK in the last twelve months. One article caught Robbie's eye. An early report about the "suspicious" death of an "up-and-coming actor" Jason West.

The name sounded familiar, but Robbie couldn't recall why.

Lured by the report, he read on, despite the constant stream of advertisements that had to be clicked through, to the most recent article, which concluded that Jason West had been murdered by exposure to peanuts, and by the removal of the allergy antidote from the EpiPens in his flat.

No flash of comprehension or heaven-sent revelation pushed Robbie to connect the EpiPen in David's bathroom to the death of West. But the memory of a coffin in David's scrapbook with the name Rooke/West on it *did* burst into his head.

Reeling from the possible connection, Robbie unconsciously clicked on another pop-up link that promised stories of more "unusual" deaths.

Topping the list were the recent murders of J-MO the gossip columnist, ironically killed with words, and a personal hygiene sales manager, Mr. Taylor, who had been murdered with cleaning products. The "sadistic" murder of Billy, tied to a tree with a dog leash, filled Robbie's computer screen.

Then his mom's footsteps sounded from the hallway. Robbie switched off the power bar to kill the computer and scurried up the ladder and into bed.

A weak shaft of light stretched across the room and backlit his mom's stealthy approach to his bed.

Feigning sleep, Robbie felt his mom tuck a blanket over his shoulder, stroke his head, and whisper, "I love you."

When the door closed behind his mom, darkness claimed the room. Swirling thoughts of murder, mixed with images of EpiPens, the word *gosip* on a scrap of paper, hazardous material labels, burglar masks, and skinny greyhound dogs pummeled his mind.

Notes in his book, about coming and going, bags of clothes, sounds in the night, and the lies David had told Jenny and his mom, jockeyed to be heard and sorted.

Confusion wracked Robbie's brain. He didn't understand. He didn't *want* to understand. But he could not avoid the conclusion any longer: David was a murderer.

He had killed all those people. The stuff in his book and his flat proved it.

Frightened, Robbie sat up and peered around his room. A toilet flushed. Tap water ran. His mom's bedroom door closed. The sudden silence amplified distant street noise. Down from his bed, he stepped lightly toward the bedroom door.

His mom was in danger. He must tell her about David. Who, and what, he really was. They should tell the police, too.

With his hand on the handle, Robbie paused. A different thought, of a melon split and crushed under the blow from Troy's axe handle, slipped in and complicated his fears.

David was a bad person, but Troy was a bad person, too, and he had really threatened to hurt his mom. David had never done anything to his mom. In fact, David was good to his mom, and to him.

Maybe, reasoned Robbie, *David only killed bad people.* Isn't that kind of what the police did? They didn't kill them, but they caught the bad people and locked them up, forever sometimes.

Letting go the door handle, Robbie stood in the darkness and wrestled with several questions.

What had David meant in the shop when he had told his mom that he would take care of Troy? Hadn't he heard his mom and Debbie moan and complain that the police never did anything about bad people like Troy? And hadn't he heard his mom tell Debbie that she "just knew" that Troy was the person who had attacked the old lady on the green?

Once back in his bed and tucked tight under his blankets, Robbie's vibrant, adolescent imagination constructed new images of David.

David as a superhero. David as Batman. David as Sherlock Holmes. David as Iron Man, or Spider-man, or Wolverine.

Then, finally, Robbie understood. Just like David had written in his own scrapbook, he really *was* a prince. A prince who would ultimately save his mom, so they could all live happily ever after, just like they did in the movies and stories.

FIFTY-FOUR

Murdering Crawford had been an impulsive act, full of rage. Early media reports indicated foul play, and questions from the police about David's whereabouts on the Friday night and Saturday morning had been a problem.

Forced to admit that he had indeed gone home, because he had a day off, had led to intense and persistent questioning from the police.

Fortunately, there had been no witnesses to place him near Crawford's home, or on the path beside the brook. Even more fortunate had been the discovery, and subsequent interviews, by the police of the group of drunken kids that David had hidden from on the path.

While reliability had been an issue, the group all remembered seeing Crawford, but were certain no one else had been on the path with him.

Eventually, without any evidence, the police accepted David's story that he had simply gone home to remember and had done nothing except sit and sleep, wrapped in his own sadness.

A few days later, when the pathology reports revealed Crawford's staggering blood alcohol level and the absence of any unusual trauma, the media story changed. Instead of being a murder victim, his death was ruled the suicide of a remorseful alcoholic who could no longer live with his conscience after killing two people while driving drunk.

Only when suicide became the official version did David's self-delusion reassert itself and fabricate the rationale he needed. There had never been any chance he would be caught, because Crawford's death *was* justified. The man had taken innocent lives, and therefore he had forfeited his own life.

David had merely been the "chosen" instrument of justice.

Not only that, but his original thought that pushing Crawford into the water had been impulsive had been wrong. To serve justice, David's aim had been to seize an opportunity, rather than be impulsive.

Building on this revision of events, David's subconscious added the "fact" that he had once again played his part extremely well, and that seizing the opportunity was the hallmark of a good actor who knew how, and when, to improvise.

He further cemented his delusional construct by adding the successful strangulation of Billy the lout with a dog leash.

So complete was David's revision of events, that the disappointment that he hadn't heard or seen the audience express their love and gratitude for the brilliant improvisation replaced his fear of discovery and capture.

While his delusion and rationalization continued, David researched and prepared for his upcoming role, to punish the man who profited from other people's misery: Philip Thompson.

~

The Inland Waterways Association website provided David with his idea for how to kill Thompson. In 2015, over one hundred and thirty fires were recorded on narrow boats, and one had been fatal.

The website also provided advice on the need for fore and aft emergency exits, and repeated warnings that barred windows for security could easily become death traps.

David, who had noted the bars on the windows of Thompson's narrow boat, relished the appropriateness of the man trapped and screaming behind bars.

Having decided on how and where to kill Thompson, David visited a used clothing store and a theatrical makeup shop and assembled a new costume. This time, he added a longhaired wig and a stick-on goatee to an ensemble of trendy, dark-colored clothes that he hoped resembled the appearance of London's middle-aged hipsters.

Next, thinking of his attack on Peanut's home, David struggled with how to carry a gallon of gasoline. Approved containers were necessarily bright red or orange, and the gasoline weighed over six pounds. No matter how hard he tried to tighten the container, there was always an odor of gasoline.

The solution came from a local outdoors store, Home Counties Camping Centre, which sold one-liter bottles of highly flammable Coleman camp fuel. The bottles were sealed and had no odor until opened.

More importantly, David could fit two bottles in the pockets of the three-quarter-length coat he had purchased for his costume. And with a little modification, he could fit two more in the lining.

The coat hung a little awkwardly, but David didn't expect a lot of scrutiny.

With the accelerant problem solved, he turned his attention to the most difficult problem with his plan to set Thompson's narrow boat ablaze: how to get in the gated boat area.

The eight-foot-high metal gate could not be climbed, at least by David. The walls that bracketed the gate were equally high and topped with broken glass.

Three circuits around the buildings that enclosed Wenlock Basin revealed no obvious way to access the area. Frustrated, David briefly considered access from the water. Aside from not owning a boat, or knowing how he might get one, he could not swim well and quickly dismissed waterside access as an option.

Resigned that the only option was to enter the gate behind someone else, David decided that he would simply have to wait near the entrance and try to reach the gate before it swung closed after someone entered. Of course, this all had to be synchronized with the need for Thompson to be home on his boat, or at least in the pub, and expected to be home.

In preparation, David loitered and walked past the gate to Wenlock Basin for three nights. On the first night, many people used the gate, but each time he was too far away to reach it before it clanged shut.

The second night yielded similar results, and on the third night, an elderly resident, who David had seen enter the gate on the first night, challenged him and told him to "bugger off" before he called the police.

The only positive outcome from his three fruitless evenings was that, on two occasions, he had seen Thompson: once going into the pub, and the second time, standing outside smoking.

Despondent that his plan would not work, David brooded for several days until his delusional subconscious provided the most obvious answer to his dilemma. Was he not a preeminent actor? Had he not, during the last few months, successfully, and to great acclaim, acted out numerous, complex, and demanding roles in the application of justice?

Succumbing to his own narrative, David made a new plan. He would orchestrate a chance encounter with Thompson in the pub. In disguise, he would drink with him and manipulate the man to invite him for a nightcap. Then he would pretend to leave, but instead, set Thompson's boat on fire.

However, his excitement at the opportunity to display his acting talents in a direct confrontational life-and-death role was tempered when a twinge of uncertainty spoiled the moment.

Thompson, cautioned David to himself, had a menacing aura. He sat with his back to the wall. He was used to observing everyone and everything. And he seemed to appear and disappear from the bar without David noticing. In addition, on more than one occasion, Thompson had muttered something about "old habits."

He wasn't sure why exactly, but he suspected Thompson might be more robust than Billy the lout, the gossip, or even the drunk driver.

David needed an edge. The one he gave himself turned out to be a can of Safehaus Mini Self Defence Spray.

~

Three tense evenings passed before Thompson appeared in the Narrow Boat pub. On Saturday, Sunday, and Monday, David, in disguise and calling himself Edward, had entered the pub around ten p.m. and ordered a drink while he scanned the room for Thompson.

The pub, like its name, was barely fifty feet in width, and aside from a few recesses caused by oddly angled walls and obstructive support pillars, only seconds were needed to cast an eye over the pub and its patrons.

Saturday night had been hot and claustrophobic, with less than thirty or so people making the pub appear full. Sunday's trade centered on perhaps fifteen customers, and on Monday, David shared the pub with fewer than ten patrons.

Without Thompson, David had engaged with the bartender and simply "rehearsed" his character.

On Tuesday, the fourth night, David didn't have a chance or need to scan the pub. Only one person required the bartender's service.

Thompson, seated on a stool at the bar, took the initiative, and greeted David with a hearty and slurred salutation.

"Thank god, another committed drinker. Matt," he said to the bartender, "give this man a drink on me."

Startled by Thompson's unexpected engagement, David stammered as he struggled to compose himself into his character.

Thompson, in a friendly mood, motioned for David to take the stool beside him. For the next hour, they exchanged opinions on football, politics, food, beer, and many subjects common to newfound acquaintances.

At eleven p.m., as Matt prepared to close the pub, he asked if Thompson and his friend wanted to stay for a couple of extra drinks while he tidied up. They continued to drink until midnight, when Matt announced he was all done.

Matt sold Thompson a half dozen bottles of beer and Thompson invited David to his boat for a nightcap.

As Thompson unlocked the metal gate that led to Wenlock Basin, a euphoric satisfaction and sense of destiny swarmed through David. In his mind's eye, the audience, who had witnessed his complete deception and manipulation of Thompson during the past few hours, held its collective breath in anticipation of the next act.

Preening outwardly, David congratulated himself and mentally prepared for the archetypal confrontation between good and evil, and the culmination of the play.

"Watch the cobblestones, Edward," Thompson said as he held the gate open. "They're pretty slippery."

Following David down the path from the bridge to the gravel track beside the canal, Thompson turned to him.

"You know, I don't usually do this kind of thing, Edward."

Something in Thompson's tone sounded off to David.

"Oh, er, me, either."

Thompson stopped on the gravel path and continued.

"In fact, Edward, I haven't been this reckless for a long time. How about you?"

"Me? No, um, not at all," David managed as a sudden sliver of doubt and fear pricked his confidence.

"Come," Thompson commanded, as he pointed with the hand that carried the six beers in a cardboard travel carrier. "Let's have a beer on the bench over there by the water."

David's imaginary audience murmured a sense of foreboding as they suspected the proximity to the water's edge might become the scene for the climax of the performance.

David, too, felt the anticipation, but more of an apprehensive dread that something was wrong.

"You sit, Edward," Thompson said with authority as he placed the cardboard box on the bench and withdrew a bottle, "while I open us a bottle, eh?"

David heard the snap before he saw the glint of the blade.

"Jesus!"

"Oh, sorry, mate, didn't mean to startle you. Old habits, you see."

"What?"

"From the Falklands War. Didn't I tell you? Used to be in the army. Very handy, this knife. Opens cans, pops beer bottle lids, and will slit a throat with no problem."

The audience, uncertain which way the plot would go, tensed.

David watched Thompson deftly pry the bottle cap off and extend his hand for him to take the beer. Shaking slightly, David accepted and lifted the bottle to his mouth.

"Thanks, and cheers."

Thompson, standing with his back to the dark water of the canal, opened the second beer, took a long swig, and placed the bottle on the bench beside David.

The knife, a Fairbairn-Sykes, seven-inch, double-edged fighting knife in Thompson's right hand, moved up from his side and stopped a foot in front of David's face.

Thompson, his body and voice swaying a little from the drink, gestured at David with the knife as he smiled and spoke.

"You're a good-looking man, Edward. And very bold to come down here on a dark night with someone you've never met before. How did you know?"

"Know?" David asked, confused and unable to tear his eyes away from the knife.

"No need to be coy, Edward. Like I said, you're a good-looking man. However, I must insist on discretion. Can't have you talking about this with anyone. Wouldn't be well received by my comrades in arms."

An inkling of comprehension flashed in David as Thompson continued.

"You seem a little nervous. Let's go to my boat, and we can get comfortable."

David's inkling then turned to fear, as he fully understood Thompson's suggestive proposition. Flustered and script-less as the plot twisted, his composure slipped.

"Oh, no, no. I'm not like that. I mean, I'm not looking…"

"Really, Edward?" Thompson teased as he leaned in closer. "What *are* you looking for, then?"

Forced to lean back against the bench, his body temperature rising rapidly, along with his heartbeat, David floundered.

"I'll tell you what I think, Edward," Thompson continued, as he edged the point of the knife under David's chin. "Or should I call you David?"

In David's head, the audience sucked all the air from the stage with such force that the back draft shattered David's confidence.

Jeers, cat calls, and boos followed, demanding David respond. The words from his high school drama teacher Ms. Cook bellowed in his head: he needed to "improvise, adapt, and overcome."

"Well, David?"

"Yes, you're right," he finally answered. "How did you know?"

With the confidence of a trained man, Thompson withdrew the knife from under David's chin and explained the amateurish nature of his charade.

"First off, I saw you last week loitering up and down the street, trying to sneak into the basin. I also clocked you when you poked your head into the pub while I was there. Then, the last few days, my mate Matt the bartender told me you had come in each night at ten and stayed for one drink, while looking around for someone. Tonight, at exactly ten, you show up again, and right away I can tell you're wearing makeup and that your little goatee is as fake as your bloody hair."

Trapped against the bench, David remained rigid and fought the panic knotting his stomach and tightening his chest.

"Listen, David, I've been around the block a few hundred times, and I've seen and done more things than you can even imagine. I'm trained in surveillance and countersurveillance, and your attempts at disguise really are pathetic. While we're at it," Thompson added in a hard voice, "let's have the bottles from your pockets and the liner of your coat."

"I don't…"

"Don't bother, David. How many times did you go to the bathroom? What do you think I did while you pissed away the beer I brought you, eh?"

When David didn't reply, Thompson raised the knife as he barked out a command.

"Empty your fucking pockets."

Unable to quell his fear, David's hands trembled as he withdrew the four bottles of camp fuel and placed them on the bench next to the unopened bottles of beer.

Thompson, eyes fixed on David, took a step back and wagged the knife back and forth as he spoke.

"That's nasty stuff you have there, David. What's it for?"

"Nothing. I'm taking my nephew Robbie camping on the weekend and picked some up…"

"You lie about as well as you use a disguise. Shall I tell you what I think? *I* think you were planning to burn me in my boat tonight. Now, I've seen people burnt before, and it's a fucking terrible way to go. While I'm pissed enough that you want to kill me, David, I'm even more pissed that you want to burn me. The question is why. Why do you want to kill me, David?"

Paralysed by the realization that Thompson had seen through his disguise, and more importantly, his act, David's eyes glazed over and his head lolled backward, trance-like.

Within himself, he felt the tension run through his audience as they waited and willed him to announce the crimes and sins for which Thompson must be punished. His ego and subconscious goaded him on, while his consciousness screamed for contrition and survival.

Sweat, hot and abundant, suddenly burst from David's body as the internal battle raged.

A slap, delivered sharp and hard by an impatient Thompson, revived David in time to hear Thompson repeat his question.

"Why do you want to kill me, David?"

"Because," David answered, his voice strong as he harnessed the strength of his audience's belief, "you are a parasite. You exploit the weak, the hungry, and the poor for your own benefit. You record all that suffering and inhumanity just so you can take holidays in the Mediterranean. You are worse than the people who commit the crimes. And you deserve to die."

"I'll tell you what I deserve, David," Thompson spat, as he tensed and moved closer. "I deserve a fuck of a lot more than I got for what I've done. Listen to me you self-righteous little prick. I gave twenty years of my life to help the weak, the poor, the starving, the raped, and all the rest of the shit that people do to each other.

"I've been all over this fucking world with the army. I saw it all, and I wasted my life. I have no friends, no wife, and no family. Most of the men I served with have PTSD and take shitloads of drugs to keep the nightmares away. Plenty of them couldn't take it and swallowed a bullet. And you know what my country, my government, the fucking *world* gave me for my service? A miserable pension that would keep me in a one-bedroom flat with enough for a week's holiday on the coast once a year, and a meal out once a week."

"What do you expect? That's more than a lot of people have. You should be…"

"What? Grateful? You've no idea what I've seen. What I've done. And I get the same pension as a fucking government desk jockey. Well that's not good enough for me. The way I see it, all these people I've spent twenty years trying to help, well they owe me now. So what if I take a few photographs and take the money that bleeding hearts like you send to help? It never gets to the people anyway. Everyone, from the international organization right down to the local village chief, tribal leader, and even the goddamn priests, takes a cut before the last piddling amount is actually spent on any kind of help. No, David, you're not going to judge *me* from your idealistic moral high ground."

Thompson, done with his self-justification rant, stepped back, waved his knife dismissively, and laughed as he continued.

"Go on, David, piss off home. You don't have the balls to take me on. Jesus, how the lads in my unit would laugh at the idea that a fucking waiter, dressed up in a wig and makeup, could take me down."

The voices in David's head compelled him to stand and lunge at Thompson, but with years of training, he easily sidestepped, grabbed and twisted David's arm behind his back, and held him fast.

With his mouth to David's ear, Thompson whispered, "Last chance, David. Now fuck off."

As he eased his grip and thrust David back toward the bench, he continued.

"You know what else gave you away, David? You fucking stink."

David stumbled, and his forehead struck the edge of the bench. He gasped as Thompson's words registered. Years of humiliation and suffering welled up in him to demand retribution.

Braced against the bench, with his back to Thompson, he grasped the neck of the half-finished bottle of beer in his right hand. Pivoting to his right, in a blind backhand motion, he swung the bottle with the strength and determination of a discus thrower.

Unexpected by Thompson, who had already dismissed David as a threat, the bottle hit just above Thompson's top lip and slid upward into his nose, to shatter teeth and crush cartilage.

As Thompson staggered back toward the canal, David pulled a small black can from his trouser pocket, pointed it at Thompson's blood-covered face, and pressed the dispense button on the top of the can.

A powerful blast of self-defense anti-attack spray leapt at Thompson's face, moving past and through his hands and fingers, and into his eyes, mouth, and open cut.

Despite the assault, Thompson stepped into David, swung blindly, and caught him on the left cheek, knocking him to the ground. Unsure where David was, Thompson kicked and swept one arm with the knife around as he held and rubbed his eyes with the other.

Shuffling back out of Thompson's reach, David stood, re-aimed the can, and sprayed again as he stepped forward. The spray forced Thompson back, but aware that the canal was likely behind him, Thompson fell to the ground and covered his face with his arms.

While Thompson attempted to regroup, David seized a full beer bottle from the bench and crashed it down on the top of Thompson's head.

Thompson crumpled for a moment before he rolled instinctively away from the attack.

Still enraged, David pursued him and landed repeated kicks on Thompson's torso until he screamed and disappeared over the edge of the canal bank into the black, cold water.

A light flicked on in a narrow boat halfway down the basin, followed by a male voice shouting, "What the bloody hell is going on?"

David, standing still and holding his breath, waited. A soft lapping sound crept up from the water. Then a door banged shut and the light blinked out.

City sounds murmured in the dark. A crescendo of applause roared through David's skull, and he turned and bowed deeply to accept the accolades and worship of his fans.

Calmly, as though exiting a stage, he straightened his costume, picked up Thompson's knife, and walked with pride away from the canal, up the gravel pathway, and out through the metal door.

FIFTY-FIVE

The euphoria of another great performance lasted until David arrived home and looked in the mirror. Blood, dried black and smeared by several unconscious backhanded wipes, spread across his forehead from the cut inflicted when he'd hit the bench beside the canal.

Below his forehead, his left cheek and eye socket had puffed and swollen red from Thompson's punch. Grass and mud stains from the damp ground soiled his clothes. Worse, the anti-attack spray he had used on Thompson contained a red dye, and the tips of three fingers on his right hand were bright red.

Shocked by his appearance, and the evidence of his actions, an involuntary scream tore from him and reverberated off the stark bathroom tiles.

Clutching the sink for support, more dark thoughts stoked his growing fear. What if Thompson was alive? He said he'd been in the army, in the Falklands. Surely, he could swim. What if Thompson was coming for him now? No, he didn't know where he lived. But how long would it take him to find out?

Frantic, David splashed and rubbed water on his face and winced aloud. The pain stimulated more thoughts. What about fingerprints on the beer bottles?

Where was the can of spray? How had he got home? Who had seen him?

"No, no, no!" he shouted to his reflection before he slid to the floor and wrapped his arms around his knees.

The smell of shit greeted David when he woke hours later. Shit, and the sheepish stare of his cat, Shadow, as it scraped cat litter over its feces and urine in the box beside David.

Drenched in sweat and trembling, David uncoiled, stripped, and stepped into the shower. Half an hour later, after calling work to explain he had tripped over his cat in the night, banged his head, and couldn't come in, he sat naked on a chair with his fan on maximum.

By seven a.m., though still sweating, David had begun to rationalize and manage his fears and worries with the aid of his subconscious. First, it emphasized David's impeccable acting. How he had deceived Thompson. How it had been David who had manipulated Thompson into inviting him to the boat for a drink. That David had actually sensed Thompson's strength and skills, and had allowed himself to be pushed to the bench in order to catch Thompson off guard.

Second, his subconscious changed David's panicked attack on Thompson into a choreographed and calculated assault, and emphasized his deft movements, improvised weapons, and cold brutality.

Last, his mind assured him that the dye used in the spray had been intentional, as it would identify Thompson as the criminal he was, and portray him as the aggressor against someone who had to use spray for self-defense.

With the support of his subconscious, David recovered from his initial shock and recalled that he had used liquid latex on his fingertips to avoid leaving prints at the pub or anywhere else. He conceded that DNA would be left, but without fingerprints to narrow the search, police would never make a connection that would lead to DNA sampling.

In addition, most of the red dye on his fingertips had been removed when he'd peeled off the latex. Next, his concerns about who had seen him coming home bloodied and bruised were erased by the rational thought that at two a.m. in London, such a sight wasn't that uncommon. Besides, how many people who would actually care, or remember, could there have been?

Two days later, media reports bolstered David's narrative construction.

Thompson's body had been pulled from Regent's Canal near the Narrow Boat pub. Identification dye on the face and hands, together with bruises and a head injury, suggested foul play. An ongoing investigation, and an appeal for witnesses was concentrated on an E-Fit portrait of Edward, as supplied by Matt the bartender.

The final revision of his performance centered on a conscious and subconscious recollection—and vivid reliving—of the rapt worship and massive enthusiasm heaped without restraint on him by the audience for his performance.

So complete, unquestionable, and irrefutable was the reconstruction created by the combined conscious and subconscious collaboration of his mind, that David, as is the nature of the beast, was unaware that he stood on the precipice of absolute psychopathy: a condition for which there is no cure.

FIFTY-SIX

Fighting sleep with sporadic success, since his mom turned off his light at 9:30 p.m., Robbie rubbed his eyes and pressed the light button on his Iron Man watch. Two a.m. Resigned he couldn't stay awake any longer, he scribbled the time in his notebook and added that David "hadn't come home yet."

Driven by a mix of hope and fear, Robbie cocked his ear one last time. Scrapes; first of feet on concrete, then a key inserted into a lock, jolted him upright.

Too late to see from his window, Robbie crept from his bed and pressed an ear to the floor. A second key scrape, followed by the unmistakable sound of David entering his flat, confirmed his arrival.

Changing position from the center of his room to a spot near the wall that Robbie had figured was directly over the hallway that led from David's kitchen to the bedroom and bathroom, Robbie held his breath and listened.

The scream, clear yet hoarse, frightened him. Afraid at what might be happening below, he jerked away from the floor. A pipe groaned as water moved through the system, pulling Robbie's ear back to the floor in time to hear David shout, "No, no, no!"

Uncertain what to do, Robbie kept listening. After ten silent minutes, he crept back to bed and added details to his notebook. Despite violent dreams and restlessness, he finally slept.

At seven a.m., he woke to his mom's gentle touch as she whispered in his ear.

"Hey, Robbie. You OK? You're all hot and sweaty."

"Yeah, Mom, I'm fine."

"You can take your time getting up because you don't need to visit with Shadow this morning."

"Why, Mom?" Robbie asked. "What's wrong? What's happened to David?"

"Nothing, Robbie. David just called and said he's not going to work today."

"What? Why not? Is he sick again?"

"No, not that. He wasn't feeling well last night, so he stayed home and went to bed early. But he woke in the middle of the night to use the bathroom and tripped over Shadow. He banged his head and bashed his face. So, he's staying home, and there's no need to visit the cat."

"He stayed home last night?"

"Yes. What's wrong, honey?"

"Nothing, Mom. I, um, just hope David's alright, you know."

"He said he was fine. I expect we will see him later. Now, why don't you rest for a half hour while I make some bacon?"

"OK, Mom. Thanks."

Rest was the last thing on Robbie's mind. David had told another lie. He had been out until 2 a.m.

And falling over Shadow? Robbie just *knew* that was another lie.

But what had David *really* been doing? Had he "taken care of Troy," or another bad person?

He needed to check David's flat.

FIFTY-SEVEN

Troy, with three disciples in tow, tumbled from the McDonald's on the corner of Bedford Lane and High Street in Feltham. Between bites of hamburger and fries, crude, sexist, and vulgar expletives, all delivered with unnatural loudness, dripped from their mouths.

Each carried a plastic Tesco grocery bag, the imprint of "tall-boy" beer cans clear on the strained plastic.

David, sitting on the knee-high wall of the abandoned church on the opposite side of the road, tugged the collar of his black overcoat to the bottom of his ears.

The cuts and bruises from "falling over his cat" had faded, and secure in his delusional construct, David pressed on with his latest rehearsal.

Despite the damp, cool evening, Troy wore trademark chav clothing and accessories.

With relief, David noted that he was not wearing his long coat, which meant he would not have the axe handle Clair had told him about.

Perhaps, thought David, *this was a sign.*

With one-finger salutes and "fuck yuhs" to cars and drivers, the group ignored the crosswalk, crossed Feltham High Street, and turned right.

David, about a hundred meters behind, stood, stooped a little, and shuffled to follow them.

In addition to the earlobe-to-knee black overcoat, he had purchased a flat cap, clear glass spectacles, and a thick wooden cane to legitimate his adopted stoop and shuffle.

He didn't need to hurry or keep close to the men. He knew Troy's destination.

For six nights, two Thursdays, two Fridays, and two Saturdays, David had stalked Troy and rehearsed. Tonight marked the seventh night, and the third Saturday. Despite six nights of observations, he had yet to figure out how he would kill Troy.

The thug might have survived David's attention, even though he had likely robbed Mrs. Chapman, but his intimidation of Clair, first in the Bell, and then in the shop, together with his threat to harm Robbie, could not be ignored.

Especially as Clair was increasingly determined take her suspicions about Troy to the police.

As David ambled, he sensed impatience from his audience. They had accompanied him on his surveillance and rehearsals, but now they wanted some action and resolution.

Off to the side of the theatre, to David's horror, a few patrons actually made ready to leave. Pleading silently for more patience, David quickened his pace.

About two hundred meters along High Street, Troy, as expected, turned left and led his boys to Feltham Green. Commissioned in the 1800s, it included a pathway overlooking a large pond fed by water from the nearby Longford River.

With a line of oak trees, bench seating, gravel paths, and a war memorial, the green, during the day, was a popular place for walks and rest. At night, it became a haven for drinking, drugs, sex, and violence.

Two young women, each pushing a stroller with a child, had the misfortune of bad timing.

Troy, chest puffed, blocked the women's path while the others formed a circle to corral the women and children.

To David, who had hung back on the street, the words were unintelligible, but the acts of intimidation and innuendo were clear as the women endured the unwanted attention.

Fortunately, Troy, according to habit, hadn't yet consumed the contents of the Tesco bags, and the women were "let go" with promises of his attention at a later date.

Done with the women, he took up residence on a worn wooden bench underneath a large oak tree.

As on previous evenings, David watched from a safe distance as Troy consumed cans of beer, smoked cigarettes and joints, and verbally abused anyone who was foolish enough to venture close.

As David observed his prey, he wrestled with the same problems that had prevented any direct action so far.

Troy was violent, aware, and strong. He was similar to Thompson, and he had underestimated the photographer. It could easily have been David who'd ended up in the canal—and dead.

Troy was also rarely alone. He had been easy to follow, and David found his home on the first night, but he shared a council house with two others, and people constantly came and went.

Checking the time, David figured he had about an hour before Troy finished the beers and headed over to the Moon on the Square, a Wetherspoons franchise pub on the High Street.

Despondent, he left his observation point on the edge of the green and headed along Staines Road to Subway for a sandwich and a coffee.

Halfway through his meal, he wanted to go home. He had had been up since four a.m., and another night of watching Troy get drunk in the Moon before he staggered through the streets chanting, kicking cans, and throwing things on the way to his house for more drugs and alcohol held little appeal.

On the cusp of giving up, an invisible yet palpable energy buffeted and jostled David. Sweeping from the audience like a tidal wave, the energy provided encouragement and support.

Perhaps he could go "off stage" for a while. Maybe home for a rest, and then back for his final act. Accepting the opportunity supplied by his audience via his subconscious, David hailed a taxi.

Out of the taxi, a block from his flat, he straightened, took off the cap and wedged the walking stick under his coat. Home, and lying on his sofa, David set an alarm for eleven p.m. and immediately slept.

~

At 11:15, after a rude electronic wakening, a hasty wash, and a short walk to catch another taxi, David returned to High Street and entered the Moon on the Square.

Inside, he easily spotted Troy and his cronies, who had monopolized a corner of the bar. Maintaining a distance between himself and his prey, he ordered a pint and watched.

Troy had one hand holding onto the bar. The other was holding a pint of lager, which spilled as he spoke and gesticulated. He appeared drunk.

More drunk, thought David, *than usual.*

While David sipped his beer, Troy fumbled with his cell phone as he answered a call. Although unable to hear the exchange, he could see Troy's body tense. The snippets of conversation and body language suggested the call had not gone well.

Without warning, or speaking to his boys, Troy slammed his half-empty pint on the bar, staggered to the door, and fled into the night.

Rushing to follow, David forgot to stoop and shuffle.

Outside, with no sign of Troy on High Street, David turned right and paused at the beginning of the pedestrian thruway that connected High Street to the public parking lots at the rear of the outdoor shopping center and the Asda superstore.

Shops, signs dimmed for the night, and doors and windows protected with metal shutters lined either side of the thruway. Concrete waste bins, overflowing with the day's garbage, flanked graffiti-stained benches and neglected flower boxes. Discarded beer cans and takeout food containers littered the grime-and-gum-splotched concrete and asphalt.

Three figures, hooded and huddled, smoked and drank on a bench. Off to the left, a couple groped and groaned.

In shadow, David skirted the three figures, scurried along the thruway, and stopped at the corner, where it turned left.

Distorted shouts echoed.

He hesitantly peered around the corner. Fifty feet away, Troy stood before three men.

One faced him and spoke quietly, while the other two flanked him, silent.

Troy's voice was loud and belligerent as his words slurred.

"I 'aven't got it. I need another week, a few days…"

The man opposite, his height and weight equal to Troy, made a slight adjustment to his stance.

"You've had an extra week, Troy. It's time to pay."

The two men flanking him stepped closer.

"Look I'm skint," Troy bleated uncharacteristically. "I 'ave noffin right now."

"You're skint," the man snarled as he flexed black skintight gloves over bunched fists, " 'cause you've been on the piss all day. Pay up, or you know what's gonna happen."

Troy shuffled his feet. Then, in an attempt to distract, spoke as he lunged forward.

"Fuck you!"

The man sidestepped his charge, doubled him over with a punch to the stomach, and pushed him into the arms of the two men. With an arm each, they held Troy up as the leader leaned in and whispered something that David couldn't hear.

Troy, not as winded as he had seemed, head-butted the man, who fell back, cursing. Troy laughed and taunted the man again as he struggled to get free of the men holding him.

"You're all mouth when you've got your little monkeys here to help you. Come on. One on one. You and me, and I'll kick the shit outta you."

Without warning, the man stepped into Troy and punched him in the stomach. By the way the man held the blow against Troy, the scream that followed, and the jerk of his body, David knew it had been more than a punch.

Then the man stepped back, the two henchmen let go, and Troy fell to the ground. Without speaking, the men looked left and right up the alleyway.

David pulled his head back and listened. After a few muffled grunts and quick footsteps, he inched his head back around the corner.

Troy, on his side in a contorted fetal position, groaned and rocked on the hard concrete.

Torn between flight and opportunity, David moved slowly toward him. With two steps to go, the groaning stopped.

"Troy," David whispered.

He vacillated between a desire to run, or hasten Troy's death.

Once decided, David grabbed Troy's shoulder and rolled him off his side.

"Arrg," Troy roared as pain stimulated action and he leveraged David's pull, put weight on his left knee, lunged and wrapped his right arm around David's legs.

David stumbled, fell to the ground, and Troy rolled himself onto David. Instinctively, David put his hands on Troy's chest to push him off.

But Troy, high on the body's massive release of survival adrenaline, rolled back to his knees, glared at David, and pulled a knife, buried to its hilt, from his stomach. Raw and desperate, his scream ricocheted off the shuttered buildings.

Blood sprayed like a geyser.

Troy screamed and thrust at David with the knife. The thrust went wide, and David grabbed Troy's knife arm and punched him in the face. Troy's grip on the knife loosened.

David pried the knife from Troy's hand, rolled away, and stood up a few feet away. Disoriented, he froze when a voice started shouting.

"Police! Put the knife down!"

FIFTY-EIGHT

David had called Jenny, who had called Robbie's mom at two in the morning. Woken by the phone, Robbie had badgered his mom until she had told him that Troy had been stabbed to death and the police had David.

Troy was dead. David had killed him. His mom was safe, but the police had David. What would happen now? What would happen to him? It wasn't right. Troy was a bad person and David had saved his mom. He had to help David. But how?

Round and round his thoughts spiraled and confused Robbie. Still in his pajamas, awake since two, and unable to eat the tea and toast his mom had made at six, he stood up from the table.

"I'm going to check on Shadow."

"I don't think so Robbie," Clair mumbled, her chin on her palm and her elbow on the table. Not today."

"But why? David's with the police, and Shadow won't have any water or food."

"I know, but I don't think it's a good idea to go in David's flat, what with all the…"

"Why, Mom?" Robbie challenged her. "David's a good person. He took care of Troy like he said he would, didn't he?"

Startled by her son's statement, Clair, exhausted from a night of worry and stress, roused herself.

"What do you mean, Robbie?"

"In the shop. When Troy smashed the melon. David said he would take care of Troy."

"But, Robbie…"

"But, Mom," he replied as he reached for the key to David's flat. "Troy was a bad person, and David saved you. Now we have to help him, and look after Shadow until he comes home."

Clair was still fearful. Even if Robbie was right, and David *was* a good person, he might still be a murderer, and she was *not* going to let her son go in a killer's flat.

"No, Robbie. Leave the key alone. I don't want you in David's flat right now."

"But what about Shadow?"

"Shadow will be fine. It's much too early now, anyway. Let's wait a few hours, until the usual time. Maybe David will be home by then."

"You think so?"

"I don't know," Clair admitted as she reached out and hugged her son. "I really don't, but I can't believe David is a murderer. It's just a mistake, a mix-up."

"Mom?" Robbie whispered tentatively. His eyes were downcast as he thought of all the things he had learned about David, and the deaths of the other bad people.

"Yes?"

"What if, you know, David is a murderer?"

"Oh, Robbie, he can't be. Come on, sit down and try to eat some breakfast."

"OK."

Clair's eyelids were flickering with fatigue.

"I've been up all night, and I have to lie down for a few minutes, alright? You should go back to bed for a while, too."

"OK, Mom. I'll just eat some toast first."

Her face gray from exhaustion and her shoulders slumped, she shuffled to her bedroom and collapsed on the bed.

Robbie, certain David was a good person and that taking care of Shadow was the right thing to do, dipped toast into his tea and stared at the key to David's flat.

He couldn't wait a few hours. He would just wait until his mom fell asleep, and then he would go down to David's flat. Just for a moment, to take care of Shadow.

FIFTY-NINE

It wasn't much. But then, suspicion didn't need much. And once suspicion set in, anything could happen. From there, twenty-five years to life would become a distinct possibility.

At 6:30 in the morning, on the way home from the police station, David mentally tallied the things he had to get rid of.

To a casual observer, the wigs, makeup, and notes on character mannerisms could be passed off as preparation for auditions and voice-overs. But for the police, especially that persistent Detective Mills, David would need appointments, bookings, and all manner of supporting material to substantiate any claims.

Material he didn't have.

The pair of shoes and the coat he had worn to kill Mr. Clean would have to go, as well. He had kept them because they were good, and he needed them.

Three wigs, several metal containers of makeup, assorted brushes, two pairs of glasses, and one pair of shoes would easily fit in two plastic grocery bags.

The coat, David decided, he would wear over a lighter jacket.

Those were the circumstantial materials that might lead the police to suspicions, and that would then lead to a demand to corroborate and explain.

Just like the list he had made on how killers are caught, David thought.

He chastised himself repeatedly for not following his own advice, but the one critical item investigators need to start the ball rolling was a motive.

But this, David was certain, was lacking in the murders.

All the other stuff, which was out in the open, simply had to go: West's EpiPen, J-MO's business card, Billy's greyhound race program, Thompson's knife, Crawford's flask cap, and even the empty bottles of bleach and chlorine.

He had been foolish to keep them, but the compulsion to have a souvenir had been too strong. Also, he hadn't hidden them because his tiny flat had few places to hide anything. He'd also wanted to be able to see them.

And of course, no one else would have thought twice about seeing them there—until now.

~

As the unmarked police car approached his street, David thought about the last six hours, and especially the lead investigative officer, Detective Mills.

The crime scene to police interview room had been a blur of noise, flashing lights, a brief examination by a medical person, and a series of rapid questions.

Once seated, Detective Mills had been blunt.

"Why did you kill him?"

This theme of enquiries continued until CCTV camera images from the alleyway and those covering the huge Asda parking lot aligned with David's account.

Fortunately, both cameras were linked to Feltham Police centralized surveillance system, and footage had been easily accessed by the police.

After Mills conceded that the evidence from the CCTV corroborated David's account, he had foolishly thought that he was free from suspicion.

But Mills' questioning had changed tack.

"Why were you in the thruway? What were you doing there? You live off Staines Road, near the Bell. Did you often go to the Moon?"

With little to offer beyond saying that he had fancied a change, David stuck to his story.

Then Mills had changed tack yet again.

"Where were you going? The thruway leads to a parking lot. You don't have a car. And it's not a place to get a taxi. It's also in the opposite direction of your flat."

To his audience's delight, David managed to turn Mills' arguments to his advantage with his reply.

"You're right. I don't go there often. I was a little tipsy, and I turned the wrong way out of the pub. I was about to turn around when I heard shouting, and I peeked around the corner."

David realized that it was only a matter of time before the police made the connection to the Troy incident in the pub between Clair, and then himself.

Plus, David had taken a taxi from the Subway to a side street near his flat, then another one back again at eleven p.m. A silly time to go, when it closed at midnight.

Then how long would it take the police to learn about the deaths of his parents, and that despite evidence, he had been within a few hundred meters of the place where Crawford had died?

It would be enough, David thought, *for the police to take a closer look. And from that closer look, who knew what might be discovered?*

The plainclothes police officer insisted on seeing David to the door of his flat. When David opened the outer door to the common hallway, Robbie, who had just come downstairs to take care of Shadow, hesitated behind the door to his flat and listened as the police officer spoke.

"Shall I come in and make you a cup of tea?"

"No, thanks," David replied, rebuffing the clumsy attempt to gain entry to his flat and no doubt poke around.

"Are you sure? It's no trouble. To tell you the truth, I could use one myself."

"Yeah, well, there's a cafe on Staines Road. Opens at seven," David said in anger.

When the police officer finally left, David went inside and quickly collected the souvenirs he should never have kept and stuffed them in the pockets of the overcoat he had worn for Mr. Clean's murder.

On the verge of going out, he ran his tongue over his teeth and sniffed his body. The stink would have to wait, but the fur on his teeth would have to go.

In the bathroom, pursued by Shadow, who he fed and watered, David squeezed out toothpaste and began to brush.

Done, he rinsed his brush and noticed dried blood under his fingernails. Reaching for a Q-tip, he wet it before working the tip under and around his nails.

From the hallway, a familiar sound caught David's ear.

SIXTY

Knock, pause, knock, knock, pause, knock.

Blood, dried black and hard to get, resisted coming out as David wiggled and rubbed the wet Q-tip under and around the chipped nail on the little finger of his left hand.

Knock, pause, knock, knock, pause, knock.

Reluctant, but concerned by Robbie's "secret" knock, David rinsed his hands, pulled the sleeves of his overcoat down, and opened the door to his flat.

"What's wrong?" asked David, noting Robbie's pajamas and flushed face.

Robbie brushed moisture from his reddened cheek with a knuckle. Then he visibly swallowed and pushed out an explanation.

"I'm… I'm just glad you're home. I was worried about the police, and what would happen to you and my mom."

"It's alright, Robbie," David soothed as he squatted down to eye level. "There's no need to worry. It's all sorted. Go back to bed before your mom wakes up."

Unmoved by the assurance, Robbie shuffled his feet and fixed his eyes on the worn doormat. Snorting mucus into his nose hesitant words slipped out.

"I, I, want to say thanks, as well."

"Thanks for what, Robbie?"

"For, you know, getting rid of Troy, and saving my mom."

Raw and desperate, Troy's scream ricocheted off the shuttered buildings as he pulled the knife from his own stomach.

Pushing the image and sound from his mind, David spoke softly.

"I didn't do it, Robbie."

"But I was in the store, and I, I, heard what you said."

"That," David said, thinking back to the confrontation, "was just talk, Robbie. I didn't want your mom to worry."

Dull gray snot had escaped Robbie's nostril, and he dragged the cuff of his pajama sleeve across his nose and mouth as he spoke.

"What about the other bad people?"

Confused, David lowered his voice.

"What bad people, Robbie? What do you mean?"

"It's all in my books."

"What books?"

"The books about the neighborhood. And you."

The wide-eyed innocence of Robbie's young face did little to calm David's sudden apprehension.

"What do you mean? What books?"

"Well," Robbie replied, confident about his achievements, and pleased that David wanted to know. "For the neighborhood, I make notes on people and things that happen. I look out for spies and terrorists, or burglars, or people watching the house. You know, suspicious stuff. And I put everything in my books in case the police need to know."

"Oh," David sighed, momentarily relieved, as he thought of Robbie's well-developed imagination. "But you said you have a book about me."

A shiver shook Robbie's body as the cool air of the unheated entranceway to the two flats leached through his loose-fitting pajamas. A tooth pressed his bottom lip as he debated with himself. If he told what he knew, then David and his mom would know he had snooped in David's flat. But David was a good person, because he had saved his mom, Robbie reasoned.

He decided to confess.

"You know, stuff like when you come and go. What clothes you are wearing, or anything different. When Jenny comes over, and the stuff in your flat. I'm sorry."

"What do you mean, the stuff in my flat?" David asked, with more force than he realized.

"Um, like the new stuff. And the odd stuff that you've been collecting. When I come to play with Shadow, I take photos and put them in my books. I didn't mean to spy on you."

David's right hand slipped into the pocket of his coat. His fingers closed around the smooth plastic cylinder of the spent EpiPen. Past the plastic, he caressed the sharp edge of a business card and the coarse thread on the inside of a metal cap that once closed a hip flask.

With his left hand, he checked the Fairbairn-Sykes, seven-inch, double-edged fighting knife wrapped in a program from a greyhound dog race.

Feigning a smile to hide his anxiety, David whispered his next words.

"Why would you do that, Robbie?"

With pride and confidence in his skills, and unaware of David's tense body, Robbie didn't hesitate to reply.

"To protect Mommy. Now I know you are a good person, so I won't do it anymore. I promise."

A dark grimace flickered across David's face, and Robbie stepped back.

"I won't do it again. Really, I won't. I, I guess I should go now."

"It's OK, Robbie," David consoled the kid, as he adopted a soft tone and relaxed expression. "I understand. It's great that you look out for your mom so much. She told me things have been bad in the past."

Assured by David's calmness, Robbie raised his eyes.

"You're not mad at me, then?"

"No, not at all. Tell me, where do you keep the books?"

"Some on my desk, but the, you know, secret ones, in my treasure chest."

Behind the mask of calmness, David's mind hurtled into a state of uncertainty and fear. He knew Robbie went into the flat every workday morning to feed his cat, Shadow.

What did the kid know?

He would have had plenty of time and opportunity to see things. But Robbie was a twelve-year-old kid, and there was nothing really to see.

On the verge of discounting his anxiety and sending Robbie off to bed, David's subconscious lunged and took control.

The kid's a snoop. He has a telescope and a camera. He's been in your flat alone, every day. He's seen everything.

To strengthen its call to paranoia, his subconscious added a restless murmur of agreement from the imagined theatre audience that had, in David's mind, followed and adored his resurrected acting career for the past year.

Now sensing the expectation of the audience and caught in the glare of the stage lights, David succumbed.

"Hey, Robbie. I'm heading out to Bedfont Park. Do you want to come?"

Eager that David wanted him to go, Robbie agreed, even though he had only been to the park before with his mom, or with his mom and David together.

"Yes, please! I'll get dressed right away. Can we go to the lake, as well?"

"Yes, of course. I'll make a flask of tea and a snack."

As Robbie started through the door to the stairs to his own flat, David, prodded by his subconscious, called out quietly.

"Hey, Robbie, I'd really like to see the books you made. Why don't you bring them, and we can look together?"

"OK, I'll bring my school bag."

"And Robbie?"

"Yes."

"Is your mom awake?"

"No, she's dead tired from, you know, being up all night."

"Let's leave her to sleep then, eh? There's no need to tell her where we're going. We'll be back before she's up."

"OK, David."

SIXTY-ONE

Moisture, heavy and dense, hung in the cold morning air and obscured the entrance to the two paths that meandered through Bedfont Lakes Country Park.

"Can we take the long one that goes by the lake?"

Yes, yes, that's a wonderful idea. You can dump him in the lake.

"OK, Robbie."

The audience, quiet and difficult to see in the bright stage lights, murmured its uncertain approval.

David sensed something was wrong. Was his audience displeased? But how could that be? Hadn't he deceived the bumbling Detective Mills? Hadn't he turned the man's questions against him?

"I'm really glad you let me come. I've never been this early before. The mist is a bit scary, though."

The mist and fog will work. No one will see.

"That's one of the reasons I come early. When you can't see so far, you hear more things."

"Look, David, there's the dock. Can we walk out and sit on the end, like we did with Mom that time?"

"Yes, that was a good day. Do you remember the birds?"

"Yes, and the frogs. They were really loud."

That's good. Keep the boy happy. He will suspect nothing.

A low rumble disturbed the air. Alarmed at his audience's disquiet, David peered through the mist.

At the gravel, before the wood of the dock, David abruptly stopped.

The knife. Use that. No, wait, not the knife. Better if it looks like an accident.

"What wrong?" Robbie asked, already on the dock.

"Nothing," David replied, his eyes vacant as his hand pressed the hard metal in his pocket.

"Come on," Robbie said, smiling as he tugged at David's sleeve.

Very good. It'll be easy now. Wait until the end of the dock, where it's nice and deep.

"Let's sit down on the edge and swing our legs."

"Robbie?"

"Yes, David?"

"Can I see the books now?"

Robbie unzipped his school bag, pulled out two spiral notebooks, and explained the entries with a sense of pride.

"Everything is in date order, but some places have extra notes on different dates, when, you know, I um, got more information. The photos are all dated, as well. I'm sorry again. I didn't mean anything bad. I just wanted Mom to be safe."

Do it now. Push him in. Hold the little spy under until his lungs fill with water.

"That's alright, Robbie," David replied absently as he opened a book.

His life for the past year and a half—since Clair and Robbie had arrived—unfolded with each turn of the page. There was four neat columns: Time, Action, Comment, and Unusual. His comings and goings, impressions of his mood and appearance, and random observations and questions were all recorded in Robbie's adolescent handwriting.

What are you waiting for? Bash his head on the dock, like he slipped, then throw him in.

Photographs, some full size, some reduced to fit four or six on a page, punctuated and supported the point-form narrative and erratic question-and-answer format of the record of David's life.

Robbie's initial uncertainty about David's character and intentions toward his mom, along with his fear for her safety, eventually gave way to gradual trust and belief that David was a "good person."

Pride and fondness for Robbie swelled inside David to coincide with a wave of affirmative emotion from the audience, as it appreciated and supported the actions of a child toward its mother.

Don't believe a word of it. It's a trick to make you weak.

David turned another page. As he read, his face tightened and his breathing stalled. He didn't need the date to know what week Robbie had recorded.

On the page, the kid had noted his view of the Jason West incident.

Monday: Didn't answer door at 3:15 p.m. / Left at 3:45 p.m. / Came back later than usual / Looked angry / Why?

Tuesday: Didn't go to work / Heard him moving around—didn't answer door in morning—didn't see Shadow / Didn't see him / Knocked on door—but he didn't answer / What's wrong?

Wednesday: No work again! / Checked in after school, but didn't let me in to see Shadow / Didn't open door—said all OK / Jenny DID NOT come for dinner!!!

Thursday: Left for work as usual / Fed Shadow / Flat smelled of fish / Checked in after school—he said hi, but not like normal / No date with Mom for their quiz night / Why?

Friday: Left for work / Fed Shadow / Still a bit fishy smelling in flat / Didn't see him / What's going on?

Saturday: David home / Didn't answer door / Why?

Sunday: 9:00 p.m. / Mom goes to see David / I fell asleep.

Back at the current day, Robbie read his most recent entry.

Monday: 8:00 a.m. / Fed Shadow / Mom quiet / Said we will talk tonight after school.

Driven by the need to "see" the results of his judgments, planning, script writing, plot development, directing, and—above all—his acting, David flipped the pages faster and faster.

His rehearsals, costumes, duplicity, ingenuity, adaptability, and improvisation stared back at him. All he could see was his bravery and righteousness. His emotions flooded and overwhelmed him.

Engulfed in self-admiration and the rapture of his audience as they shared the memories of his performances, David's ears rang with applause and the calls for more.

Stop it, you fool. Destroy the book, and the boy. Now!

The internal battle between his subconscious command to destroy and his need to feed off the accolades of his imagined audience contorted his whole body.

Robbie was frightened by David's face and body twitches.

"Are you alright?"

"Who else knows about the book, Robbie?"

"No one."

"Your mom?"

"No. I keep it in my box, and it's always locked. Like your box, in the bedroom."

You see? He broke into your box. Your *private* box. You can't trust him.

"Why are you a prince, David?" the kid asked with soft innocence.

A hush settled over the audience at Robbie's question. Eager for an explanation, the crowd waited. Aware of the audience and keen to perform, David puffed out his chest and proffered his distorted interpretation of Machiavelli's fifteenth-century political treatise.

"A prince is a good man. A man who decides what is right and wrong, and judges what is best for society. For everyone. Those who choose to do evil, or live bad lives, must be punished."

"Is that what you do?"

"Yes. When I was younger, I was bad person. Then I became an actor and I discovered through Shakespeare's plays how to be a prince. You've heard of Shakespeare, right?"

"Um, yes. I guess so. I think we study him at school next year."

"That's good. Shakespeare understood what it means to be a prince, and how to make the right decisions to punish the bad people. *The Prince* was a book written five hundred years ago…"

"Oh yeah, I know that. I found it on Google. Something about politics."

"Not just politics, Robbie. It's about how to conduct one's *life*. How to be good and righteous."

You're talking too much. Get rid of him now. Quick, before someone comes.

"Troy was a bad person, wasn't he?"

"Yes."

"And the others? The ones in the news that I read about? And that man who killed your mom and dad? They were bad, too, right?"

"Yes, Robbie. Very bad."

"Is that why you killed them?"

"Yes," David said as he pulled his hands from his coat pocket and set the contents on the dock beside Robbie.

Get rid of them now. Throw them in the lake, along with the boy.

"What are you going to do with the books, Robbie?"

"Keep them, I guess. Maybe one day I could write a story. Maybe I could make you a spy, or a man who fights evil men, like Troy."

The boy is deceiving you. He knows too much. You must kill him.

David stood up abruptly and moved behind Robbie.

"It's beautiful here, isn't it? The sound of the water and the birds, the smell of the earth and grass and plants."

"Yeah, it is. I could stay here for ever."

You will.

"I'll never tell anyone. I'm good at keeping secrets. I want to be like you, David. We could be a family, and Mom never needs to know."

Robbie leaned back against David's legs, looking backward and up at David as he spoke.

"Could I be a prince, too?"

NOW!

On reflex, David's legs tensed, thrust forward, and tipped Robbie off the end of the dock.

A roar, angry and raw, erupted from the audience. Shouts of, "No, no, no!" echoed across the lake.

Good, David. That's it. Don't listen to them.

Through the light, hundreds of people waved programs and called out, "Enough, enough! Stop, stop!"

"Help, David! Help," Robbie cried out as his arms flailed under the weight of his clothes and coat.

Push him under with your foot. Stamp on his fingers.

Up on their feet, the voices of the audience coalesced into one. In unison, they called out, "Save the child. He is innocent!"

Ignore them. You can't trust him. How many people has he told about his books? Kill him now. It's either the boy—or you.

Losing the fight against his waterlogged clothes, Robbie spluttered as more water seeped into his mouth and lungs.

"Please, David! I, I love you."

The bright stage lights dimmed as Robbie began to sink. Without the glare, David watched in horror as the audience, suddenly silent and abhorred by the murder of an innocent child, turned their backs on him, one by one.

The disgust of his audience slammed into David. Reeling under their rejection, he realized that all he had done and accomplished would be erased by this last performance.

He would not be remembered as "a prince," but a hated child killer.

A sense of calm, like the slowing of time, engulfed David. He now realized what he must do to complete his transformation into the real, ultimate prince.

Didn't Machiavelli maintain that "every Prince should desire to be accounted merciful and not cruel"?

Now David understood everything. Robbie had simply been a test of his virtue. His fitness to be a prince.

And he had almost failed.

No, no, no!

With a nod to his audience, who in the silence of suspended time had begun to turn back toward him, David jumped off the dock and reached out for Robbie.

Using the last of his strength to pull and push the kid up on the deck, David kicked backward, away from the dock. Then he spread his arms and legs wide to make a star and closed his eyes.

In his mind, a bright blue and reddish-orange kingfisher dived for fish. A stoat, its yellowish-white underside visible, stood in search of prey. A red fox and a tern joined the stoat. Together they hunted. The weak overcoming the strong.

Clapping, loud and constant, drifted across the water.

His legs, pulled by the water, drifted downward. Cool and refreshing, it trickled past his lips. Then his breathing slowed.

Using the oxygen from his last breath, David recalled one final Machiavellian maxim: "He who defines his role has more freedom, for people become their roles."

EPILOGUE

Robbie sat in his bedroom. It was much bigger than the old one at the flat above David's. His desk, also bigger, and with drawers, wasn't under his bed anymore.

He had his own flat now. So did his mom.

Every Wednesday, just like Jenny had with David, Robbie went to his mom's for dinner. Dinner on Wednesdays had been good at first. But Mike, the man his mom now lived with, had started to upset Robbie.

More importantly, Mike had also upset his mom.

The truth had taken a while to come out. Months, in fact. But Robbie had been patient, and his mom had finally showed him the bruises on her back and legs.

Never on the face or arms, where they might be noticed.

Using a pen, Robbie made notes in the black, spiral-bound notebook that lay open on his desk.

Done, he closed the book and placed it on the shelf above the desk. Flanking the book on the left, stood an EpiPen, a worn business card, and a metal cap. On the right, a Fairbairn-Sykes fighting knife rested on a faded program from a greyhound dog race.

Mike, Robbie had decided, was a bad person. And as a new prince, Robbie knew that those who "chose to do evil, or live bad lives, must be punished."